FIFTH DRAGON

D KANE

CUMULOS CAPERS

BOOK I

Fifth Dragon
Copyright © 2016 by D Kane

No part of this publication may be reproduced, distributed,
or transmitted in any form or by any means, including
photocopying, recording, or other electronic or mechanical
methods, without the prior written permission of the author,
except in the case of brief quotations embodied in critical
reviews and certain other non-commercial uses permitted by
copyright law.

Tellwell Talent
www.tellwell.ca

ISBN
978-1-77302-468-4 (Hardcover)
978-1-77302-305-2 (Paperback)
978-1-77302-306-9 (eBook)

FIFTH DRAGON

CUMULOS CAPERS

Chapter 1

I really thought I'd gotten it. I mean, how hard can it be? Levitation without a broom is pretty basic, right? I'd done well practicing in my living room over the past two weeks. At the moment however, I hurtled earthward from my tenth-story balcony making frantic efforts to recall the process. Although my fall was slowed, it was still too fast. I'd passed the sixth floor and cars expanded at an alarming rate.

What the hell! This wasn't supposed to happen! According to all the fairy tales, magic was supposed to be reliable!

Levitate! Levitate! Whose goddamn stupid idea had this been anyway?

Right … mine.

Maybe if I changed my nightgown into a parachute! Good idea. Too bad I didn't know how to do that either.

Floor number three!

With shocking suddenness, something clamped onto my ankle and I was jerked skyward. A good thing considering the circumstances, but it had the effect of spinning me upside down which caused my sleeveless nightgown to slide off my arms to flutter like a ghost on the updrafts. I was grateful to be wearing more but mortified it was only a tiny lace thong. I'm not sure how I could be embarrassed when someone had just saved my life but there it is. Women are not logical creatures.

The hand gripping my ankle belonged to a young man with wavy black hair and a broad smile – and he was astride a broom!

"I should go fishing here more often." He looked like he couldn't decide whether laughter or astonishment was the better response.

I hung for what seemed an eternity trying to wrap my head around the fact that I wasn't dead. Since I was as limp as a trout, the guy's comment about fishing was apt.

"Umm … I'll pull you up and drop under at the same time," he said, swallowing his mirth. "You're getting heavy."

Heavy? I was heavy?! Reality returned. Who the hell was he to call me fat? With lightning speed, the logical side of me choked the erupting emotional response. *Shut the hell up! He can call you whatever he wants while he's the only thing between you and a splat on the sidewalk!* Good point. Perhaps I was being a tiny bit irrational. I'd blame that on almost being killed.

I looked up and nodded, which felt strange considering my inverted position.

There was a jerk on my ankle and, as I rose, he dropped beneath until I was seated on his lap. My thick, extra-long black hair didn't cover enough, and the ends of his lips quivered as he shrugged out of a denim jacket to place it around my shoulders. I pulled it snug in an attempt to cover my body which brought me too much attention at the best of times.

My teeth had begun an awful clattering that soon included the rest of my body. I'd heard of people going into shock after such an experience and decided I didn't like the sensation. My mouth wouldn't work well enough to thank my rescuer.

"Are you okay?" Brown eyes were inches from my own. He did a quick scan of my much too visible skin, looking concerned.

I shook my head but couldn't speak because of violent tremors.

"I'll take you back to your balcony," he said, and the floors began to drop.

My balcony? He knew where I lived? Who was he? And did he just happen to be in the neighbourhood? Not that I was going to object since he'd saved me from certain death due to personal incompetence. But the man was riding a broom! All these years I'd believed I was alone in the things I could do. My paradigms were smashing with alarming speed and I wasn't coping well.

When in doubt, go with a good offense. "Do you have to do that?" I growled, grateful and mortified at the same time.

"Do what?"

"Stare like you've never seen a naked woman."

"I'll admit I've seen a few but never under such circumstances. It usually involves some privacy." I tugged the jacket tighter. "I expected you to pop back up on your own and didn't realize you were in trouble until almost too late."

He maneuvered onto my balcony until our feet touched. At the speed of light, I shot for the bedroom where I jammed myself into the baggiest sweat pants and tee shirt I owned. I didn't know whether to be more embarrassed I'd been seen screwing up a basic levitation spell or caught naked by a gorgeous stranger. I took a quick peek in the mirror to ensure bright green roots didn't show at the front of my hair. Strange thing to inherit – a wide swath of bright emerald I dyed black to match the rest.

My tremors had subsided by the time I peeked from the bedroom door. He was seated on a stool at the kitchen counter, arms crossed; broom leaned against the balcony door. Looked like he wasn't going anywhere. I took a deep breath and forced my feet to move.

He glanced my way. "Don't care for the new look," he said with a quirk to his lips.

"How I dress is none of your business!" *I believe I've mentioned I don't handle embarrassment well.*

"Gee, thanks for saving my life," he said in a dry tone. "I appreciate you didn't let me die but it must be your fault my clothes fell off." He spread his hands. "Look! I get you're embarrassed. It isn't the way I'd have chosen to meet but that's the way it happened. Can we move on?"

My arms were gripped over my chest and I felt mulish. Not only had he saved my life, on top of that he was too damn sensible. Odd for someone not over thirty. But I could see I was going to have to suck this one up. His melted chocolate eyes regarded me.

I let out a gust of air. "Would you like tea?" Not waiting for an answer, I started getting stuff down.

"Love some."

I noticed him watching me and stopped what I was doing. "What?"

"I'm surprised you have blue eyes and such light skin considering your hair color."

I shrugged and resumed making tea. "My mother is Irish and Scots. Black hair and blue eyes is common there." I seemed to have forgotten something. Right. "By the way!" I snapped. The teapot hit the granite counter with a rattle. "How did you know I lived here?"

"I've been watching you."

My eyes narrowed. "You're a stalker?"

"You're the first person I've seen other than me who can do the things we do. I needed to be sure you weren't part of a trap."

"I don't follow."

"It's a long story."

"So, why are you here now?"

"After … you know . . ." He gestured to the balcony. "I don't believe you're involved in anything manipulative."

"Why not?"

His cup became fascinating.

Understanding flashed and anger flamed my cheeks. "It's because I'm not good enough isn't it? Nobody would send somebody so … incompetent!"

He crossed his arms and returned my accusing stare. "Beautiful women have been used to lure men in the past."

"I don't even know you!" I must've still been in shock because even I could perceive I was on an insane rollercoaster of emotion.

"Look," he said with a placating gesture. "The stakes are high for me. I had to be sure. I've spent my whole life hiding who I am and what I can do."

"And what the hell do you think I've been doing, advertising on the Internet?"

"I think you're like me – magic. And you're learning to use it by trial and error just like I am."

How do you keep up a good head of steam if the other person doesn't rise to the attack? I was doing all the work here. And he was starting to make sense again. "How long have you been watching me?" I demanded.

"A few weeks. You see, meeting someone like you would be so incredible, I just couldn't believe it. I kept waiting for the other shoe to drop. What was wrong with this picture? How could a beautiful woman like you be like me?"

That shut me up for a bit. How do you argue with that? After an ineffectual attempt to say something intelligent, I extended a hand. "I'm Cheryl James. You can call me Raven."

His grip was warm and strong. "David Stanford. You can call me Dorian."

I dumped tea leaves into a strainer. "How did you spot me?"

"I caught your shadow against a building one evening. I had it narrowed to a couple of blocks when I saw you lift off one night. Once I knew where to look, it was easier. I'd planned to introduce myself soon anyway."

I turned the stove on to heat the kettle. "Is there somebody in particular you're afraid of?"

"It's … complicated. Maybe we'll talk about it someday."

And someday we did.

Chapter 2

I've always enjoyed my apartment in Denver, Colorado with one exception – a ten-year-old monster named Reginald Clugg who lives below me with his single mother. As her days are spent glued to a computer screen in an attempt to put food on the table, the kid has a lot of alone time. Not sure what her business involves, but Reg roams the halls of the building far too often and, the more I get to know this blot on humanity, the more inclined I am to think we should follow the example of sea turtles and reproduce by laying eggs in the sand of some distant shore.

For some reason, Reg has decided I'm a witch and I ride a broomstick at night. This might be true but I'd rather the kid didn't broadcast that little factoid. I'd obviously been slow on the invisibility spell one night and, ever since, he's had me on his radar, spying and making me crazy. He told his mother I was a witch and a ghost because he'd seen me fly past his window in a white gown. *Yes, that would be the night I was rescued by Dorian.*

Well into childhood obesity and looking at a diabetic future from all the crap he ingests, he sports nondescript orangey-red hair, has prominent teeth with a big gap between the middle two, and always wears the same tee shirt with red and white stripes around his middle. He looks like a rubber ball on legs. Pale greyish-blue eyes are magnified by heavy dark-rimmed glasses.

My life wouldn't have intersected with his but for the vending machines in the hall outside my apartment which draw him like a fly to honey.

One afternoon as I fumbled for my key and juggled shopping bags, I got an itch between my shoulder blades. "Hello, Reg," I said, stepping up the search for my key.

He stared through those owl glasses, lips not quite closed.

"Nice chatting," I said as the key slid in.

"What do you do for a job?" he blurted.

"Why do you want to know?"

"My mom says people who don't work are criminals."

"Sounds simplistic."

"What does simplistic mean?"

"Never mind; and I'm not a criminal."

"I don't think you're a criminal either. I think you're a witch."

I set the bags on the counter and leaned against the doorway. "Although it's none of your business, kid, some people have what's called an inheritance. My father gave me money so I don't need to work if I don't want to."

"Good thing you got money 'cause you don't seem very smart."

"Smart enough to be a witch, aren't I?" Shit! Had I said that?

His eyes got huge. "Moooom! … Moooom! She *is* a witch! I knew it!" And he charged towards the stairs.

Maybe I should be thankful he was such an unpleasant little sod no one would take him seriously. Still … I should learn to control my temper and look on the good side – he wasn't mine.

I'd put the groceries away and some extra-rich chocolate ice cream was calling my name when a disk in the shape of a happy-face materialized next to the fridge. It was replaced a few seconds later by a sketch of two figures flying through the night sky astride brooms. I passed my hand over the disk and added "8:00 p.m." to the invitation which disappeared with a quiet "pop."

Since meeting each other more than a year previously, Dorian and I had spent a lot of time together. That first night, it was a simple exchange of phone numbers. I remember pacing the living room the following week as I stared at his number scrawled on a slip of paper, and it was an hour before I summoned the courage to call.

How could a man who was so perfect – gorgeous and magical – not scare the crap out of me? How did one resist that? One misstep and I'd be heartbroken and alone again with my magic. Somehow I'd have to resist a romantic attachment. Friendship was safer.

Apparently he felt the same. We'd developed such a distrust of others during our lives that it'd taken time and talk before we relaxed around each other.

I glanced at the mountains that formed the western border of the mile-high-city where mid-June bits of snow clung to granite peaks. I never tired of the sight my tenth-floor corner apartment afforded of both the mountains during the day and city lights at night. As the air cooled on summer evenings, I'd relax on the balcony that wrapped around the southwest corner, sip something cool, and admire the view.

Denver, Colorado was a nice city. Looking to the east gave me a sense of freedom and ease while a glance at the mountains felt secure and homey – a perfect balance.

Born in Vanderhoof, British Columbia, Canada, I'd been attracted by the shorter winters and lovely country – besides the fact my mysterious father had insisted I move there – or somewhere like it. I hoped to meet him someday.

I decided I had time for that ice cream and slid a small bowl from the cupboard which is my way of restricting junk food. Two small bowls are less than one large one. That was my scientific theory.

As I dug into rich chocolate, I contemplated the evening ahead. I admit it was still exciting to have met Dorian. We'd developed a deepening friendship based on our shared lack of magical understanding and, though it had taken months, Dorian's story had eventually come out.

Ordinary people called him David but his mother had confided his real name was Dorian. She'd said it was magical and never to tell a mortal. She'd stroked two silvery locks that painted the front of his thick black hair and told him he had royal blood and that one day they'd return to Altaria, land of his birth. Until then they must remain hidden amongst the humans. Dorian, as heir to his father's throne, represented a major threat to his uncle Gargeran's growing power.

On his twelfth birthday, she'd pressed a key into his hand and told him to keep it with him always. It would open secrets she'd hidden but, since only a grown man could survive what needed to be done, any attempt to open the lock before he was thirty would damage some of its critical content.

After her murder six weeks later, he'd overheard police forensics whisper about strange burn marks. He'd clutched the key in his pocket and said he was going to his room. He'd retrieved his emergency pack and a bag of gold coins then went to the window and climbed down the fire escape. His instructions had been drilled into him. If something happened to her, use his magical abilities to do what needed to be done to survive but no more. Do not attract attention. Above all else, do not attempt to open the lock until his thirtieth birthday.

After hearing Dorian's story, I felt better about mine. My parents hadn't wanted a strange daughter, especially in a conservative town like Vanderhoof. What would the neigh-bors think? After the scolding I received for materializing a coat for my mother on a cold afternoon when I was six, I'd learned to keep my mouth shut and my abilities to myself.

One night in my seventeenth summer, my parents had returned from a party at which flagons of wine had been a factor. My father, a stalwart man going to fat, had collapsed into bed without a word. I'd always wondered why my beauti-ful and intelligent mother had attached herself to such a man. Bill wasn't bad just… uninteresting. Work, eat, watch television, sleep.

She'd looked long into my eyes and come to a decision she wouldn't have made had she been sober. "Cheryl my girl, let's talk," she'd said and, with each step down our long driveway, my life had changed.

When my mother had been my age, a young man with longish honey-coloured hair and teasing blue eyes had begun showing up near her home. He never came in or met her parents but they'd go for long walks and talk for hours. Of course she was soon crazy in love. One morning she threw up – and on successive mornings until a couple of weeks later she was dumbfounded to discover she was pregnant. Only later did she realize there were gaps of time when she'd been with him.

Bill, eldest son of a neighboring family had always had a crush on my mother. He was a stolid, quiet kind of guy who really should've gotten out of Vanderhoof to expand his world. Her parents talked with his. The marriage ceremony was small, the pregnancy never discussed. He'd been an adequate if unimaginative and distant parent who'd put food on the table by working at a local garage.

The shock of learning about my true parentage was followed by a shot of resentment at having been misled my entire life. To say I was relieved not to have been sired by Bill was an understatement but, deep down, I wasn't surprised. No wonder we'd never bonded. He wasn't interested in a child not his own. Perhaps my mother resented that he took so little notice of me. Regardless of the reason, the fact that I had no siblings now made more sense. Bill was a nice enough guy, but he exhibited the voluntary ignorance of many who never leave their home towns. He had no interest in learning anything that wasn't of immediate necessity.

My unusual parentage also explained the swath of bright green that my mother dyed to match the rest of my hair. To say I was shocked that she'd known where my magical abilities had originated was an understatement! Here was this woman who, my entire life, had insisted it was all my imagination!

Of course I'd wanted to talk some more the next morning but my mother had refused. The subject was closed.

The day I turned eighteen, a note written in a flowing spidery script had appeared on my mother's pillow after Bill had gone to work. A bank account had been opened for the two of us containing two million dollars for us to split. It was to buy her freedom or to use in any way she chose but I was to leave Vanderhoof and go anywhere as long as there was a city nearby.

Denver, Colorado had always interested me and was as good a place as any. As we'd waited in awkward silence in the Vancouver airport, my mother had blurted, "White Raven. Your name is White Raven. Your father came to me the night of your birth and insisted on the name. If I hadn't been so preoccupied with labor pains, I'd have demanded an explanation. He said I'd understand some day. It was the last time I saw him. I've called you Cheryl to help you fit in." Her mouth had twisted into a wry smile. "You know how small towns are."

I did.

I shook my head at the memories and licked the remaining ice cream from the spoon. Since meeting Dorian, the enigma of my past had become more urgent. Who was I?

I wasn't going to figure it out tonight. I glanced at my watch. I had a date. At least it seemed like one even though Dorian had never hinted at anything other than friendship, and I'd never risk the loss of his companionship by pushing for more. Soaring through the clouds alone in the moonlight had always been fun but having someone to share it with was awesome!

Tonight we planned to explore New York until the police helicopters buzzed around. They couldn't see us but sometimes we made a blip on their radar.

As I scurried into the bedroom to change, I caught a glimpse in the mirror and dove for the shower. Maybe I should spruce up a bit.

Wrapped in a towel, I was braiding my hair when the scent of wildflowers drifted through the room. Since I was ten floors from the ground, I shrugged and applied mascara. The scent faded. Must've been a glitch in my sense of smell. Putting it from my mind, I squirmed into a clean pair of jeans. Oh, oh! The clasp was tight. Time to get back to the morning jog. I hate running but I hate being fat more so I slug it out.

Five minutes later as I buttoned a light jacket, I was stopped in my tracks by the unmistakable scent of lush forest. Coming from British Columbia, I knew the scent well. I looked around. Nothing. Now that was strange! Chewing the inside of my cheek, I stepped onto the balcony and lifted into the evening air, looking forward to some time with Dorian.

In retrospect, I realize I should've paid more attention.

Chapter 3

I spotted Dorian where he waited near a stream in Rosamund Park. As I skimmed treetops, I felt a stir of excitement. We'd never tried to go as far as New York. This would be fun! Imagine hovering over the flame of the Statue of Liberty – watching one of the busiest cities in the world from above!

Dorian spotted me, straddled his broom, and we shot into the air. As I caught him, we spread our hands, palms down, to pull magic from the ground, a new process we were working on. The country-side blurred and we were stunned to be at our destination in less than an hour. Some of the things magic could do were flabbergasting.

City lights reflected from a low cloud cover. That was disap-pointing. We'd hoped for a clear night. Since the moon was full, we decided to trade landscape for skyscape but, having no desire to be splatted like bugs against an aircraft windshield, we skimmed low over the Atlantic. Minutes later we shot up into a grey haze. I formed a shield to keep out the cold wetness until we popped through tumbling piles of shadowed cotton silvered by a brilliant moon that turned Dorian's chocolate eyes to black – our own magical world.

An unusual cloud floated above in an otherwise clear sky. I couldn't put my finger on it but it seemed odd. I stared at its unusual solidity and, almost against my will, it drew me.

"I'm enjoying the flight, Raven," said Dorian, pulling up beside me, "but this thing is weird and you seem to have a destination in mind. Care to enlighten me?"

"I've no clue why I'm here."

A deep male voice came from behind. "Tha' would be me. I wished te meet ye."

We spun and my jaw dropped. Floating before us, also on a broom was a muscular man with curly red hair. He wore a kilt and sporran and a broad grin. Never in my wildest dreams could I have imagined such a sight.

As Dorian slid between us, the newcomer boomed in a thick Scottish brogue, "I'll not harm ye. I've come te invite ye te tea."

Seriously? "Who are you?" I blurted.

"Name's Angus MacBride, head o' the tribunal o' Cumulos. Ye can call me either Angus or MacBride as ye choose."

I'd have made a response if I could've thought of one.

"Come along. We'll chat where tis more comfortable … and warmer."

Dorian and I exchanged a look – but we weren't about to miss an opportunity to meet other magical people. We followed our host and, minutes later, a mist parted to reveal a glittering castle in the center of the enormous cloud. Windows glowed and a courtyard was ringed with flickering sconces. A picture of Lichtenstein Castle if it were constructed of crystal popped to mind. Lights refracted into moving colors wherever they met with thin slices of stone and tiny rainbows flickered in and out of existence. Moonlight outlined a jagged mountain that framed the castle from behind. Mountains could float? Rolling grassland surrounded the castle and I spotted the lights of a village further along the mountainside.

My mouth opened but only a thin squeak emerged as our guide drifted to a flower-filled courtyard then climbed some stairs and marched to a heavy set of rose quartz doors. They inched open on their own to reveal a wide hallway. Maybe they had motion sensors.

"Turn right at the next set o' doors," he said, stepping aside. "I'll nae be long." Then the kilt-clad Scot disappeared. Literally. I blinked and scanned the area. Nope. Gone.

Curiosity won over caution as we climbed the remaining stairs and entered. Our footsteps echoed against a slate floor. A monstrous set of double doors swung open at our approach and we stopped at the threshold of a room a dozen times the size of my apartment. Warmth blasted from a gigantic fireplace carved from what looked like a solid chunk of hematite. Clear spheres enclosed golden flames that floated throughout the room casting a gentle glow amongst comfortable-looking divans and low tables.

Didn't seem to be any electricity in the place. In spite of crystal walls, thick scatter rugs and colourful tapestries made the room inviting and cozy. I snapped my mouth closed, noticed each table had been set with a silver teapot, cups, saucers and small plates.

A side door popped open to admit three gnome-like creatures bearing trays of food. As they passed, one gave a nod and a grimace that, generously speaking, might've been a smile. They distributed their burdens with quick, stubby fingers, and departed the way they'd come.

As the room regained a quiet expectation as rooms do, we approached the blazing warmth of the fire and waited next to a life-sized statue of a winged horse. A number of other animal carvings, each on its own pedestal, were scattered throughout. There was a cat with oversized pointed ears, a dragon, a creature that was half goat/half man, and a number of other mythical beings.

I jumped as our host burst into the room and gestured towards the repast. "Do ye prefer coffee or tea?"

"Coffee, please," I said.

With a grimace, he waved a hand over a tall coffee-pot. Steam issued from the spout and the welcome aroma of fresh coffee drifted to us. The heat was penetrating so I slipped off my jacket, laid it over the back of a tartan divan, and settled next to Dorian as our host poured.

As delicate china cups filled, he said, "I'd appreciate it if ye could spend some time with us after tea. I'm hoping the two o' ye can help with something."

I heard Dorian mumble some kind of response but my attention was caught by other … beings that arrived in twos and threes to take their seats. I saw an eyebrow or two go up as we were spotted. An enormous soldier ducked his head, squeezed through the door with difficulty, and lowered himself onto a bench constructed of solid wood. I now understood why it had remained unoccupied. He'd have crushed any other furniture in the room.

His arms were like tree trunks and he clanked with weapons that hung from a variety of leather straps. I chose to assume the nod he gave us was courteous as the canyons on his face made it hard to identify an expression.

As Angus rose to his feet and moved to an open spot close to the fireplace, I felt a tightening in my solar plexus, imagining his green kilt exploding into flame (at least it would solve the mystery of what Scots did or did not wear beneath their kilts).

"Good evening, everyone," he said, when the last whisper had died away. "We've visitors from below today – Dorian and White Raven."

Where had he learned our names? Curious whisperings ceased as Angus continued. "As ye know, the spyders have become a considerable threat so I've invited our guests who are strong in Gaia energies. If they agree te help us, I'd ask some o' ye te assist in their training."

My ears pricked. *Help? Training?* I wasn't sure I liked the sound of this. Angus grinned and gestured to the tables. "But first we eat!"

He returned to our table, slid onto a chair, and passed me a plate filled with hot scones. The thought of juicy gooseberry jelly mixed with butter slathered onto the hot pastries made my mouth water. Fresh air always makes me hungry. Besides, there were all sorts of tasty treats.

Dorian slanted a glance at my heaped plate.

"What? There's lots of food! I'm hungry!"

He gave a quick shake of the head, speared a sliver of ham, three cucumber slices, and a scone. I looked at my plate. Hmmm. Probably should've spread it out a little. Maybe taken two small plates. Ah, well, too late now. I slathered a scone with gooseberry jelly and took a huge bite. Mmmm. Delicious! I added two spoons of sugar to my coffee and washed it down. Even better!

Twenty minutes later, I sat back with an agonized groan. "I ate too much!"

Dorian has one teensy fault. He's perfect. "It isn't necessary to overeat," he said in a tone that seemed to carry the slightest flavour of condescension. "Put your fork down sooner." *So speaks someone who never does anything wrong. Have you ever met anyone who's perfect? Drives you crazy, doesn't it?*

As I set my empty cup down, Angus made a gesture and the remains on the tables vanished. I put that on my list of things to learn. No more dish-washing.

As the room emptied, Angus invited us to his study where we found two others – a beautiful woman named Fabiana Frost who preferred to be called Frost and a small figure with a patchy coat of mauve fur and oversized ears that reminded me of a lop-eared rabbit.

Frost, in a floating, glittering gown, gave us a gracious smile. I learned later that she was an accomplished witch from Transylvania who, in the past, had been the victim of an enemy's spell. Ever since, her age made slow revolutions between fifteen and fifty. Stunningly beautiful, her current age was about forty and regressing. Angus had been vague about the spell but had mumbled about needing to watch out when she was between eighteen and thirty. As a member of the ruling tribunal with Angus and Talon, Frost had resided in Cumulos for two decades.

We greeted the woman with polite nods and turned to the little purple creature. At first glance, it seemed cute as a bunny – that is, until one noticed the huge slanted purple eyes magnified by goggles had a distinct chill. The goggles were held up by a hooked nose with narrow nostrils and an elastic band around its head.

It reminded me of a grey alien with a fungal disorder. He was introduced as male, his name was Talon, and he floated with longish skinny legs cramped into the lotus position, thin arms folded. The unfortunate shape of his floppy ears gave him a slightly stupid appearance – stupid and bad tempered. Triple-jointed toes had an off-putting tendency to twitch.

I'd been working on reserving judgment and here was a good opportunity to practice. Perhaps his appearance was deceptive. Maybe he was wise and gentle. After all, people who meditate are supposed to be enlightened, right?

Then Angus introduced him, he opened his mouth … and I was ready to throw him into the fire. His wide, thin-lipped mouth flattened further.

"They're a waste of time, Angus," he said in a raspy voice, ignoring our polite greetings. "They can know less than nothing."

I jerked erect as Talon's purple gaze swept over us with supreme contempt. I was tempted to ask him what his problem was but thought I might be at risk of adding unnecessary adjectives. As we moved further into the room, I approached the little mauve creature, stared into his eyes. I've been told my icy blue gaze can be intimidating. Apparently he'd not been informed. In fact I was the one who experienced a definite chill.

Angus handed us each a flute of clear liquid from a tray on a side table and gestured towards an arrangement of comfortable chairs before the fire. Even though it was spring, the crystal castle was cool and the warmth welcome. As our host settled into a leather chair with dark wood carving, I took an experimental sip, not surprised I didn't recognize the delicious taste.

"Tis made from the nectar o' the Meadowfair flower that grows on the hills behind the castle. Tis quite difficult te acquire as the ground gnomes are fond o' it and they'd prefer te keep it for themselves. Fortunately for us, one of our herbalists is good with ground gnomes and always manages te get enough."

At this point, I wondered how anything could grow on a cloud. Turns out that with magic, a great many things are possible. Cumulos was only surrounded by cloud. It was solid earth (not that this information was a solution to the mystery).

"Now," continued Angus, "we've a few questions for ye if ye don't mind."

After Dorian and I explained what we knew of our magic, Angus returned to the point of the evening. I remembered the word *spiders*. I don't like spiders. They're squirmy and twitchy and make me itch just thinking about them. I thought I'd tell him right off.

"I don't do spiders."

"These're nae the spiders you're familiar with, lass. They've the same name but tis spelled with a 'y.'"

"I don't care how it's spelled. I don't do spiders." I scratched my neck.

"Allow me te explain. We'll not force ye."

I surged to my feet. "Good. Since I'd only do spiders by force, thank you for the food. It's been a slice. We should do this again sometime." I turned to Dorian. "Time to go." I gestured for him to get up but he didn't move. I've noticed Dorian has an unfortunate tendency to do his own thinking.

He placed a hand over mine. "Let's hear what the man has to say."

Don't you hate hearing that statement? It never leads to anything good.

Chapter 4

Firelight reflected from crystal walls and the crackle of logs
radiated a welcoming glow. I sipped a delicious drink and
relaxed in the warmth of the cozy, pleasantly-crowded room.

Angus floated before stuffed book shelves looking for
something. A complex gyroscope balanced on a corner of
an enormous oak desk made slow rotations to some unknown
rhythm. Magical gadgets, few of which I recognized, rested
on every available surface. Although the flickering spheres
that drifted throughout the room lent an air of mystery and
shadow, I wondered why they didn't hire an electrician, buy
a generator and install some lights.

Row upon row of books stacked around the tower walls drew my attention. How I'd love to peruse those musty old volumes! The mind boggled at the hidden secrets.

I envisioned a fourteenth-century-style laboratory filled with black cauldrons and jars of desiccated bat carcasses, newt's brains, and goat's eyes hidden somewhere in the castle. Was there a limit to the possibilities? Were the magical stories I'd read as a child real here, and was I part of that magic?

When the mage returned with a gigantic tome floating next to him, I blurted a question that'd been buzzing about with all the other stuff in my brain. "How did we get here? Doesn't seem to have been an accident."

His lips quirked. "I sent ye an invitation."

"What interest could you have in us? We've had no training in magic other than what we've been able to figure out for ourselves. There's no way we could be of any help." *You can imagine how difficult it was for me to agree with the cranky purple fuzz-ball.*

A fat black cat with white paws strolled from the shadows, sniffed Dorian's leg, glanced at me, and made an abrupt change of direction. It leaped to the padded arm of my chair where its green orbs fixed on my face, tail-tip twitching.

Angus set his flute on the table and relaxed into his chair with a sigh. "Your magic is different. The magic o' a cloud island, even a large one, is unlike that o' a continent. The Americas are old and span the earth verra nearly from pole te pole, so it pulls and mixes magic from different areas. Like all things o' the earth, there's a duality te magic. The stronger the good, the more harmful the bad. There's balance and, in that balance, is life.

"A handful o' creatures, including humans, have the power te change that balance, te grow the light without a corresponding increase in dark, but most people never realize it, succumbing te one degree or another te the pull o' the shadows.

"But creatures o' wisdom change the verra earth itself. Darkness is infused with light until, in time, duality is dissolved. In this way the dark contributes richness te light as tis transformed."

"What about bad magical people?" I asked. "I'm guessing they exist."

"They add te the dark as do those who fight against them. Therein is the issue. If we fight evil as an opponent, we become the problem. After all, the aggressors throughout history have all believed they were in the right." His chair gave a leathery squeak as he adjusted position, retrieved the flute and took a delicate sip, rolled the liquid around on his tongue. "Wonderful stuff, this nectar!"

I tried not to notice he was careless about keeping his kilt down (another mystery solved). In a desperate attempt at distraction, I asked, "And what does all this mean to us? What can we do?"

The cat brushed my hand with a delicate paw and continued to stare. It seemed to be trying to send some sort of message. As it watched me, I had the uncomfortable feeling it wondered if this person had any intelligence whatsoever.

From long habit with childhood pets, I stroked its back where-
upon it closed its eyes and set to purring like a lawn mower.
Mission accomplished.

"Some o' the creatures that add light te the world are
the giant unicorns. Twice the size o' a horse, they're scattered throughout the world in small herds, the largest in
Northern Scotland, a remnant from before the flood. Their
presence modifies the weather and restores balance though
they're seldom seen. People don't believe they exist so canna
see them."

"Has something happened to the unicorns?" *At this point
I wasn't discounting the possibility of unicorns being real. After
all, I was in a floating cloud castle.*

"They're disappearing and we don't know why. We hope
ye may be able te help."

"What can we do?"

"With proper training, ye'd both be formidable mages."

I couldn't wrap my head around that concept as I recalled
a great many explosions, singed hair and foul smells over the
years. My magical history had pretty much been a train wreck.
"We don't even know what there is to learn."

"Then you're in the right place."

Chapter 5

One of the stocky gnomes who'd introduced himself as Mr. Stonewall paced along the top of a low quartz partition. He wore baggy grey trousers, a black vest over a white shirt, and a squishy knit tam perched on white curls that made him look like an ugly child in a nightcap.

Dorian and I watched him pace. Angus had said the little man would evaluate our magical skills which we looked forward to as we hoped to solve some of our questions.

"Let's start with something simple," he said in a gravelly voice. He pointed a thin reed at seven lights that floated in a row to create a rainbow. Each time he pointed the stick at a light, a tone would sound. I recognized the tune of "*Mary had a Little Lamb*."

"Now, you try it," said Mr. Stonewall.

Dorian and I looked at each other. "Come now," said the gnome, "let's get started!"

"Um … what's the stick for?" I asked.

Stonewall's face went through a startling number of contortions before settling on incredulity. He held up the stick. "You can't mean this?"

"Yes. What is it?"

It seemed I'd sprouted two heads without warning. "Are you serious?!"

As the bulldog wrinkles on his face deepened, I got the niggling feeling I'd said something wrong and groped for a clue. Although my mouth opened, nothing came out.

"I imagine that's a wand," said Dorian, stepping close. "Helps to cast magical spells. Probably directs energy. Didn't know they were real."

Stonewall teetered. "Didn't know they were *real?*"

"Mr. Stonewall," I said with a touch of defensiveness. "We grew up without benefit of a magical education. People in North America don't believe in magic and we've never seen a real wand!"

He sniffed and mumbled something that might've been unflattering.

"What was that?" asked Dorian.

"Nothing … nothing." He waved short arms.

I winced and ducked as the stick passed close to my face. "Would you like to lower that … device?" I asked, retreating from harm's way.

"What? Oh … oh yes, of course." He eyed us as if we were an insuperable undertaking. "If you don't even know what wands are, we'd better visit the library." With a deep sigh, he stepped off the partition and my heart lurched as he strode into midair. Unlike the crash I expected, he floated to the grass before heading toward an arched door, heels clacking.

As we trailed in his wake, I could see why he used the wall. Two inches taller than my hip bone, we'd been informed his height was normal for a gnome. I tried not to stare but was still getting used to the idea these creatures were real.

After a trek through crystal hallways and down a set of winding quartz stairs, we came to a wooden door with heavy brass hinges tarnished with age. Stonewall waved his wand at the lock, there was a click, and the door swung into darkness. Wall sconces burst into flame.

A narrow hallway ended in a wall patterned with black hematite and rose quartz. "Don't dawdle!" he commanded in a tone which I felt lacked courtesy.

As we trailed behind, I got the feeling if he stopped without warning, I'd flip right over him but, as I expected his face to collide with the wall, a door-sized opening appeared – and he walked right through it.

Gone.

Too astonished to slow down and with the thought that if he could do it, I could too, I marched forward, closing my eyes at the last step. Can't imagine why. How could that have helped?

Imagine my surprise when I opened them to a large quiet room with a curved counter of dark wood carved in intricate patterns. Shelves of books identified it as a library. People and *other kinds of people* studied at tables throughout the room, reading by the light of skylights and numerous flickering globes that floated throughout. One ancient crone had four on a tether.

A large tattooed rat watched us from a bookshelf. A thin grey specimen with a bulgy, saggy belly, it stood on hind legs as we went by. I could've sworn it'd been reading the book open in front of it and a chill washed over me at the realization it seemed far too intelligent for a common rat. There was something odd about its fur too but I didn't have time to take a good look. It eyed me as I passed.

Due to the momentary diversion of my attention, Stonewall got underfoot and, after he was knocked to the floor, I helped him up amidst profuse apologies. When I had the opportunity to glance back at the rat, the shelf was bare. Stonewall gave me an injured glare, brushed off his clothes, re-set his tam then clacked towards the counter to climb a couple of steps provided for the vertically challenged.

A squat, toadish creature that I labeled female shuffled over to greet us – or kick us out – or turn us into something awful. She wore a faded black cloak and semi-crushed witch's hat which she pushed back to peer up at us. A look of astonishment crossed the sagging lined features.

"Good Lord! Never thought I'd see the like! Mr. Stonewall! Where on earth did you find these two?"

"Angus," grumped the gnome. "Wants me to teach them." He lowered his voice. "They don't even know what a wand is."

"Are you serious?" Bulging pale eyes widened. "But they're mages!"

"From below," he said as if sharing a dirty secret.

"Are you certain? I've always heard that mages from there were a myth. Could you be mistaken?" Her bulgy eyes continued to stare at us.

"I could be, but Angus?" Stonewall shot her a look. "What are the chances of that?"

The stumpy witch twisted loose lips. "Not good, I'll grant you that." She peered at us as if examining a new species of insect. "So what would you be lookin' for then, Stanley?"

"Thought I'd start them with basic spells. You know . . ." He whispered behind his hand, ". . . kid's stuff."

The old witch swiveled her head towards him. "That bad?"

Stonewall nodded, his expression sad. "Never seen the like."

The crone's tall hat began to slide to one side. She shook her head and somehow it righted itself. "I'll see what I've got. Should be some old books in the back."

As she lifted a portion of the counter and shuffled past, through heroic self-control, I resisted straightening the hat which had slid to one side again. Since it didn't fall off, I concluded it had to be attached with the magical equivalent of super-glue. She squeezed by a collection of odd-looking children to a shadowed aisle near the back and I followed at a safe distance.

Deeper into the shadows, I made out a few words. "Mmmm … had some old stuff back here. Not much call for it. Most people master the basics before they're five."

I chose to ignore the insult and wondered if I was supposed to be following her at all. Maybe I should stay in the light. No telling what was back there. Dorian bumped into me when I halted.

"Raven?"

"Just uh … you know . . .thought I'd wait out here."

"She might need help carrying the books."

"True. You're stronger. I'll wait."

Dorian looked down at me with an expression of disbelief then shook his head and disappeared into the spooky bowels of the library. Trying not to feel like a coward, I wandered to a window to watch my strange new world go by and wait for Dorian. I slid a look at the shadowed interior of the book shelves … *if* he came back.

I tapped my fingers and stared with little attention through a dusty window. It wasn't until two bearded men strolled past and disappeared behind some trees that I realized they'd been goats from the waist down. *You're not in Kansas anymore . . .*

The drum of my fingers on the window ledge had become a machine gun before Dorian emerged from the shadows, arms filled with old, leather-covered volumes. Crap! Looked like homework.

"So," I said, following him. "Those all for us?"

"It seems we require remediation work," he said in a dry tone and dropped them with a dusty thud onto the counter.

I picked up a volume, untied the cracked leather thong that held it together, and peered at thin, spidery writing. "Is this English?"

The old crone chose that moment to rejoin us, loose lips formed into a squishy line; wobbly colorless eyes on mine. "You *can* read?"

"Of course I can read! It's just this is … you know … written by somebody with really flowery writing and a skinny pen."

As the crone and Stonewall exchanged a look that said they'd have better luck teaching a pair of chimps, I got the urge to turn her into a toad … if only I knew how. I dropped the book back onto the stack where it produced another puff of dust which made me sneeze. The old witch backed away.

"Hope that's not catching!"

I sniffed. "I'm not sick. It's dusty in here."

"Of course it's dusty! It's a library!"

She waddled back behind the counter where she turned to face us. I tried not to stare at three warts on the left side of her face which, if they hadn't been decorated by spiky black hairs, might've been not quite so mesmerizing. Her hat, with a new accumulation of dust, had another crimp and was kept from falling by nothing I could see.

As she stared at us for a long minute, I grew impatient. I was tired of being insulted; the woman was obviously nuts and perhaps dangerous. I measured the distance to the door.

Her face crumpled as if thinking was painful.

"Um … are we done here?" I asked. Her moles elicited the morbid fascination a person gets when coming upon an accident. You don't want to stare but can't help yourself.

"I seem to remember . . ." A sudden wide, toady grin split her bumpy features. If she had teeth, they weren't visible. "Ha! I've got it! My memory ain't what it used to be!"

She cackled, stumbled to an ancient chest against the back wall, dumped armloads of rags onto the floor, and scraped spider webs from the lid. With a grunt, she managed to lift it and her head disappeared into the chest's interior. Stuff flew everywhere as she dug like a badger after a ground squirrel.

As the dust storm spread to us, she extracted two books with carved copper covers. She dropped them on the counter with a thud and blew off a layer of grime which brought on a coughing fit so prolonged, I feared she'd require mouth-to-mouth.

Dorian and I glanced at one another. He wasn't any more anxious than I that our recuperative services be needed. After sucking in a deep, shuddering breath, the witch's colour returned to its former muddy pallor and I heaved a sigh of relief. At least now I wouldn't have to feel guilty for letting her die.

An uncomfortable silence stretched as she composed herself. What was I supposed to do? Ask her if she was alright when she obviously wasn't? Ask her what I could do to help? I shuddered, shut my mouth, and looked at the books. I opened one of the ornate covers to discover writing interspersed with beautiful illustrations – but this writing was definitely not English. In fact, it was like nothing I'd ever seen.

I pointed out that fact but the witch simply cackled and wandered away to the dusty bowels of the library. Guess we were finished.

Stonewall adjusted his tam and insisted we read the books in our stack before coming to him for further instruction. When I asked about wands, he pointed out that, at this point, it would be like giving loaded guns to children.

I scowled at his retreating back as Dorian and I added the copper books to our stack and picked a spot at an empty table. Maybe Angus would help us read the mystery books when we'd finished with the rest.

Later that day, Angus invited us to his study. Dorian and I, lugging our books, dropped them with a thump onto a table and settled into chairs across from him.

Angus withdrew from a desk drawer a pair of long, thin objects wrapped in cloth. He pushed one to each of us. "This might be premature but there's nae a lot of time so we'd best get started. I'll instruct ye myself in the use of these."

Dorian pulled back the cloth from his package and stared at a black wand nestled in red silk. It looked like the tree it had come from had grown under harsh conditions and been altered because of it. As Dorian picked it up, he sucked in a sharp breath.

I surged to my feet. "What?!" I couldn't imagine what would give him that expression. Had something gone wrong?

"This is amazing!" he said with a wondering grin. "It feels like … cold fire!"

"Ahh . . ." said Angus. "Interesting. I've had these wands for centuries but yesterday I had a powerful impulse to get them from storage. That one must be yours."

He gave Dorian a direct look. "Tis from the Tree of Eternal Night and is strong in the dark energies. But it draws nourishment from deep in the earth so has powerful healing as well. Only a balanced mage can use this wand without succumbing to the dark. Be careful ye never use it te harm without cause. It'll seduce ye."

Mine, nestled in what looked like dandelion fluff, was made of crystal. Colors and smoky images swirled within it. I couldn't resist.

The instant I touched it, a shock ran up my arm; a feeling of light and power filled my body.

"Ah . . ." said Angus. "There's nae doubt this one is yours. Crystal energy is strong in ye. Shows in your eyes." He glanced at the wand. "Tis the most powerful crystal wand I've ever seen. Both have been here for centuries. Had almost given up expecting anyone to be able te use them."

"What do you mean?" I asked.

"Many centuries ago, these powerful wands came into my care. Didn't expect I'd have them for so long but the wheels of time are slow te move."

Chapter 6

Mr. Stonewall was back on his raised crystal partition, the coloured lights floating before him. "Mage Angus has asked me to assist with teaching you how to use your wands. To put it in your terms, you each own a Ferrari but we'll be using first gear. Do you understand?"

At our nod, he continued. "Using a wand is not supposed to be hard work. Magic is like a river. When it stops flowing, it either builds pressure until it explodes or becomes stagnant like a swamp. Hold your focus and allow irrelevant thoughts to flow around the perimeter of your mind. Pick your position and let its energy move you where you want to be."

I wasn't sure what he meant about letting energy move me, but I stood in front of the lights and tried what he said.

I felt like a conductor in front of a silent orchestra. With thinned lips and a groan of frustration, I turned to him. "This isn't working!"

"Give it a few minutes. Don't think about what you want to happen. *See* it happening. Magic follows vision and emotion. Feel and see; don't think in words."

"Don't mages use words to cast spells?"

"Only words that have been instilled with magic. And those are dangerous to use without instruction."

Desperate to succeed at something, I tried to follow his instructions, surprised when it worked. Thoughts no longer snagged my attention as they had before. All went well until my orchestra gave off a discordant blast and fell silent. I slumped to the grass and glared at my wand. "Why's it so hard?"

The little man settled into a seated position. Short, muscular legs dangled over the side of the low wall. "It's difficult for a number of reasons, not the least of which is you've grown up as mages without instruction on how to control magic. You're fortunate you managed to grow up at all without destroying your surroundings. How did you handle spontaneous blasts as your powers increased?"

Dorian and I exchanged smiles. "We pretended to be as puzzled as everyone else," said Dorian, "and I think we were lucky."

"Perhaps your luck had help. Magic would've known of the consequences to its host."

"Are you suggesting the magic kept us hidden?" I asked.

"If you were damaged, the magic would have no host through which to work."

Goose bumps raced up my spine. "You make it sound like a parasite!"

Stonewall looked offended. "Magic is no more a parasite than your arm, your leg, or even your heart. It's an intelligent part of you. You look after your body, and your body looks after you. Magic is no different."

My temples throbbed and I dropped my head into my palms. "I can't possibly learn all this!"

It happened we were skilled in one area they were not. Necessity had taught us to sense upcoming danger and constant scans at a subliminal level had become so automatic, we were alerted when something intruded that didn't belong. Magical people who lived amongst other magical creatures never had to develop this type of awareness but Dorian and I could not only sense the presence of the non-magical, we could read their intentions. When Angus expressed interest in this technique, I experienced a sense of relief at having something to offer.

A few days into our training, Angus invited me to accompany him to Edinburgh, Scotland, his place of birth (who knew how long ago). While we were gone, the huge soldier by the name of Cash would take Dorian for a flight on a Pegasus. Dorian, who'd spent his teenage years on a ranch, had been chomping at the bit (so to speak) since his first glimpse of the flying horses.

It was late morning and Angus wore his best kilt and formal jacket. A gold circlet designed with intricate Celtic knots controlled curly red locks.

"Are ye ready, lass?" He outlined a circle in the air, a spinning maelstrom formed, and I backed away with a wary look.

"Not te worry," he said. "Tis safe." He took my arm, a step forward and, before I could object, the world spun. *Crap!*

I'd have fallen onto a grassy surface if not for the grip on my elbow.

"Are ye alright, lass?"

Perhaps my greenish hue suggested otherwise. I held up a hand in a time-out gesture and leaned forward, hands braced on my knees. *Have I mentioned my stomach, as Angus would say, is a wee bit sensitive?*

When I'd recovered, curiosity stirred and I straightened to look about. I'd never visited Edinburgh where my great-grandmother had been born so was interested in the sights.

"Would ye like some lunch? I'd hate te miss the opportunity te stop at a grand restaurant nearby."

My stomach growled. I'd scarfed down a muffin but had elected to go with Dorian to see the Pegasus instead of eating a real breakfast. I'm one of those strange people who can forget to eat if I get distracted – that is until my stomach gets desperate and sends LOUD messages at which point I don't know when to stop.

We turned into a narrow alley where a steep flight of stone steps descended into the shadows. An old wooden door creaked as we stepped into a dim room with tables scattered throughout. A horse-faced man with a long black forelock bade us welcome and held a chair for me. Leather menus materialized on the wooden table along with two glasses of water.

It seemed Angus MacBride was well-known. I felt dozens of eyes on me but each time I glanced up, no one was watching. I wasn't a native … and everyone knew it.

"Sooooo, what do humans think of this restaurant?" I asked, raising my eyebrows. "Don't they notice it's a little … odd?"

"They canna see it. Only those with magical sight know o' it."

Oh.

"What do you recommend?" I asked, trying to decipher the strange language in which the menu was printed. When Angus muttered an incantation, the menu changed to English. "Thanks."

"Ye might want te try the dragon egg omelet smothered with goat cheese and a plate o' sourdough. Tis delicious and nae too different from what you're used te."

"What are you having?"

"Bat's wings simmered in newt-belly soup. Verra nutritious." He chuckled at my expression of horror. "Ye may learn te like it."

I found that profoundly doubtful since I'd have to try it for that to happen.

After the waiter left, I examined the room. Rock walls were divided at intervals by heavy wooden support beams which were blackened with age and smoke. Small windows at street level exposed scurrying feet on concrete sidewalks connecting the magical with the mundane. Despite my earlier unease, as the murmur of conversations resumed, I found the room to be cozy. I sipped water and waited to find out why we were there.

"We'll be making a couple o' stops," said Angus. "I'd like your input on one but we'll talk later. Would ye like tea?"

He caught the expression I tried to hide. "Ahh . . ." he said. "From the Americas. Yer drinks o' choice will be hot chocolate or coffee."

I nodded. "Tea seems kind of . . . ummm . . . thin." Concerned my preference could be construed as offensive, I added, ". . . but I'm sure I'll get used to it."

He chuckled. "Ye nae need te get used te it, White Raven. Drink what ye like. I've heard they also make pretty good coffee here."

When the odd waiter brought my coffee in a teacup, I sipped with anticipation – then peeled my tongue with difficulty from the roof of my mouth. An ominous brew, I was beginning to comprehend why coffee wasn't popular in the British Isles. It gave the word "bitter" new meaning.

After a glass of water had restored my taste buds, I tucked into a delicious omelet while trying to avoid looking at Angus' bowl. His stirring caused the batwings to look like sharks searching for a lunch of their own.

Later as we climbed the stairs to street level, I cursed myself for overeating yet again. Maybe we had a good long walk to wear it off. I wore a periwinkle blouse cinched by a corset over loose black trousers tucked into soft leather boots and, at that point, wished I hadn't tied the corset so tight.

"So where are we off to?" I turned away in a surreptitious effort to stretch the corset and marvel at the fact that women a couple of centuries ago mustn't have needed to breathe.

"Te visit an old friend. His village is next te an old stone castle that's been renovated into a hotel."

That sounded odd. "There's a village *in* the city?"

"In a manner o' speaking." He waved his wand, a rectangle of light appeared … and we walked though.

On the bright and busy street corner that appeared, I experienced a moment of panic as a passerby walked right through me. Apparently we were invisible – and non-physical as well. Took some mental adjustment.

Then I noticed the castle … I tipped my head back and sucked in a breath. Although tall stone spires and enormous arched windows revealed its great age, the castle was magnificent. Made me want to take a tour.

A brass mailbox stood beneath an ancient oak whose branches reached over the sidewalk providing shade for passersby as it had for centuries. A squirrel chattered from a lower branch and flicked its tail. It could see us.

Angus stepped onto the grass beneath the tree. "Stay close," he said. "And don't worry, we'll nae be seen. I've cast a weak spell over us. We'll look like shadows."

I was less concerned with being seen than I was with where this village was supposed to be. I flicked a glanced at the squirrel that kept up a tirade of scolding. "Why can the tree rat see us?"

"Animals see what's there. Humans see what they expect te see and, since most believe magic is impossible, it takes only a nudge for them te ignore us. Their eyes see us but their brain filters out the image because o' their beliefs. Tis the brain that sees, nae the eyes."

"How did that guy walk through me?"

"Matter is made o' vortexes o' empty space so, since the human knew no one was there, he could walk through ye."

"Seriously?"

His bright blue eyes twinkled. "Ye passed through him as well, did ye not?" Before I could ponder that, he grasped my wrist. "This could get a wee bit bumpy."

And I was jerked into a maelstrom of energies that squeezed and spun me through some kind of tube. Couldn't they make these things bigger?

I staggered as a street materialized beneath my feet but my head continued to spin. I sucked in a few deep breaths. "What was that?" With hands on knees, I told myself I didn't need to vomit.

"Twas a short-cut."

"Could we take the long way in future?" I swallowed, straightened, and huffed out a deep breath. "Where are we now?"

"In the mailbox. Tis where the village is." At my dumbfounded expression, he winked and said, "Tis magic, lass."

No shit.

The narrow twisting street was lined with stone buildings that faced onto cobblestones. Some were homes, others stores and assorted businesses. Didn't look like much municipal planning had gone into the place. An assortment of people strolled along the street. As children dashed about, every once in a while one would wave its stick – *wand* – and something would materialize. The adults would smile and continue with what they were doing and, after a few minutes, the materialized object or animal would dissolve into grey mist.

It was past noon but the sun was warm so Angus picked up the pace. "Tis nae far. I'm interested in your observations about someone."

"What kinds of observations?"

"The person in question is unusual in Maj Block 1. He seems te be human."

My brows ascended. "What would a human be doing here?"

"And how did he get here?" added Angus. "He's at a friend's house. Tis why I was called. Ye see, the human is pretending te fit in but my friend is nae easy te fool and I don't need te explain how important it is humans don't know about us. They can't hurt us but it would be far less easy te move about in their society if they knew. Since they don't want te know anyway, tis better for all concerned if they remain ignorant."

"You want me to find out what he's hiding."

"It would be helpful if ye could. I can read magical creatures but I don't spend enough time with humans te read their thoughts well. I imagine you've had much more experience if only for survival."

"Dorian and I are both sensitive that way. What do you want me to look for?"

"We'll be wanting te know how he got here."

"Can't you ask him?"

"My friend gets the feeling the stranger's nae telling the truth. O' course, it might've been an accident. Could be he's scared te death and afraid te admit it."

We came to a wrought-iron gate set into a high stone wall where a tinny voice filtered through the bars. After Angus had confirmed his identity, the gate swung open. We marched along a narrow path through a bewildering variety of flowers that nodded in a refreshing breeze that was confined to the yard. As I inhaled the bouquet of scents, I imagined it would be a wonderful place to spend an afternoon. A swinging bench, a mug of coffee and a book.

We were greeted by a man with longish grey hair, plaid trousers, and a white shirt open at the neck. Angus introduced him as Gord Gruenwalden. Backless slippers slapped against bare heels as we were led through a dim hall to a bright and airy kitchen that was cool despite sunshine which poured through tall windows.

A thin-faced blonde individual with long fingers sat at a table tapping a cup of tea. Pale grey eyes evaded mine as we shook hands. His name was Ted and he was pleased to meet us.

As I subsided onto a wooden chair with a tied-on blue cushion, I opened my awareness to the stranger who certainly *was* hiding something. But he didn't feel sneaky. Perhaps Angus had been correct with his first guess; the guy was lost and scared. After all, he was a non-magical person in a magical realm. His arrival could've been a mistake although how that could've happened was beyond me. How would he have gotten through the mailbox?

I could tell by his repeated surreptitious glances at Angus that he was curious but afraid to ask. After all, the mage didn't look like your average dude. The solid gold circlet alone would evince curiosity.

Gruenwalden brought Angus and me tall, cold glasses of iced tea and settled at the end of the table. I was across from Ted.

An uncomfortable silence fell – uncomfortable for Ted, that is. He fidgeted and loosened the collar of his shirt. Angus glanced at me with a lifted brow. I nodded. Ted knew this was somewhere very strange but had no clue where he was.

"Are you a … a . . .," he stammered. "I mean; are you an actor or something?" His accent was New York.

Angus gazed at him. "I'm nae an actor."

"Then … then . . ." He trailed off.

"Would ye tell us how ye got here?"

"I … don't know. I was taking the garbage to the alley when I heard a couple of men whispering. I was behind a hedge and about to step into view when I heard something about collecting unicorns. Now ain't that a damn silly topic for two grown men? But one said it wouldn't be long now. When they had enough, they'd kill them all and, without them, the dark energies would take control of the world.

"Didn't make sense to me but, by then I wasn't so sure I wanted them to see me. I ain't got no patience for crazies." He made a circling motion with his finger at the side of his head. "I couldn't get by without them seeing me so I waited, hoping they'd leave."

"You're from New York?"

"Of course." His expression said, *Is there anywhere else?*

"Well, you're nae in New York now. What happened next?" His attention had, of course, been snagged at the mention of unicorns. My senses confirmed Ted was telling the truth. He didn't understand it though.

"I … I ain't sure. They looked around kind'a sneaky like; one brought out a thin stick and waved it in the air. This whirlpool of light started spinning around them and … it somehow caught me too." He looked around. "That's when I found myself here … which is where? Have I been in an accident and I'm in a hospital high on drugs? Because I'm seeing things here that just ain't possible! This can't be real!"

"There are many ways te define *real*." said Angus. "Can ye tell me more about the unicorns? Did they say anything else about them?"

Ted looked at the table and licked his lips. I could feel confusion and fear but not subterfuge. He just wanted to go home. "They said the herd was starting to cause changes in the area." He looked up. "I've no clue what that means. He said they wouldn't be able to hold them much longer and the window of opportunity to kill them was closing."

He looked at Angus. "How do you kill a made-up creature? I mean, everybody knows unicorns ain't real, don't they?"

"Did they say where they were holding the unicorns?"

Ted closed his eyes with the effort to remember. "They did say something … didn't make sense. They said the mountain meadow wouldn't hold them much longer … and something about Switzerland."

He looked at the rest of us. "That's it. Hope it makes sense to you because it don't to me. Now, I've answered your questions, you answer mine. Where the hell am I?"

"Ye were caught in a transportation vortex. Tis nae necessary ye understand the phyics o' it. Think o' it as a controlled mini-wormhole and will be close enough. The spin comes to a halt in the centre, leaving room te travel."

Ted's laugh was part scoff and part incredulity. "What is this place? *Magic!*"

"Just so," said Angus. "But ye'll not find it again and your friends will nae believe ye. Ye'll think 'twas but a dream but I'll ask ye not te mention it, especially the part about the unicorns. The wrong people may hear ye and know it was nae a dream. They'll have little regard for your welfare, especially if they knew ye'd overheard their conversation. I canna stress enough that ye keep this te yourself for your own safety."

Ted could stand it no longer and gestured to Angus. "Why are you dressed like that? Are you in a Scottish band or something? I thought they wore tams, not that gold thing around your head. What's it for? And how come you know how I got here?" He looked around the room. "Wherever *here* is."

Angus almost smiled. "Tis nae necessary for ye te know. Step outside with me and I'll send ye home. Ye'll take a wee nap and think it all a dream."

"No it won't! You can't make me think this place is a dream!"

"Perhaps." Angus gestured. "Shall we?"

Ted took a final swallow of his iced tea and, with hunched shoulders, stepped out the back door. There was no such thing as magic … but still … The door closed, there was a brilliant flash, and Angus returned alone.

"So that's the end of it?" I asked. "He seemed genuinely lost."

"He'll think twas a dream, especially since a lot of it couldn't possibly be true … and he will nae talk about it."

An hour later, the sun still high, we closed the wrought-iron gate behind us. Angus stopped to ask, "How well could ye read the human?"

"Very well. He was confused … scared."

Angus frowned. "Then tis fortunate we met him – and I don't believe in coincidence." He turned away with an abrupt motion. "I need te talk te Cash. We'll keep our second appointment and return te Cumulos wi' all speed." As he strode away, I scrambled to keep up.

Chapter 7

Our second stop was a three-story house. The first floor was built of stone, the rest of weathered wood. A dwarf with dark hair shot with grey and wearing a loose shirt answered Angus' knock. As we stooped to get through the door, I had the unique experience of feeling tall as my hair brushed the ceiling.

Our host gestured toward a living room filled to bursting with overstuffed furniture. As I stooped beneath the low doorframe, it reminded me of a friend's doll house when I was seven. I settled onto a sturdy wooden stool next to a bristled broom which leaned against a plastered wall. Angus lowered onto a cushioned couch, stretched out long legs and crossed them at the ankles. I noticed he wore old-fashioned Scottish footwear with ties crisscrossed around the calves.

"Mr. Dandicolt, I'd like ye te meet White Raven, a visitor from the Americas."

Dandicolt startled but caught himself and extended a hand in greeting. "Tis a pleasure te meet ye, Miss White Raven." His voice was rough and scratchy, his hand hard like a human labourer's. If fact, it was larger than most men's, no doubt a result of tunnel-digging ancestors. His stocky build would support the theory. I shook his hand and declined an offer of tea as did Angus who wanted to return to Cumulos with all speed.

The dwarf settled into an easy chair patterned with bright red poppies, arranged his squashed visage into an expression of polite interest, and waited for Angus to speak.

"I need te collect the mirror I left with ye a few months ago," said Angus. "I appreciate ye storing it but tis time for it te be used."

Dandicolt's dark complexion paled. "Are ye sure, Angus? Twill nae cause any problems down there."

"Thank ye, Mr. Dandicolt, but ye've taken the responsibility long enough. Tisn't even your burden, tis mine. Disturbing things are happening and we'll need all the help we can get before tis too late. The Scrying Mirror of Grodonon must be used no matter the consequences.

Our host held Angus' gaze a moment longer then nodded and slipped off the chair.

"Come with me."

As he marched on short, strong legs to the back of the house, Angus motioned me ahead of him. I ducked through a rounded doorway that led to a stone tunnel that sloped downward in a slow spiral. Sconces on the walls burst into flame at our approach.

"What's the Scrying Mirror of Grodonon?" I asked with a glance over my shoulder.

"A normal scrying mirror allows ye te see what's happening anywhere ye wish. Ye set your intent and the image appears in the shadows o' the mirror. The Scrying Mirror of Grodonon does the same but also creates a transportation corridor – a mini-wormhole if ye prefer. Ye can use the mirror te travel anywhere, but the person you're scrying may see ye, and they can use the corridor te travel in an instant te wherever ye are. If you're scrying a dark magician, he could use it te attack ye and take the mirror for his own."

"Sounds dangerous."

"Just so. The Scrying Mirror of Grodonon has been hidden for so long most mages think tis just an old legend. And that's a good way for it te stay."

"If it's so dangerous, why are you using it?"

"I'm nae going te use it … *you* are."

I stumbled, hoping I'd misheard. My stomach spasmed.

"What do you mean, *I'm* going to use it?"

"Tis possible ye and Dorian may be able te view with the Grodonon mirror without the observed person knowing."

"Why would that be?"

"I'll explain when we return te Cumulos." And he wouldn't say another word.

As we spiralled down, claustrophobia closed in. *Have I mentioned I don't like small places?* The tunnel got narrow and steep. Just as my thighs began to knot and burn, the tunnel leveled and we approached a heavy stone door about four feet high. Dandicolt made a gesture then inserted a heavy iron key into the latch and pulled the door towards us.

As I ducked through the opening, flashes illuminated absolute blackness, making me catch my breath at the sight. Small doors were cut into the walls of a cavernous circular stone room. There must've been hundreds, none of which had handles. Only magic spells would open these vaults. The mind boggled at the hidden secrets.

Dandicolt trudged across the room to the far side, stopped and pointed to a door that looked like all the others. "There. Number ten-fifteen. Needs your spell te open it."

Angus muttered something too low for me to hear and, with a scraping sound, a cylinder of stone slid from the wall. The mage transferred an object wrapped in red felt to an embroidered bag slung across his chest. Dandicolt's expression was grave but he refrained from comment.

At a wave of Angus' wand, the shelf retracted into the wall and I heard it lock with a soft "snick." As we retraced our steps, I asked. "Why would you show me the mirror and this place? You don't know me that well."

Angus slanted a look at me as I preceded him through the door. "If ye do anything that makes ye feel guilty with regard te the mirror or this storage vault, all memory o' it will be erased from your mind. I trust twill not be necessary."

I trusted not.

By the time we emerged into Dandicolt's living room, I was winded and my thighs burned, but Angus and Dandicolt never even took a deep breath. Another gap in my knowledge, it seemed. All my huffing and puffing were embarrassing.

"Would ye like te rest a few minutes, Raven?" Angus asked.

I rubbed my thighs and sighed. "Better to keep moving. Might stop my legs from cramping up."

Angus smiled. "We return te Cumulos." He bowed to Dandicolt. "When we've finished with the mirror, I'll return it for safekeeping. My thanks for your guardianship."

Dandicolt dipped his head. "'Tis my pleasure te serve. May ye walk in safety."

"And ye."

Minutes later, we were beneath the giant oak. The squirrel had moved further up the tree but peered at us out of black shoe-button eyes, scolding as loud as its little voice could manage. An irritating little tree rat. Angus surveyed the peaceful street and waited while my stomach recovered.

"Am I ever going to get used to that?"

"In time."

I looked up from my stooped position with hands on knees. "How much time?"

"Hard te say." Angus waved his wand, the street wavered, and we materialized in the dim light of the Cumulos courtyard where the setting sun cast long shadows as it sank towards the horizon.

Dorian was accompanied by the pungent aroma of horse when he arrived later that evening followed by Cash who had what I hoped was a grin on his terrifying visage.

"That was incredible! I may never go back to a broom!" Dorian flopped onto a comfortable chair before the roaring fire and began to describe the long flight of the day, a rare glow of relaxed happiness in his eyes.

I wondered if Denver would ever again be enough for either of us. As their deep male voices carried on, I gazed around the circular quartz room whose ceiling disappeared into the dimness. Thick, warm rugs in tones of red warmed the room and a sideboard held leftovers from the evening meal.

I was surprised to realize that for the first time in my life, I had a sense of peace and safety. *So this was what it felt like.*

The evening flew and, after the fifth smothered yawn, I gave up and staggered for the stairwell. Dorian was close behind and, as we parted to go our respective ways, he kissed me on the forehead.

"Sleep well," he said, and was gone.

I was frozen to the spot at the unusual gesture of affection. Cumulos was having a profound effect. A smile tugged at my lips as I began the long climb.

Chapter 8

Over the following weeks, Dorian and I lived and breathed magic, astonished at the ways it could be used. Angus remained in his study except for the times he'd burst from it to deluge us with instructions on the use of our wands for countering black magic.

One grey afternoon, the sound of rain dripping onto the window ledge interfered with my focus on his monologue about the Grodonon mirror. I must admit I was uneasy about the ominous device. Instructions over the previous few days had been quite graphic about spells gone wrong and I wasn't eager to use the thing.

My gaze rested with a lack of focus on the mantelpiece until I noticed something looked back at me. I yelped. It was the over-sized rat I'd seen in the library; hunched down, rat belly bulging at the sides. I suddenly realized what had seemed odd about it at first glance – it was bald except for twitching whiskers – and its body was covered in tattoos!

I have to say, it has not once occurred to me to wonder if rats have wrinkled skin. Who in their right mind would care? Now, I knew far too much about what was under their fur. Other than a multitude of tattoos, this one sported one item of jewelry – a spiky collar with a crystal pendant.

Most unsettling though, was its focus on me.

In a calm manner, I interrupted Angus' lengthy explanation of something I was supposed to be absorbing and pointed to the mantelpiece. "What's that?"

Dorian, with a pained expression, covered his ears. "For god's sake, Raven! You'll burst our eardrums!"

Angus stumbled to a halt. "What on earth's the matter, lass?"

"That … that rat! It's watching me!"

Dorian glanced at the mantle. "What rat?"

I stared at him, dumbfounded. "How can you miss it? The thing's the size of a god damned cocker spaniel!" I turned back to the rat, stunned to see an empty shelf. "But … but it was there seconds ago! A huge, bald, tattooed rat!"

Dorian folded his lips together in what I knew was a valiant effort to keep from laughing.

"It's not funny, Dorian! It was there!"

Dorian and Angus exploded into guffaws until tears spilled from their eyes. To say I was not amused is the understatement of the century. I locked my jaw, crossed my arms, and tapped a rapid beat with my toe.

When Dorian could speak, he spluttered, "Are you hearing yourself, Raven? *A huge, bald, tattooed rat?*" He burst into laughter again. "Where do you get this stuff?"

My eyes were mere slits and I shoved my nose in his face. "Keep it up, funny guy! My question is, why didn't you see it?"

"Raven," he said, wiping tears from his eyes, "when I start seeing things like that, I'm going back to Denver!"

I growled and turned to Angus who'd gotten himself under control. "What the hell was it you wanted me to do?!"

"One o' the unicorn herds grazes on a series o' meadows near a remote northern loch." As Angus waved a hand, a hologram of steep hillsides appeared above the table. "Fix this image in your thoughts as ye look into the mirror."

"You're sure it's safe?" I glanced at Dorian for moral support but he was leaned against a nearby pillar, arms and ankles crossed, eyes narrowed, miffed that Angus had asked me to go first. I'd have accused Dorian of pouting if I'd ever seen him do it.

"If I suspect a threat, I'll disrupt the conduit."

A disturbance of the thin film of water poured onto the mirror was supposed to break the connection. I took a deep breath, held an image of the meadow in my mind, and gazed into the reflective darkness.

I saw my own face.

Angus instructed me to allow my eyes to glaze and focus beyond the image. If I persisted, three-dimensional images would appear in real time.

At first I was afraid I'd see something but, as time dragged on, feared I wouldn't. Angus encouraged me to persist. After all, he said, it was my first try.

After a half hour and the beginnings of a headache, I was ready to tell Angus where he might put his mirror when something caught my eye. I could've sworn … there it was again! A movement in the exact center … My eyes adjusted in and out of focus and, as I learned to ignore my reflection, perceived movement beneath the surface. I didn't need encouragement now.

A pastoral scene of a dozen unicorns emerged. One jerked its head up, stopped chewing, and stared before going back to grazing. I caught my breath at the realization that these were real creatures!

Something dark moved – a shadow amidst darker shadows. I thought my eyes were playing tricks when I perceived a man in a dark cloak on a smoky horse. They moved towards the herd. The unicorns became restive, ears flicking but it was obvious they couldn't perceive the intruder. The rider approached the animals, made a circular motion – and the nearest faded from view. I watched as the process was repeated twice more.

I was so wrapped up in the image I was shocked when a thousand spiders skittered up my back. Metaphorical or not, they freaked me out. The shadow-man had frozen as if listening. In slow motion, the hood of his cloak turned towards me, the aura of menace staggering. I couldn't move.

With lightning speed, Angus whipped the surface of the water and the image vanished. I sank onto the nearest couch, light headed and cold.

"Who the hell was that?" My voice was hoarse.

Angus tipped the water out and covered the mirror with its red cloth. Lines appeared on his forehead as he paced. "Surely it canna be," he mumbled. "It canna be . . ."

Dorian plopped down beside me, arm around my shoulders, brown eyes anxious. "Are you alright?"

"I think so." A violent shiver rippled through me. "But I'm really, really … cold."

Dorian pointed his wand at the fireplace until flames roared. As a wall of heat slammed into us, he selected a plaid coverlet from the couch, wrapped it around my shoulders, and pulled me against his chest.

"You're like ice," he said, shooting an accusatory glare at Angus.

The oblivious object of his ire paced around his desk. I imagined how many times in the past he'd done just that, hands clasped behind his back, eyes on the floor, thoughts miles away. But Dorian's warmth felt so wonderful I didn't care how long it took for Angus to return. I'd never been in Dorian's arms and it felt every bit as good as I'd thought it would.

Eventually the mage dropped into a chair to peer at me from beneath bushy red eyebrows. "Are ye warmer now?" I nodded. "We had a verra narrow escape if that's who I suspect it was."

"Who'd that be?"

"A dark mage I thought te have died many centuries ago, one o' the verra few who came into this world with evil in his heart. If there hadn't already been dark energies, he'd have invented them."

Angus nodded to himself. "Yet it makes sense. He'd remove anything that threatened his domination, and the unicorns would be at the top o' that list." His brows drew together. "If he killed them himself, their essence would contaminate his evil. Also, someone might discover their remains, and no magical creature would ignore the mass murder o' sacred unicorns. He'd have te remove the creatures te where they'd never be found, have someone else do the murdering. What Ted overheard must've been his helpers who hold the unicorns captive."

"Who is this mage?" asked Dorian.

"His name is Mydryth!"

"What does he want?" I asked.

Angus looked like he'd eaten something sour. "The destruction of all. He sees it as Nature's way."

"But science has discovered neg-entropy. Without it Earth would be barren rock," said Dorian.

"Mydryth would see it as another evil."

I raised an eyebrow. "Neg-entropy?"

"Entropy is the constant breakdown o' physical matter," explained Angus. "The theory is that the universe started with a finite amount o' energy and tis running down like a wound clock.

"Neg-entropy, on the other hand, is the opposite. Take a plant in a pot in the sun. Sow a tiny seed in, let's say, five pounds o' soil. Only water is added but soon the seed sprouts and begins te grow. In a few weeks, the plant has dozens o' leaves, a fine healthy stalk, and flowers bloom.

"Where did all the matter o' the plant come from? What are the flowers made o'? Not the soil because, other than a few miniscule amounts o' mineral absorbed by the plant, the soil is still there. So it didn't turn into the plant. How about the water? If ye were te measure all the water ye poured into the plant and compared it te the water that evaporated, ye'd find verra little missing. And the plant is obviously nae water although it uses water for its processes. By now it consists o' trillions o' specialized cells each doing what it was designed te do.

"The only other thing is sunshine. The plant has transmuted the energy o' the sun into matter. 'Tis true alchemy. A tree weighing thousands o' pounds is built o' nothing but sunshine. If that is'na magic, I don't know what is!"

"I don't imagine explaining it to him would do any good," said Dorian.

"Mydryth is all about self-indulgence and control. He's nae interested in reason."

"What can we do?"

"Our most powerful weapons are ye and White Raven. If I'd been scrying Mydryth, he'd have sensed my presence in an instant. Even so, as ye could see, he suspected something."

He jumped to his feet. "At least now we know who's stealing the unicorns, we can come up with a plan but it'll nae be easy." Angus gave us a hard look. "Never challenge him yourselves. Ye *will* lose!"

I shivered and leaned into Dorian. "Don't worry!"

"Thank ye for your help. Ye've assisted more than ye can imagine." He glanced at an ornate hour-glass on a carved wooden pedestal. I've got studying te do." He moved to a wall of books, lifted into the shadows, and began searching the titles of ancient tomes along the top rows. As he waved a wand, two of the old books slid from the shelf to float to his desk where they settled with a puff of dust. Soon, half a dozen more were piled in an irregular stack and Angus had forgotten us.

As I was beginning to sweat, I moved away from Dorian's embrace which was feeling all too good anyway. "Thanks," I said, avoiding his gaze as I re-folded the coverlet with exaggerated care. "We should probably go practice…something."

The next day, we worked on memorizing spells until my brain felt ready to explode. I was levitating a chair whose wobble hinted at a lack of control when we received a message that Angus wanted to see us again.

"Thank god!" I said, letting the chair fall with a crash. "Let's go!"

The mage was immersed in a huge volume when we tapped at the open door and he gestured without looking up. Head still spinning from the day's exertions, I sank down with a sigh of relief and a hope that he wouldn't have any complicated issues to solve. I wouldn't be of much use if asked to think.

Silence settled over the room as Angus traced a column of writing which was interspersed with drawings of magical beings. He gave a grunt of satisfaction and looked up.

"Thank ye for coming. I may have something." He leaned back with a squeak of leather. "Since ye're both different enough te be hard te detect, it should nae be difficult te cast an invisibility spell around ye."

He opened a desk drawer and withdrew two amulets on silver chains which he handed to us. The amulets were flattened spheres containing what looked like quicksilver in the shape of a galaxy deep in the darkness.

"How does it work?" I asked.

"Te become invisible, ye squeeze the amulet for a couple o' seconds. Te return, repeat the process."

I slipped the chain over my head, grasped the object, and squeezed. As the light in the room made a subtle shift, I realized I could no longer see my body. Even strands of hair and the shadow of my nose were gone. A second squeeze and everything returned to normal.

Dorian examined his. "What's in there?"

Now, I believe this is a basic difference between the sexes. My first concern was *if* it worked, and his was *how* it worked. Maybe it's a man thing.

"Enchanted quicksilver in dark matter."

"Isn't dark matter in space?"

"That's what makes it difficult te collect. The Phoenix is the only creature that can fly high enough te capture miniscule bits at a time from the edge o' the atmosphere. What ye see in the amulets has taken over a year te collect."

"And you want to give them to us?"

"Ye'll need them."

By the time Angus was satisfied we could use the amulets, I was smothering yawns. It'd been a long day and I thought with longing of my cozy bed in one of the towers.

"Ye'll not be able te evade Mydryth without protection," I heard Angus say through fuzzy attention. "Tomorrow I'll teach ye more spells te guard against the dark energies." Sharp eyes peered at me. "I apologize for keeping ye so late but time is verra short. I received word today the unicorn disappearances are increasing."

After another jaw-cracking yawn, I pushed to my feet. "I need to sleep. We'll have to rescue the unicorns tomorrow."

As we walked to our rooms, Dorian gestured to our surroundings. "There's so much information on magic here! A person could live hundreds of years and not learn it all."

"Maybe that's why mages live so long," I mumbled. "They have to."

We chuckled at that, Dorian lit his wand, and we began the long climb to our chambers in relative darkness. All these stairs should keep me in shape, but what I wouldn't give for an elevator!

We were half-way up the fourth set when I suspected we'd taken a wrong turn. "Please tell me we can get to our rooms this way."

Dorian brightened his wand and peered into the darkness. "Guess we'll find out."

We resumed climbing until we found a long hallway I'd never seen. "This way," said Dorian. As if he knew where he was going, he turned to the right and marched away with a confident stride.

I swiveled my head both directions but could detect no difference. Perhaps Dorian's theory was, "When in doubt, make a decision – any decision." I scampered after him, lit my wand, and grumbled about the lack of electricity.

Dorian stopped before a narrow hallway that intersected from the left. "This goes the right direction. Let's try it."

Plan B was dark and narrow but, if it was going to lead to my chambers, I was willing to chance it. Glued to Dorian's side, I followed his lead until we came to a solid wooden door hung with iron hinges. "This should be the tower stairwell," said Dorian.

"Which tower?"

"Hopefully the one with our rooms."

Hopefully?' Selecting the wrong tower would mean *a lot* of backtracking.

It was locked but, at Dorian's incantation, the latch lifted, and it swung towards us. My stomach went into an instant spasm at the pit of blackness.

"We should go back to the main stairs," I blurted, and spun in my tracks.

Dorian's hand clamped onto my wrist. "It's not far." He stepped onto a landing. With a brilliant flash, a blue-white light shot from the tip of his wand.

I sucked in a breath. It was like staring into infinity. The stairs wound in a spiral along the inside of the wall.

"It's only a few more floors," said Dorian, starting upwards with my wrist still in his grasp.

You see, I've always had this fear of heights. Ironically, I'm not the least bit afraid of flying on a broom. It's only in relative proximity to the ground that I get worried. Perhaps I'm afraid of being hurt. Falling from a broom would make getting hurt implausible. Being dead was ensured. Whatever the reason, this situation activated my vertigo.

I slid against the wall and tried not to look over the edge. It would've been helpful to have a handrail, but old castles hadn't been built with safety in mind and only an inky blackness met my gaze. It didn't seem to bother Dorian as he chugged along like a machine. To him, it was a fun adventure.

The endless steps caused my legs to burn and I was grateful when Dorian stopped at an old wooden door near the top of the tower. As expected, it was locked. I grumbled that it was locked for good reason as I couldn't imagine a more dangerous set of stairs.

As the door swung open, I had a flash of premonition and stepped to the side in a reflexive movement. A dark shadow slammed into my shoulder. If I hadn't moved, it would've catapulted me into the abyss. As it was, I was off balance and fell back. Terror gripped me and my arms flailed. One foot found purchase – but the other met only air.

A scream escaped as I tipped into blackness . . .

75

Chapter 9

Time stopped in an eternal instant of disbelief and terror. This couldn't be happening! I wasn't falling to my death! How Dorian would laugh when I told him what I'd imagined! As blackness closed, my thoughts were coherent enough to notice something powerful had clamped onto my ankle and, through a haze of horror, perceived Dorian's white face over the edge of the stairwell.

"Raven! Stop squirming! I can barely hold you! Keep your wand bright! I dropped mine!"

I hadn't realized I still had it. Too terrified to do otherwise, I hung immobile as Dorian pushed to his knees then, with a powerful heave, brought me even with the landing.

"Give me your hand!"

I waved my arm in his general direction until I felt my wrist clamped in a vice. Another heave and I was on the stairs. With a tight grip on me, Dorian scuffled backwards until we were against the wall. My arms were around him like a baby monkey, plastered to his chest in a failed effort to control the violent tremors from the adrenalin that surged through my veins. Funny how something like a near-death experience clears the head. I was no longer sleepy – and I could check that off my list of life experiences I'd have preferred to avoid.

I don't know how long it took for the tempo of Dorian's heart beneath my ear to return to normal and the barrage of tears washing my face to slow. It occurred to me I may be as important a companion to him as he was to me. There was no one else for us – at least so far.

The grip of his arms and the feel of his cheek pressed against the top of my head were incredibly comforting. Along with the co-mingling of our breaths, there arose a sense of intimacy we'd never known, a newfound and delicate sensation neither of us wanted to disturb.

Although I'd have preferred to stay wrapped in Dorian's arms forever, the real world intruded with rude insistence as the chill of stone sucked heat from my body. I glanced at the abyss and shuddered. "Let's get out of here!"

I was surprised at what seemed his reluctance to let me go.

"Wait," said Dorian as he loosened his hold. "My wand is on the stairs and it's not coming to me so the magic must be disturbed." He pushed me against the wall and rose with care. "Stay here!"

"Don't worry," I said, wrapping my arms around raised knees and pushing against the cold stones. "I'm not going anywhere."

The planes of Dorian's face were harsh as he descended a half dozen stairs, scanning the darkness. As soon as he'd grasped the wand, he sprinted back and grasped my upper arm, pulled me to my feet. "Let's go. Stay close." Like I was going to wander off!

Although the door had re-sealed, it yielded to Dorian's unlocking spell. He pressed me against the wall with one arm while peering into the inky maw. Keeping a tight hold on my wrist, he shot a brilliant light down the corridor to reveal curved crystal walls that narrowed to a point. Dorian's hair would brush the ceiling. We eased into it.

"Should be an entrance soon," he muttered a few minutes later.

When a narrow door appeared in the wall, Dorian released my wrist long enough to try the well-oiled latch. A sigh of relief escaped us as it swung open to the equivalent of a living room where a cheerful fire crackled. Couches and overstuffed chairs were scattered about in conversational groupings, several pulled near the fireplace. The door merged into the wall behind a coat rack which supported a weathered Macintosh and blue plaid scarf.

I shivered and scampered to the blazing fire, palms out. For the second time that day, I was chilled.

"I'll make hot chocolate," said Dorian, going to the sideboard. He passed a hand over a tray, and a silver urn with two cups appeared. He brought them to a low wooden table then pushed an overstuffed chair close to the fire. After retrieving a green plaid throw, he pushed me onto the couch and draped it around my shoulders.

"Drink this," he commanded as he gave me a steaming cup. "It'll help."

He pulled another chair opposite mine, scanned the room once more, and reclined into it. Firelight cast moving shadows along the planes of his face where I noticed faint stubble, and the silver streaks in his hair reflected red from the fire. Long legs stretched toward the heat, elbows propped on the padded arms of the chair, cup balanced in both hands. Flickers reflected from eyes that stared into the flames.

I sipped in silence, tried to comprehend that someone or something had tried to kill me – and whatever it was had dissolved like mist into the well of darkness.

After a long silence, Dorian blurted, "That was no accident, Raven."

"I know."

"If you hadn't stepped aside . . ." He closed his eyes. "I hate to even think about it."

"Yeah … me too."

He glanced over. "I'll sleep with you tonight."

My heart thudded but I tried to keep my expression neutral. "What?" My voice had a distinct squeak.

"I mean, I'll sleep in your room. Don't worry. I can behave myself." One side of his mouth quirked.

Sigh. Speak for yourself.

I pondered yet again how Dorian and I avoided a closer relationship although I knew we were both afraid of the risk.

My head felt fuzzy. I'd have to think about it tomorrow. I swallowed the last of my drink, pushed from the chair, and headed to the stairs. "I'll appreciate the company. See you up there."

Dorian shot to his feet, gave a quick wave at the dishes which floated to the sideboard where they stacked themselves. "Wait here while I get my stuff."

After he was gone, the room felt emptier … and scarier. It was frustrating that he could make me feel safe. *Perhaps because of the fact he'd just saved your life?* I scanned the room for shadows that might spring to life and was listing defensive spells when Dorian stepped into the room with a canvas bag over his shoulder. He raised an eyebrow at me, back against a wall, wand out.

I hated the tremor in my voice. "It … feels a lot more dangerous by myself."

"I know what you mean." His eyes softened. "You look beat. Let's go to bed." For some reason that sentence brought a rush of warmth to my insides that I thought it best to ignore.

We followed a narrow spiral staircase that led to a circular tower room containing two four-poster beds with green privacy curtains. Thick warm rugs were scattered over the crystal floor. Shafts of moonlight outlined puffy cushions and shadows flickered along the wall from a small fire.

Dorian tossed his bag onto the bed nearest the door as I drew curtains around the other and changed into sleepwear borrowed from Frost. I was chagrined to realize they were all sexy negligees with plunging deep necklines. I sighed, folded the clothes I'd worn that day and set them on the chair next to the bed. Soiled clothing would be cleaned and returned by morning and the fire would be burning when we awoke.

I opened the curtains to let in the heat then slipped beneath the covers hoping Dorian hadn't noticed all the exposed female flesh. For a few seconds and from a muzzy distance, I was aware of quiet movements as he readied for bed. Then nothing.

I jerked awake, heart pounding. The moon had moved on, the shadows that flickered along the walls the result of a low fire. My fingers curled around the wand beneath my pillow as I searched the shadows and recalled with a shudder my narrow escape of a few hours earlier. I inhaled a deep breath, tried to relax the tension that interfered with the performance of spells. Dorian's soft breathing carried to me, his solid form a comfort beneath a patchwork quilt on the other bed.

Could I have heard the ground gnomes that cleaned the castle? Not likely. Like invisible ghosts, I knew there were dozens in Cumulos but rarely saw one. My clothing was gone and the fire had been tended.

I froze in the hope an intruder would assume I was asleep, extended my awareness, searched for the threat. A sinister presence intruded into the room as a dark mist flowed beneath the door. I waited until it had formed a shape beside Dorian's bed then hurled a spell as I shot to my knees. At the same instant, Dorian rolled to his feet, wand in hand.

The resulting confusion of spells caused the dark mist first to freeze into a man-shape then dissipate.

I groaned and Dorian cursed as he came to sit on the side of my bed wearing only shorts. His muscled body snared my attention. My mouth was dry and I could see this sleeping in the same room wasn't going to work.

He expelled a deep breath and scanned the shadows before turning to me. "What woke you?…Raven?" He passed a hand in front of my eyes. "You okay?"

I dragged my eyes away from his chest and nodded. "Ahh…yeah. I…ah. I'm not sure what woke me. I thought you were asleep."

"I felt it outside the door," he said. "I thought *you* were asleep. You were pretty exhausted." His eyes roved over my sleep-tumbled hair and…lower. He swallowed and his eyes darkened as his gaze lingered on my exposed feminine curves.

"You look . . ." His hand moved as if to touch me but he stopped. He trailed off. "Look…ah . . ." He ran a hand through his hair, shot to his feet, and turned away. "I'll keep watch the rest of the night. We'll report this to Angus in the morning." He got up, tugged on jeans and a shirt, and moved to a chair in front of the fire. "I'll be here."

Feeling stupid, I burrowed under the blankets and slipped my wand back under the pillow. Why hadn't I done something instead of sitting there like an idiot? Why hadn't *he*?

Maybe it was time to re-think this whole hands-off relationship with Dorian. We were obviously attracted to one another. What was in our way now? As the vision of his incredible form danced before my closed eyes, I couldn't think of a single obstacle.

Chapter 10

Frost and Talon joined us in Angus' study after breakfast. We'd been introduced to the other two members of the tribunal but had seen little of them. Talon perched on a statue of a winged horse, spindly legs cramped into a meditative position. Bloodshot eyes hinted at a bad night and his mauve fur, ruffled in places and flattened in others, made my fingers itch to give him a good brushing. Our old dog sometimes got to looking like that.

Frost, dark hair in an intricate style and aglitter with jewels, was attired in a lot of flowing golden fabric. She lounged on a loveseat next to Angus whose size thirteens were propped on a bronze statue of a giant toad.

"Talon tells me the gnomes were disturbed last night," said Angus. "Kept saying the shadows were moving. They're still upset." He gestured towards Talon. "Tell us again what ye found."

Talon described how the proximity alarms had made a terrible racket in the middle of the night but had faded to silence in minutes. He'd spent the remainder of the night traversing the castle halls.

Frost had been awakened near midnight by the soft glow of her wand. After a few minutes, the glow had faded so she'd decided to wait until morning to report it.

About the same time, Angus had caught a glimpse of a shadow in the depths of the scrying mirror which had vanished the instant he'd performed a spell to reveal its identity.

After Dorian and I related our experiences, Frost said, "From now on, you'll stay with me, Raven. It's too dangerous for the pair of you to be without protection." She turned to Talon. "Perhaps our gentleman guest could stay with you?"

Talon twisted his mobile face into a grimace. "I work late so Mr. Drughorn would be a preferable host. His chambers are protected by spells and dozens of magic-sensitive plants."

"Verra well," said Angus. He no doubt realized Talon would make a less-than-friendly roommate anyway. "Frost, will ye speak with Mr. Drughorn?" At her nod, he continued. "Only a mage o' great power could get into Cumulos at all. We were lucky he set off the alarms. Although tis unlikely Mydryth identified us from Raven's scrying, Cumulos is a logical place te start."

He glanced from one to the other of us. "Tis fortunate ye woke in time. We'll ensure you're better protected in future. Talon, see what ye can find on Mydryth's history. There are bits o' information in these old books but details are difficult te come by. Perhaps ye have other sources?"

"Last week I acquired a rare copy of *'The Black Magicians, Volume II,"* said Talon, puffing his little purple chest. "In addition, there are other sources. I'll inform you when I've got something." He floated into the air, spindly legs still in a meditative position, and skimmed from the room.

Angus turned to Frost. "Could ye check for other incidents? We may have te call a general meeting."

Frost nodded. "Of course. Raven can accompany me and meet some of the other residents." She glanced toward Dorian. "Come along and I'll introduce you to Mr. Drughorn."

Dorian gave her a polite tip of the head. "Of course."

Angus glanced at the giant hour-glass and rose. "I've an errand te run." He moved towards a carved hematite wall and gestured in an arc. A swirling maelstrom of colors appeared into which he stepped and ... vanished. Seconds later, the wall again reflected the flickers of the fire. I wondered how long it would take to learn that.

"Come," said Frost as she swept toward the door. "We've work to do."

Mr. Drughorn, short and sturdy with mutton-chop sideburns, wore a faded baggy grey suit. As we entered his workshop, he was taking cuttings from some mature vines. It would've been easier if the foliage hadn't been so high.

Dorian reached a long arm over Mr. Drughorn's head and pulled down a thick tendril. The plant must've been tough as Dorian gave a few grunts before it got to Drughorn's level.

"This what you need?"

"Yes, please," said the small man as he lopped off a tendril.

Frost and I waited while Drughorn placed the cutting into one of many glasses of water that littered the room. This must be the source of all the flowering vines that climbed the castle walls.

After Frost had provided Drughorn with a rundown on the situation, he bobbed a silvery head. Of course, he'd be happy to have Dorian as a roommate. They'd retrieve his things as soon as he was finished with the plants.

Frost and I left them to their work and headed to Cash's place where he lived with his girlfriend, Basia, whom I hadn't met. If anyone knew of an intrusion, it would be Cash. We summoned our brooms to float up the steep hillside behind the castle.

The sun was in the process of dissolving the mist that had gathered in hollows overnight. As I stared at the gorgeous view, I collided with one of the tall obelisks that encircled the area. As my forehead and nose slammed into sandstone, I was lucky my broom caught me.

After the tears stopped, I perceived a forty-foot Egyptian obelisk carved with Celtic runes. Odd. One would think they'd be hieroglyphs. I can't imagine why I hadn't noticed them before. They were all over the place.

As I rubbed the bump that erupted from my forehead and explored the bloody scrape on the end of my nose, I asked Frost what on earth they were doing there.

It seemed their origins were lost to the mists of time but were the reason Cumulos was invisible. Together they anchored a dome of magic that sealed the floating island from the outside world. Although Cumulos castle was made of crystal, the obelisks were of sandstone. How, why, and by whom they'd been constructed remained a mystery.

I mused over this information as we approached Cash's rambling cottage. We touched down on a winding path and climbed a set of quartz stairs to a solid verandah where Frost tapped on the heavy wooden door with her staff.

Shuffling sounds came from inside along with a rumbling that might've been a voice from deep in a cave. The door, which I was sure couldn't be opened by an ordinary man, swung wide.

I'd had little to do with Cash to this point and was reminded that he was the biggest and ugliest man I'd ever seen. I tipped my head back to get a better look at his face. There was a lot of it topped by a shining bald head bigger than my exercise ball back in Denver.

I'd like to be generous but I doubt his own mother would've called him handsome. He'd gotten a double dose of testosterone though. He was eight feet of pure bulging muscle. Dressed in trousers and a vest, he clanked when he moved due to weapons that hung from leather thongs and belts.

Talk about intimidation! The guy scared the crap out of me! I kept a tight hold of my broom, only lessening the stranglehold when it squirmed. *Just so you know; you need to squeeze pretty hard to choke a broom.*

The rumbling began again. "Well! This is a nice surprise, Frost!" he said. "And you've brought White Raven. Come in!"

We stepped into an enormous kitchen where I watched him clank to the cupboards, lift down three huge cups for us, a truly monstrous one for himself, and set them on a scarred wooden table. Basia must've been expected to join us.

He dug out a dented metal teapot the size of a five-gallon pail which he filled from a tap that would've made a fire truck proud. Then he busied himself setting out cakes and honey as Frost and I climbed onto chairs that made me feel like Goldilocks.

"Now," said Cash sometime later as he finished pouring tea and reclined into an oversized chair made of tree trunks. "To what do I owe the pleasure? Want me to kill someone?" At my look of shock, he laughed until dust fell from the ceiling. "Just my sense of humour! What can I do for you?" He swallowed a quart of tea.

Besides being in charge of Cumulos' small army, Cash helped Basia who tended the gardens and fish ponds within the castle. A huge atrium provided food when the cloud community moved into northern or southern regions and the outside temperature dropped. I was assured that didn't happen often.

An interior door swung open and a chubby, friendly-looking thing trundled in trailing a line of dirt. Shy, twinkling dark eyes disappeared when she smiled and, when Cash introduced us, she shook my hand. I retrieved it along with a streak of mud across my palm. I'd have told her not to worry but it seemed she didn't. Conversation didn't seem to be her strong suit as she didn't utter a word the entire time.

As Basia settled beside Cash and helped herself to an outsized piece of cake, Frost asked him about the previous night.

His face twisted in concentration. "Now that you mention it, there *was* something odd last night! I was helping Basia feed the evening swans (they like to eat about midnight), when a colony of the biggest bats I've ever seen flew toward the castle. We didn't think much about it since bats are nocturnal creatures but, now I think about it, I've never known bats to be that big. I didn't notice because we don't normally consider wildlife as a military matter."

We spent the next half-hour discussing ways to sneak into Cumulos. There weren't many. When I'd polished off my pound of pound cake, I dragged my overstuffed body to the door as Cash sent message birds to the troops. I hoped my broom wouldn't object to added weight.

We spent the rest of the morning talking to local residents, most of who were surprised to hear about the intruder. Of course, they wanted an update from Angus so we arranged for discussions at the castle that evening.

After we'd returned to the castle, I headed to the eating area where I found Dorian in the dining room off the kitchen.

He was deep in a discussion with Drughorn. I took a chair next to him as gnomes delivered dishes of aromatic food. It seemed the cake didn't have much staying power as I was already famished. There were several pieces of fried chicken and some kidney pie on my plate when Dorian looked over and shook his head in disbelief.

"What? I'm hungry!" I said around a mouthful of chicken.

"I can't imagine why you aren't two hundred pounds." He did a double take. "What happened to your face?"

"Mmm … nothing."

"It looks like somebody punched you! There's a purple lump on your forehead and blood on your nose!"

Sigh. I'd been in such a hurry to eat, I hadn't thought to look in a mirror – which wasn't my fault. You have to look forever to find a mirror in Cumulos. I don't know what the deal is.

I pulled a lock of hair over my forehead. "There. I'll clean up later."

"I thought you were going to *talk* to people!"

"Are you going to eat?" I growled and, for a while, there was only the clinking of utensils.

"So … how'd it go?" asked Dorian, making another effort. "Besides the . . ." He gestured to my face.

"You could find out first-hand if you took over for the afternoon. I'm exhausted. Didn't get much sleep last night."

"And I did," he said with a slanted glance.

"I know you didn't either, but you're so much tougher than I." I even said it with a straight face.

As Dorian laughed out loud, people turned to look. He choked back guffaws and turned to me, chocolate eyes dancing. "Would you be willing to put that in writing?"

"No."

He chuckled and picked up a forkful of potatoes. "I said I'd help Drunvold finish trimming vines this afternoon so you'll have to struggle on."

"Who's Drunvold?"

"Drughorn."

I stopped with a forkful of potatoes halfway to my mouth. *"Drunvold Drughorn?* You're joking!"

"Nope. That's his name."

"His parents should've been sterilized."

After an exhausting day, we stepped into one of the gathering rooms to attend the evening meeting. It was filled with people and a low mumbling roar. Most had never heard of Mydryth, and Angus was deluged with questions. Talon floated at his shoulder offering opinions and I was miffed to realize Talon was more congenial to his fellow residents than he was to Dorian and me – well perhaps it was turning out to be mostly me.

The meeting continued late into the night. Everyone was to take whatever precautions they could. The castle cats, who scoured every inch of the grounds, were to be given collars with black magic sensors. Hyper-hounds, strange creatures that reacted with a baleful howl at the slightest touch of dark magic and looked like anemic greyhounds, would be set loose at night, and I'm sure Angus had other plans to which I wasn't privy.

It was close to midnight before everyone dispersed and I blinked dry eyes. "I've got to get to bed before I collapse."

Dorian slanted a look at me. "Kind of fading myself. Sleep tight." He chucked me under the chin then strolled away to his new quarters.

As I watched his retreating back, I worried at the disappointment I was feeling. Perhaps it was just that I wasn't used to spending so much time with him. Back home we led our own lives, got together when we felt the need to be with someone who understood.

On the one hand, I was glad to move in with a master witch like Frost but, on the other, perhaps we would've worked out whatever was developing if we'd had the privacy to talk and … well …

There was movement at my shoulder as Frost sent a knowing glance in the direction of my gaze. Angry with myself and horrified to feel heat in my cheeks, I fell into step with my all-too-perceptive companion.

Dim firelight flickered on the walls when I opened my eyes to Frost's darkened guestroom. What had awakened me? Surely not another attack already! I curled my fingers around the wand beneath the pillow, scanned the room without moving.

I felt eyes on me.

As I inched to a sitting position, a shadow moved. With a shriek, I scrambled behind the bed and, after a couple of botched attempts, activated the globe lights.

A bald, skinny, tattooed rat sat on its haunches on the nightstand, little front paws hanging over a disproportionate belly. Little rat eyes watched me, the crystal that hung from its collar reflecting flashes of firelight. A faint memory rose from the fog of sleep. Where had I seen this specimen before?

We seemed to be at a stalemate. I watched it as it watched me. Finally it heaved a little rat sigh, thin chest flexing.

"Good evening, Miss White Raven." Though its voice was thin and nasally, it sounded male and like it could be an English speech instructor.

I held my wand between us and scrambled further back. "Who … what are you?"

He spread his little arms (front legs?). "I'm obviously a rat, Raven. An outstanding specimen but definitely a rat."

"What do you want?"

"I made a recent move to Cumulos Castle in search of a new challenge. Imagine my surprise when I spotted you earlier? A completely uneducated magelet! How could I refuse?"

"Refuse what?"

"Why, the opportunity to become your familiar, of course!"

"My familiar *what?*"

He pursed little lips. "Do you know what a witch's familiar is?"

I searched my memory. "Aren't they animal companions, black cats or something?"

"That is correct." He tilted his head to the side and twitched his whiskers. "I have decided to become your familiar," he repeated.

I must've gaped as my brain froze. I stuttered. "Wh…why?"

"You are in need of one even though you aren't a witch."

"Well, you aren't a cat either!"

"True." He straightened and gave his tattoos a loving stroke. "You'd never see a cat with the likes of these!"

I agreed. No self-respecting cat would deface itself in such a manner.

"So, what does a familiar do?"

The rat settled back onto its haunches. "He lives with and teaches his witch. Since I believe it is my destiny to exceed normal limitations, I've decided to link to a mage, but I never imagined I'd have the good fortune to find one so adorably clueless. It will be a wonderful challenge that I expect will bring greater satisfaction in the end. Just think of me as your Professor Higgins."

I couldn't remember the name of the story, but knew it had to do with bringing a young woman from the streets of London and training her to speak like a well-bred society woman. It confirmed my original observation of his perfect speech patterns.

I narrowed my eyes at him. "I recall Higgins was ready to toss her back into the street after he'd won the bet!"

His whiskers twitched and he gave a little condescending laugh which showed tiny pointy teeth. "I've no intention of trying to pass you off as upper class, my dear. That would be too amusing."

"Then what the hell *do* you want?" My back teeth ached. I noticed he was about the size of a football and envisioned a perfect punt down the hall.

"To bring an under-educated stray to realize her potential, of course. It has always been my dream to perform the impossible."

My eyes were slits. "You pompous, arrogant little … Wait a minute. . . You said, *lives with?*"

"Of course, Raven. That's how it works. How could I teach you otherwise?"

"No you don't! I hate roommates! I'm selfish and messy, up at all hours, and I'm told I snore."

"Who told you that?"

"None of your business!"

"Not to worry. I can fix that. Familiars are magic, after all." He swiveled his little head. "That spot by the fire looks warm. I'll bring my things from the library."

Of course! I did a mental head-smack. The rat in the library! But that didn't mean I wanted the arrogant creature to become my new best friend! In desperation, I raised my voice. "I don't want a familiar, either cat *or* rat! I need my solitude!"

His round black eyes turned back to me. "By the way, the name's Cyril. See you in the morning." And he was off.

I sent him a parting shot. "Don't think you'll be sleeping in *my* bed!"

Chapter 11

Dorian and I huddled beneath an overhang a couple of days later as I cursed a downpour reminiscent of the biblical flood. Puddles ran together to create little streams which gathered into a small river that rushed through the broad front gate. I shivered and pulled my cloak tight.

"How the hell are we supposed to find unicorns in this?" I was cranky that I'd exchanged a roaring fire for the deluge of the century.

"The weather could be different where we're going." Dorian gazed at the flood-waters with a disturbing degree of optimism.

I don't understand men. Dorian didn't have the slightest difficulty leaving a warm castle to go for a ride in a storm. It seems things like weather conditions don't compute in the male brain while I'd rather have waited for the torrent to abate. But I'd agreed to collect the unicorns so here I was.

An errant blast of wind dumped a pint of icy water down my neck which trickled beneath my cloak and soaked my shirt. Wonderful. My boots were wet through and my patience was wearing thin. Where the hell was Angus?

A side door popped open and he trotted out in kilt and a Scottish shawl of some kind. Now, this is one of life's mysteries. Why is it that Scotsmen can wear skirts and shawls; their hats are tams with pompoms on them, and everyone moons over how masculine they are? Try that with any other kind of skirt and see what happens!

In the moments it took Angus to dash through an open area, he was soaked through. Ignoring the streams running into his eyes (the man thing again), he handed us each a small ivory disk carved with alien inscriptions.

"These will bring ye back." He gave us a simple incantation. "Envision Cumulos and ye'll return."

I grimaced at the flooded yard. "Got any weather spells?"

"This weather will hide ye better."

I sent a sour look at Cyril who crouched on a low stone wall beneath a leaf that acted as an umbrella. I got a perverse satisfaction at seeing him shiver. Guess the arrogance of exchanging fur for tattoos had its drawbacks.

I'd almost resigned myself to Cyril's presence in my life since Angus had informed me that once a familiar chose its companion, it would never give up, so I might as well.

I narrowed my eyes at the little creature. "Are you coming along on the grand adventure?"

He blinked. "It's raining."

"So I've noticed."

"I don't like to get wet."

"Neither do I."

"Seems I've made a better choice."

Angus interrupted my retort by handing us each a small glass vial containing a brush. "Touch each unicorn with a dab o' this enchanted quicksilver, but keep your wits about ye and be quick. Mydryth will be there in a heartbeat if he thinks anyone's messing with the beasties. "Are ye ready?"

I would never be ready.

I nodded – and was sucked into a dark spiral that made me feel like I'd been dropped into a washing machine on spin cycle. I'd lost all sense of control when there was a blast of light and I was flung into the air ass-over-teakettle as my grandfather used to say. My broom whisked me into the safety of an overcast sky where at least it wasn't raining.

It took a minute for my eyesight to recover before we shot across a meadow bordered on three sides by dark forests and a rocky outcropping swathed in blackberry bushes on the fourth. A stream meandered through the meadow until it became a narrow waterfall that plunged into a lush, broad valley … where hundreds of unicorns grazed the tall grass.

They were pure white with heavy long manes and tails and, though I'd been informed they were twice the size of an ordinary horse, I was stunned at their size.

After closing my jaw with a snap, I skimmed over the long waving grass, wand in one hand, paintbrush in the other. The unicorns glanced as we approached but then ignored us even as we touched their silky coats. Back and forth we sped, targeting each flank as my sense of time pressure increased.

It'd reached the point of desperation (probably my subconscious mind screaming at the closed door of my inattentive brain) when I felt the arrival of … *evil*.

One of us had flown over a sentinel stone – the magical equivalent of a proximity sensor. I tried to warn Dorian but he'd dropped over a shallow hill.

As I topped the low rise, a shadow formed behind him. I was reminded of a drawing of a harpie I'd seen in one of Angus' books but it was bigger and, if possible, meaner. Black leathery wings sprouted from something kind of human-looking except for a heavy sectioned tail that curved over its back towards its head.

Goddamn! Who the *hell* decided to create a flying human scorpion?!

So much for invisibility. The creature could see Dorian, there was probably more than one, and that meant they could see me … Tendrils of evil made the hair rise on the back of my neck and the temperature inside my body plummet.

As every instinct screamed to flee, a corner of my mind realized the unicorns took no notice, too pure to conceive of evil. Also, I imagined the scarpies (as I'd christened them) would be unable to hurt them as few beings could harm a unicorn without having the attack rebound.

The creators in the Ancient of Days had distilled pure innocence into the creatures and, though the corollary to such innocence was invincible power, unicorns could never be drawn into conflict. Few wars happened with a herd in the vicinity. Negative energy dissolved and people returned to their daily tasks without understanding they may have had a narrow escape. No wonder a war-monger like Mydryth was desperate to remove them. You couldn't get a good war going with all that positive energy in the way.

I put on a burst of speed and dove towards Dorian as two more scarpies closed behind him. Wind whipped tears from my eyes and Dorian must've thought I'd gone mad when I shot by the nose of his broom. At his startled expression, I held out the medallion and pointed behind.

After one glance, he shot straight up; I saw him reach into his shirt as a supernatural cold washed through me. A menacing winged creature was closing in, my arms were heavy, and it took all my strength to clutch the medallion and mumble the incantation as I envisioned Angus' study.

After a lurch that felt like I was being turned inside out, I skidded across a polished wooden floor to crash into a solid wall. Three more crashes followed as Dorian and our brooms arrived.

I groaned, put a hand to my head and used a table to leverage upright. Every bone in my body hurt and I felt like I'd been frozen from the inside out. Angus hurried to help me to a soft chair.

"Easy does it, lass."

Dorian climbed to his feet, staggered to a couch, and dropped his head into his hands. "Man, I feel like I got kicked in the head by a mule!"

After ensuring we were intact, Angus hurried to a wall of chemist's drawers to withdraw two glass flasks filled with powder. He poured a scoop of each into a small bowl and mixed them with a long-handled brass measuring spoon. Through a haze of disorientation and a pounding head, I saw him step back, mutter something, and wave his wand over the bowl. A flash of light congealed into a glowing ball which shot out the window.

"What was that about?" I asked, trying to speak low enough to prevent my head from exploding.

"It's te close the hole I made in the magic shield when I pulled ye back. Don't want te leave openings for Mydryth."

I rubbed my temples. "We need to figure out a different way to travel. My head is splitting!"

"My apologies for the rough landing. When I realized ye weren't alone, there was nae enough time te wait for your incantation." He spoke over his shoulder as he hustled towards the door.

"Where are you going?" asked Dorian, eyes squinted in pain.

Angus paused. "Te bring the unicorns o' course, before Mydryth realizes what the quicksilver's for."

Dorian and I looked at each other and pushed to our feet. This was not something we wanted to miss. We staggered down the steps that linked the study to the rest of the castle and into the inner courtyard where rays of sunshine shot through breaks in the clouds. A brilliant rainbow arched over inky clouds to the east.

Balls of light shot from Angus' fingertips to spin into a purple vortex. There was a brilliant flash – and fifty unicorns appeared, each with a luminous purple spot on its flank. I wondered if they'd noticed the change of scenery as they continued to graze.

This ignoring of evil thing seemed to me kind of naive. After all, how did you prevent being victimized? The sense of it all was less than obvious.

Angus wore a satisfied smile. "Well done! Tha' should put a crimp in his plans! The magic o' Cumulos will keep these unicorns safe." As I rubbed my forehead, Angus added, "Mr. Root will take a look at ye both and give ye a potion for the headache. We'll talk later."

I staggered to the low stone wall that surrounded the courtyard and sank onto it, winced as a bruised knee met with a protruding stone. I cursed and rubbed it, wondering where this Mr. Root was.

Dorian leaned against a pillar. "You alright?"

I gritted my teeth. "Relatively speaking. How are you?"

He rolled his shoulders. "Not bad considering how hard I slammed into that wall. Be sore for a day or so." He eased onto the stones beside me. "You know we have to go back."

I closed my eyes and groaned. "I know."

"We'll have to be fast."

I shuddered at the chill that crept up my spine. "We *were* fast."

Something brushed my elbow. "Cyril, if that's you, I don't have the patience . . ." I turned to see two lovely dark eyes with a small nub between them peering at me. One of the unicorn foals. My jaw dropped.

"Do you see this, Dorian?" I whispered without moving a muscle, afraid I'd frighten it away.

"It sees you," he whispered back.

"What do I do?"

"Hold the back of your hand out so he can sniff it."

"How do you know it's not a she?"

I could feel Dorian's inaudible sigh. "I lived on a ranch, Raven; I know the difference."

Oh.

The creature was so lovely, it made my heart hurt. Fingers relaxed, I inched my hand toward its velvety muzzle until it brushed against me, breathing in my scent. Then it glanced at Dorian, made an elegant turn, and wandered away to its mother.

"That was odd." Cyril was crouched on a dry rock; ropy tail drooped over the side.

I slanted my eyes towards him. "Why? I should be too evil for a unicorn to see?"

"No. But it takes a mage many centuries to be able to communicate with unicorns. To have one come to you is . . . astounding, especially considering . . ." He stopped short and cleared his throat. "As I said, it's odd." Round little eyes fastened on me with benign innocence.

Ripples in the stream splintered sunlight as Dorian and I skimmed along its surface watching for sentinel stones which could be hidden in the water. Huge trees lined both banks, branches intertwined in an arch. Growls and screeches echoed throughout the forest as I white-knuckled my way through narrow spots, shuddered as leaves brushed my cloak and imagination created scores of evil tendrils that whipped from the forest to rip me from my broom.

As an opening appeared, Dorian gave a thumbs-up, we put on a burst of speed – and something clamped onto my right shoulder. With what I'd like to think of as lightning-quick reflexes but was more likely reflexive panic, I jerked hard to the left.

As the grip slid away, I gave a sharp exhale. A snake-like tendril withdrew into the darkness, disappointed at letting breakfast slip away. I shivered and turned my attention to an upcoming turn.

Cattails nodded with the wind of our passing as we came to another gap in the trees and angled up a slope to view a wide meadow where a stiff breeze whipped the tops of tall grasses into waves. A herd of unicorns appeared to float chest deep in a green ocean. One flicked its ears at an annoying insect but continued with the business of grazing in the sunshine.

As Dorian sped to the far side of the herd, I ducked to the right and began to circle, targeting left handed with the brush, keeping my wand at the ready in my right.

Shiny white coats flashed by as I wound toward the center of the herd. It became kind of fun. When I came upon a mare and foal, I was careful to get them both and, within minutes, we'd tagged fifty with no sign of Mydryth. At first I was relieved ... then nervous. This had been too easy.

I'd decided we should leave when a savage wrench jerked me into nothingness.

Chapter 12

The world congealed into a damp, smelly earthen floor. I grabbed my head, groaned and rolled to my knees, squinted through one eye to perceive a ten-foot-square musty cell. Two pallets of moldy straw with dirty blankets sagged against ancient stone walls. The straw moved with a light rustling. Damn. Mice. Or worse – rats! I wasn't crazy about either. I was having limited success getting used to Cyril as it was.

By the dim light of a high, narrow window, I perceived a pile of clothing along the opposite wall. It moved and groaned. Dorian rolled to his back clutching his forehead. "Christ! I'm tired of this!"

I crawled over to him. "I don't think this was Angus."

Dorian peered around, eyes narrowed in pain. "Probably not." He rolled to his stomach, pushed to his knees. "This can't be good."

We helped each other to get vertical then worked our way around the cell, looking for weaknesses. There wasn't much to see. What I'd thought was an earthen floor was, in fact, stone covered by centuries of dirt. The door was wooden with heavy iron hinges and a small barred window.

Dorian patted a pocket and gave a snort of disgust. "They took our wands. Looks like we're on our own."

The makeshift bedding was still moving so I decided it was safer to sit on the dirt and lean against a wall. When Dorian tired of pacing, he settled next to me.

"We need a plan before Mydryth comes," I said. "Since we're still alive, he must want something. And we can do stuff without wands. We never had them before."

Dorian slid an arm around me and pulled me against him. "Could give us an advantage. This guy, Mydryth, might not know what mages from a continent can do. We don't even know what we can do."

We brainstormed until we had a shaky plan. I must've fallen asleep after that because I awakened in Dorian's arms, my head against his solid chest, listening to the regular thump of his heart. Although this was pleasant, I knew I'd heard something.

My ears perked. I opened my eyes and watched the door through half-closed lids. There it was again. Footsteps.

As I moved to get up, Dorian's arm tightened. "Don't move," he whispered. "Watch for an opportunity."

The footsteps stopped outside the door, a metal plate grated, and sharp brown eyes peered in. "Ah! They're up!"

Metal scraped against metal and the door made an ear-damaging screech. There was no pretending to be asleep after that. Dorian helped me up as a tall gaunt man wearing a silver-and-black pointed hat strode in. He had a short grey beard, wore black robes covered in silver crescents and stars, and carried a black wand. The essence of magic surrounded him like another cloak.

Three enormous ogres with hostile stares accompanied him. I swallowed and eyed their broadswords. One stayed outside while the others took positions behind the mage who stopped three feet from us. Dorian and I separated so he'd have to look at us one at a time.

"I apologize for the accommodations. I wanted to investigate your … accoutrements. Angus is a great mage and I'd be foolish to underestimate him. *You*, on the other hand, I don't know much about." He stroked his chin. "You're obviously mages but unlike any I've known. From whence do you come?"

"North America," I said.

"There are mages in the Americas?" Grey bushy brows lifted into his hair and he shook his head. "North America is far too young to have developed magic."

Dorian's expression was sardonic. "It's a continent! It didn't appear yesterday!"

Mydryth's mouth tightened. "I'm aware of that! I'm refer-ring to magical people. It takes years of practicing magic for it to sink into the very fabric of the land. The more magic in the land, the more power is available. Each feeds the other. North America hasn't had enough of those who practice true magic. Certainly not enough to saturate a continent!"

"Why would you think that?"

Mydryth drew himself up. "It's well known that North Americans have always dealt with nature, not magic."

"What's the difference? Isn't magic natural?"

"Working with nature involves understanding and working with pre-set flows. Magic is the use of deeper energies. I'm sure there are people in North America who dabble in true magic; I'm saying there haven't been enough for it to sink it into the land."

"Then where did we come from?" asked Dorian, impatience coloring his tone.

"Perhaps you're lying about being from North America."

Dorian blew a burst of air through his lips. "Did it ever occur to you that magic may've been imprinted into the land thousands, maybe hundreds of thousands of years ago? Long before living memory by a civilization that no longer exists?"

"I doubt that," snapped Mydryth. "Where would they have gone?"

"Maybe they had people like you who live to destroy!"

Mydryth's eyes narrowed. "Regardless of how you got it, you're both powerful mages and I'll give you one opportunity to join me. I'll soon rule the world and I want your magic on my side."

"Why do you want to rule the world?" I asked.

He looked at me as if I had a mental deficiency.

"Why not?"

"Don't you have anything better to do?"

"What could be better than to have every human being on earth worship me?"

"You've mistaken yourself for someone else. I believe the position's been filled."

Mydryth's face flushed. "The non-magical of this planet need someone to lead them. They're stupid and confused about the simplest things."

"If you don't respect them, why do you care what they think of you?

"I don't care, but it amuses me to play with their little lives."

"And you figure telling them what to do will make you happy?"

"It will entertain me."

I must admit; I snorted. It wasn't very ladylike, and it seemed a good time to shut up before I got him mad.

Dorian folded his arms. "We won't be joining you so, what now?"

Mydryth's eyes turned wintry. "You might want to reconsider while you can." His voice scraped like a blade of steel. "You either use your magic for my benefit or you don't use it at all."

I remembered Angus' warnings about taking Mydryth on. At Dorian's quick glance, I gave him a tiny nod and activated my magic. Dorian threw up his hands and bolts of blue light flew towards the ogres who dropped flaming weapons onto the damp earth where they sizzled and smoked. I threw a protection spell between us and our captors as Mydryth's eyes widened, jaw tightened, and his wand pointed our direction.

Dorian grabbed my hand, pulled red energy from Mydryth, and uttered an incantation we'd used often in Denver.

For a heart-stopping moment nothing happened. Then we were sucked into a spinning vortex of red that seemed to go on forever before spitting us out six feet above the ground.

Fortunately for me, I landed on Dorian.

I groaned, dropped my head onto his chest, and grabbed my temples. "There's gotta be a better way!"

Dorian blinked a few times then rolled me to the side as he bounded to his feet. I peeked through my fingers. We were on a mountain plateau overlooking a broad valley that disappeared into the distance. Early dawn; the glitter of city lights as far as we could see.

A grin spread over Dorian's face. "Denver! It worked! We're home!" He hauled me up and I sagged against him.

"I can't believe it!" I stared at the city. "You used Mydryth's own magic against him! You sent us thousands of miles!" I looked up. "I'll bet you pissed him off!"

Dorian shrugged. "Better him than me." He reached for my hand. "Your place or mine?" He smiled at my cocked eyebrow. "I don't think we should separate. He might be able to follow us."

I stuffed down the elation that bubbled from somewhere and grabbed his warm hand. "Mine. I'd like to pick up a few things."

I emerged from a heavenly hot shower and wrapped myself into a soft robe. Morning sunlight streamed through my window as I headed to the kitchen to make coffee.

Dorian dropped a folded blanket onto a pile on the couch and tossed a pillow on top. His glance flicked over my comfortable bathrobe, turbaned hair and bare feet. He didn't say anything but his eyes smiled.

In an attempt to distract myself from a growing warmth, I said, "In spite of their shortcomings, the non-magical know how to be comfortable. Electric lights, computers, central heating, television . . ."

Dorian settled into an easy chair and grinned. "Getting appreciative now you know how the other half lives?"

"Clarifies things. I'm now in love with electricity and all the things it can do. Also, there aren't any talking rats here."

"You like this better?"

"Not a chance. But I'd be a fool not to appreciate it while I've got it!"

At a pounding on the door, Dorian and I exchanged a quizzical glance. Who could know I was home? Then I got a familiar cramp in my stomach. I stalked to the door, jerked it open and stared down at a red-and-white striped figure.

"Hello, Reg." I said with a fake smile.

Reg peeked around me. "Is that your boyfriend?"

"Why do you want to know?"

"He never takes the elevator to your place. How does he get in?"

Reg's eyes locked onto Dorian's broom which had arrived and was balanced in the umbrella stand next to the balcony. "Are you a witch too?"

Before I could stop him, he'd scuttled over to the broom, grabbed it in pudgy hands, and was turning it over looking for magic buttons.

"Okay, Reg! I don't need you insulting my guest! Put that down and go home. We're in a hurry here!"

"Not till you show me how this works!"

"I could beat you with it."

He stuck the broom between his legs and galloped around the living room. I rolled my eyes towards Dorian who watched Reg with an indulgent smile.

"You can ride that broom all day and it won't fly for you," he said.

The kid stopped short in front of Dorian. "Why not?"

"Everybody knows magic brooms recognize only one master. They won't work for anyone else."

"How do I get one?"

I was ready to grab him by the collar and toss him out the door but Dorian held up a hand. He looked into the expanded eyes of the monster. "Do you believe in magic?"

Reg stared at him for a while, thinking it over.

Then he nodded. "Yea!" He pointed a stubby finger at me. "I've seen her fly on a broom, and she's a ghost too!"

"A ghost?" Dorian glanced at me.

"Reg seems to think he saw me fly in a white nightgown straight down the side of the building." I raised my brows at Dorian willing him to remember our first meeting. Reg had been younger but his suspicious nature was already in place.

Dorian nodded in understanding and grinned at Reg. "You're a pretty lucky young man to have a witch *and* a ghost living upstairs."

Reg's owl gaze turned to me. "Everybody knows witches and ghosts are evil!"

"Why do you think that?" I asked.

He turned back to Dorian with a solemn look. "My mom told me."

So, of course it was true, and that's how the stupidest ideas continue from one generation to the next. If you said anything with enough solemnity and often enough, you could make people believe pink teddy bears were gods and goldfish were devils – or anything else for that matter.

"Reg!" Losing what little patience I had with the kid, I took the broom and jerked the door open. "Go home! We're busy!"

"Are you flying on your brooms tonight?"

"Yes! Now go home so we can get ready!"

"I'm gonna watch from my balcony and I'm gonna take a pitcher so I can prove it! Then everyone will believe me!"

Great.

"Goodbye, Reg."

I double-locked the door behind him. "That kid makes a person want to get sterilized!"

Dorian gave me an odd look. "Really?"

"I … well … maybe all kids aren't as awful as that one."

"He may not have much else going for him, but he's smart as a whip."

"He's sneaky!"

Dorian chuckled. "Don't let him get to you. He's just a kid."

"Hitler was a kid once," I mumbled.

He rose. "I'll pop over to my place for some clothes while you get dressed. Be back in a flash and we'll have breakfast out. My treat."

I tried to suppress the grin that threatened to take over my face. "Ahhh … sure. Let's."

After he disappeared, I charged for the bedroom and tore a half-dozen items from the closet. *Too dowdy; too sexy; too formal; too casual; too boring.* My god! I had nothing to wear!

I sat on the bed. Get a hold of yourself, Raven! It's just Dorian. You've eaten together dozens of times. No big deal! I took some deep breaths. I was being ridiculous. I wished I'd never noticed how wonderful Dorian's arms felt. Life had been much simpler before I'd gone and done something so stupid!

I'd finished a stack of pancakes far larger than was wise when the door to the small diner opened to admit a man in a kilt. I choked on my coffee.

Dorian saw my expression and looked over his shoulder. "Angus!" He leaped up and made his way to the flame-haired Scot.

"Hello, my boy! I trust Raven is with ye?"

Dorian gestured and I gave a small wave. "Over here!" I called. "Care for breakfast?"

"No thank ye." As Angus slid in next to me, the booth became too small. Not to mention how out-of-place I felt sitting next to a man in a skirt in a diner in Denver, Colorado – especially one who didn't believe in underwear. After we'd finished our coffee and Dorian was paying the bill at the counter, I skooched over the spot where Angus had been sitting.

As we strolled down the street, I noticed people glance at us. With his kilt and flaming hair, people probably thought our companion belonged to a Scottish pipe band but, big as he was, nobody was going to comment within his hearing.

It was his first time in Denver and Angus wanted to absorb the ambiance as he put it. He was also interested in how we'd been able to steal Mydryth's energy.

We explained how we augmented our power from the surroundings. If we needed to transport farther than we felt we could, we'd draw the extra energy from a large healthy tree or stream. Since Mydryth exuded energy, Dorian, catching the mage unprepared, had been quick enough to transport us all the way to Denver.

Angus chuckled as he examined the young fruit of a crab apple tree that reached over the sidewalk. "Must've been quite the blow te Mydryth's ego!"

He sniffed the green apple. "Mmm," he said. "Interesting. The altitude and winter temperatures make significant changes te plants. This tree, tis hardy."

"Anything that grows here is hardy," I said. "We get tons of snow and cold temperatures, much colder than anything you'd have on Cumulos."

"Aye, we never let the castle get too far out of the warm zone."

"So," interjected Dorian with a quizzical look at Angus. "You never told us how you found us."

"When ye first arrived at Cumulos, I imprinted my wand with your magic so I'd be able te find either of ye if necessary. I did'na know the extent of your magical powers – still don't, but felt it might be o' use te be able te find ye. Tis how I got ye away from Mydryth two days ago." He scowled. "He seems te have pierced the invisibility spell I used. I'll have te figure out how he did that."

He gazed at the majestic wall of Rocky Mountains, jagged tips still capped with snow. "Those are magnificent!" Bright blue eyes roamed the ragged peaks. "Perhaps I'll return when there's more time." He turned back to us. "Much as I'd like te be a tourist for a while, I must return te Cumulos." He hesitated. "Will ye be returning with me?"

It was clear then why he'd come. Besides the fact that we needed him to get us there, he hadn't been sure we'd want to come back. After all, we were safe at home in Denver.

Dorian and I exchanged glances. "We won't leave Cumulos in danger," I said. "When we were in that dungeon, this was our only option. Lucky it worked. Would you've been able to find us in Mydryth's lair?"

"Like Cumulos, Mydryth's castle is protected by spells. The only way I knew ye were there is because I knew ye weren't anywhere else. I'd started on a rescue plan when my wand picked up your trail. I'm glad ye were able to get out on your own. It would nae have been easy te invade Mydryth's stronghold though I'm sure with Talon's help it could be done. That creature has an inexhaustible knowledge o' dark magic."

Not surprised.

"Mydryth will now be on his guard. We'll need te find other methods o' bringing unicorns back te Cumulos."

"Why don't we discuss it at my place," I said, "while Dorian and I get ready?"

Angus took a final long look at the mountains and nodded.

Two hours later we were again on Cumulos and I was anxious that our wands had not returned. It would be embarrassing if, after hundreds of years of storage, we lost them in a matter of weeks. But Angus was unconcerned, confident they'd be back in a few hours. So Dorian and I decided it would be a good afternoon to explore Cumulos village.

I'd learned that castles always have a village or town nearby. After all, what's the point of living in a lovely castle if there's no one to admire and envy you?

We followed a winding footpath through rolling farmland until we came to a jumble of quaint buildings with sharp roofs and sturdy stone walls. Steep roofs shed snow in winter and Cumulos sometimes got heavy snow depending on the latitude in which it drifted. Today the grass was green and a multitude of flowers nodded colorful heads in a passing breeze. People sauntered along narrow winding streets.

After exploring the village, we stopped before a building with a sign that indicated an eating establishment. I hoped it had something other than boiled frog's eyes or some other such stomach-roiling menu items. The heavy wooden door was low, forcing Dorian to duck, and it took a few moments for our eyes to adjust to the dimness.

A short, squat man with a bad haircut and rude manner led us to a scarred table. "Don't take all day," he snapped and tossed down a couple of menus.

A woman in a bent witch's hat came over to display a vast expanse of bosom for Dorian's admiration. "Don't mind him," she said, wriggling her assets as she scrubbed an already clean table. "He's half mountain dwarf. They're all cranky but he's worse. Felt cheated so I swear he's more dwarf than the pure-bloods are."

She grimaced. "Made it all the more peculiar when he up and married my sister. Wouldn't have him around the place if he wasn't related by marriage. What can you do though?" she said. "Family!" And sailed back to the bar with an extra swing to her hips for Dorian's benefit. I noticed he followed her progress.

As the server went behind the bar, Dorian glanced at my arch expression and gave me a smug smile. I rolled my eyes and began to read the menu, startled to find such delicacies as fried newt's brain, boiled bat legs and frog's eyes. There it was – *frog's eyes!* It was a real thing!

My appetite was on the verge of collapse when Dorian pointed to an item that looked innocuous – milkweed soup. It didn't sound that great, but at least it didn't have strange body parts.

I realize the contradiction here; if I can eat one body part, why not another? I don't know. I can only tell you, it matters. I cannot insert eyes into my mouth. Sorry, but there it is.

We ordered milkweed soup along with slabs of sourdough bread and fresh butter to be washed down with ginger ale made with real ginger.

By the time our orders had been written on a small slip of paper, the surly dwarf was crankier. I wondered why he didn't use a bigger sheet but refrained from asking. After Stumpy (as we'd christened him) had grumbled his way through the tables to the kitchen, we sat back to survey our surroundings.

Sunlight struggled to pierce dusty windows decorated with spider webs, the gloom dissipated to some degree by torches fitted into sconces that left dark smudges of soot. Heavy wooden beams stained black over the years supported a high, slanted ceiling along which smoke meandered until it found the chimney. The floor was of unvarnished planks worn to a smooth finish by what were probably centuries of footsteps, and the walls were slabs of smoky quartz criss-crossed by planks.

Stumpy returned bearing a tray laden with steaming bowls and two metal tankards. He dropped them in front of us as if doing a tremendous favour then stalked away, jaw set in a mulish line.

"How'd you like to wake up with that every day?" whispered Dorian.

"Not in this lifetime! I'd either have to kill him … or myself."

We chuckled and stuck experimental spoons into our soup. There was something lumpy in the bottom of my bowl. *Please let it not be random body parts!* I brought up a piece of … something. Afraid to look, I dropped my spoon with a clatter. "Tell me it's edible, Dorian!" I covered my eyes.

I heard a "hmmm. . . hmmm," but nothing further. "Are you going to tell me?" I was becoming annoyed – both with the food and with Dorian for teasing me when I heard a deep chuckle.

"It's safe to look, Raven. It's some sort of root vegetable. I may have to supplement this with a steak."

I peeked through my fingers. Sure enough, Dorian shovelled soup into his mouth. I stirred mine to examine its contents and nearly jumped from my skin when a surly voice at my elbow asked if I was going to play with it or eat it.

"Somethin' wrong with it?"

"No … ah … not at all! Just … appreciating the texture . . ."

Stumpy peered at me out of mud-grey eyes shot with brown, lips in a tight line. I wouldn't have dared complain even if I'd been eating frog's eyes. He stared for a full minute before moving to the next table where two men mopped their plates at high speed.

The ginger ale was excellent; something to be said for the real thing, and the soup passable. We spent a pleasant half-hour chatting about nothing important. As Dorian swallowed the last of his drink, our server reappeared to clear the table, an accusatory glare telling us we were now using up space.

Since we were ready for fresh air anyway, Dorian dropped coins onto the table and we worked our way to the door followed by Stumpy's complaint about a cheap tip. I hoped there were other eating establishments in the community.

We stepped onto the street where I thought I saw a shadow slip around a nearby corner. Dorian said he hadn't noticed but I felt a chill, the winding narrow street filled with ominous shadows. As I cast a wary glance over my shoulder, I longed for the safety of the castle where it would feel wonderful to curl up in front of a roaring fire. The cape snugged across my chest was inadequate against a blustery west wind that boiled from the mountain.

A warm hand found mine. Before I could process the *other* warmth that flooded me, I heard, "It's almost dark out here, Raven. I wouldn't suggest you could be clumsy, but the cobblestones are uneven and there's a lot of stuff to run into."

Crap! Buzz kill . . .

Chapter 13

Four interminable days were spent learning about dark magic from Talon – an exercise in self-control. The one positive thing about Talon was the fact that he made Cyril's presence look good, a situation to which I still wasn't resigned.

The tattooed addition to my life was the oddest mixture of intelligence, class, and creepiness. At first he'd insisted on sleeping in my room but, after dodging a number of projectiles (he's pretty quick), he'd agreed to bunk elsewhere. I was relishing my temporary freedom as he had, with profuse apologies for his absence, torn himself away from my company in order to visit friends for a few days.

After yet another attempt to transmogrify a turtle into a snake and producing only a segmented eel, I realized my temper had frayed to the danger point. It didn't help that Dorian had mastered the spell within five minutes and Talon was treating me like a defective monkey. Recognizing the danger signals, Dorian told Talon we were done for the day and took me to the courtyard to watch the unicorns.

It's difficult to put into words the feeling I get in the presence of the creatures. I believe if I was led blindfolded into a room with a unicorn in it, I'd feel its gentle, pure essence.

As my blood pressure eased, a small foal strolled over, took a cautious sniff at my hand – and looked right at me.

Dorian's eyes were wide and I must admit to a rush of excitement. This was the second time a unicorn had acknowledged me! In fact, it could *see* me! I began to croon and brushed its silky white neck with the backs of my fingers. This must be what it felt like to touch an angel.

Angus strolled over and I felt a stab of disappointment as the foal trotted back to its mother.

"Mydryth was in the village a few days ago," he said with a puzzled glance at the foal, "and warnings have been going off in the castle the past couple o' days but we haven't found anything. He's being cautious, especially since ye used his own energy te escape. He won't forgive that nor will he forget. Mydryth is an opportunist, and the chance te learn what ye two can do is something he'll nae be able te resist.

"I'm caught in the unfortunate position o' needing to protect ye but you're the only ones capable o' collecting the unicorns, and we canna wait much longer. We need at least a hundred more animals before we're confident Mydryth is blocked."

"How do we do that?" asked Dorian.

"Talon said he had an idea."

I cringed as Talon floated up to join our little circle. *I'll bet the unicorns couldn't see him.* I wondered what the purple wonder brought to the Cumulos table. I wouldn't trust him with a hamster.

"Good afternoon, Talon," said Angus.

Talon sent a condescending look my direction and turned to Angus. "I'm not surprised our new mages were less than successful with the unicorns."

"Considering we canna' do it at all, they're doing better than the rest o' us. Have ye a suggestion?"

Talon pursed fuzzy lips before spitting out, "An energy pyramid. I can be the third point. Anything within the pyramid the size of a unicorn will be transported to Cumulos, but a young unicorn is no bigger than a mage. If any of Mydryth's dark magicians are within the area, they'll be brought through the castle's protective barrier. In fact, anything enchanted will be picked up, meaning we'll need to be careful."

Angus rubbed his chin. "An energy pyramid. Tis a good idea. We could transport quite a few at once." He stroked his chin. "We'll have te ensure every magical sensor in Cumulos is active."

"If we run into Mydryth," continued Talon, "he should come after me first as the greatest threat. While he's distracted, these two can absorb local magic to send us back.

They should be able to handle that." He glanced our direction. "And don't ever use Mydryth's personal energy again as he'll have it tainted."

"You want us to transport back here?" I blurted.

He turned on a fresh scowl. "Where else?"

"We've only used it to travel to Denver. I wouldn't trust it to get us back here in an emergency."

Talon spun his little body towards me, long toes twitching. "Perhaps you could at least make the effort. After all, it is closer!" Like I was the village idiot.

My teeth grated. "I know it's closer, but we don't have the habits ingrained like we do for Denver!"

"Then perhaps Denver can be Plan B."

The three of us hovered amongst puffy clouds above the meadow where we'd found the unicorns. The stream twinkled in the sunlight as it meandered towards a distant sea and the same stiff breeze that tugged at my braid whipped the deep grass into rippling waves. Half-a-dozen deer rested in the shade of a forest. It was pastoral, beautiful, and peaceful.

And empty of unicorns.

"Could he have moved them?" I asked. Talon slanted me a look but declined to answer. "Where would he put them? Unicorns can't live just anywhere." Apparently I was talking to myself.

Talon pulled a thin flat disc from a pouch, peered into it, and moved his lips in an inaudible incantation. I made a point of ignoring him.

"Could this be a trap?" asked Dorian. "If he moved the unicorns, he'll be expecting us."

"Most likely," muttered Talon. He gazed into the disc.

"What is that?" I asked, unable to contain my curiosity.

Talon tightened his lips. "If you'd stop interrupting, I might find some answers."

I gave him a narrow-eyed look and turned away, my fingers itching to send him *the sign*. I was antsy but couldn't for the life of me see a threat. I moved closer to Dorian as my unease expanded.

"We should go back," I blurted. "Something's not right."

"Not very brave, is she?" Talon tossed at Dorian.

Before Dorian could answer, I gave Talon a nasty look. "I said, there's something wrong! See you at Cumulos! Maybe Angus can find the unicorns from there."

I shot toward the stream to gather the extra energy to transport to Cumulos – this time without slamming into a wall but, as I neared the water, it felt like I'd hit a sponge. My broom halted so fast, I almost fell off.

Dorian, close behind, fared the same. We looked at one another then at Talon still by the cloud. Could he have done something? But why? He'd return to Cumulos right behind us. We moved further along the stream and tried again. Same thing.

"We'd better talk to Talon about this," I said.

Purple eyes swiveled our way as we approached. "Thought you were leaving," he growled.

"Apparently we can't," said Dorian. "Didn't have anything to do with you, did it?"

Talon focused on Dorian. "It did not."

After we explained what'd happened, alarm flashed across Talon's fuzzy visage. He shot vertical for a few seconds, came to a halt then moved to the east where it happened again. As he floated down to us, I realized it was the first time I'd seen the purple fuzz-ball worried. Although I didn't like the creature, at this point I was glad to have him with us. If anyone could figure this out, it would be Talon.

"Contraction spell," he said, snapping little shark teeth.

"And?" I asked with raised brows and a gesture for him to continue.

"A sphere is contracting around us. When it was bigger, the outside was thin enough to let us through. Now it's contracting, the edge is more solid and, the smaller it gets, the thicker it gets."

A burst of claustrophobia clutched at my stomach. "How small?"

He sent me hard look. "Too small!"

"How much time do we have?" asked Dorian.

"Perhaps an hour. The longer we wait, the harder it will be to escape."

"Is there any way to make it visible?" I asked.

Talon waved a hand and a bright greenish sphere congealed. When it was twelve inches across, Talon gave a snap of his wand and the sphere flew away. Where it collided with the invisible trap, fingers of flickering green created a web and, in minutes, we found ourselves inside an enormous green glowing ball. Confirmation that the sphere was shrinking was accompanied by a sinking feeling in the pit of my stomach.

"Can we blast our way out?" asked Dorian.

"Such a response will add strength to the trap," said Talon.

"It must have a magical source," I said. "Where does its power come from?"

Talon's eyes narrowed. "Yes, this spell takes a lot of power. Mydryth must be drawing heavily on his magical stores."

"This will weaken him then," said Dorian.

"Not for long. You should be flattered he'd take you this seriously."

"I have to do something!" I flew in a spiral around Dorian and Talon, widening the diameter of the circle until I was near the sphere. The closer I got, the brighter it became. "It reacts to my proximity," I called. "Does that make it use more power?"

"Yes," growled Talon. "It will make it shrink faster."

Oh. I returned to the others. The bottom of the trap still encompassed a portion of the meadow. As the edge contracted along the ground, it bent trees almost flat before they sprang back. Within minutes, the meadow would be outside the sphere and the trap complete.

A dark shadow next to one of the older trees gave me an idea. "Could there be dwarf tunnels here?"

Talon shrugged. "Dwarves dig tunnels everywhere."

"What are we waiting for?" I shot to the ground, skimmed over the grass, scanned for anything that might be a camouflaged entrance. A winding hedge followed the edge of low hills and I felt a faint stir of hope. Dwarves also planted hedges so maybe there was an entrance.

I tried not to watch the movement of the trees as the contracting sphere approached. Each passing second gave us less chance to find an escape route. I flew to one end of the hedge and worked my way towards Dorian and Talon who'd gone to the other end, one on each side.

The hedge must've been old as it was larger than it seemed from above. Good. Better chance of a tunnel.

I was sweating when I spotted a pile of rocks to one side. It's convenient to hide a hole beneath rocks. Turning around for a second look, I dropped lower. Please let there be a tunnel! I'll be nice to dwarves in future even if they're cranky!

Knowing they were good at hiding tunnel entrances, I jumped from my broom at a pile of large rocks. Maybe they weren't real. I poked the handle of my broom at one – and stumbled when it passed through.

"Taloooon!"

I shot after my companions, keeping a wary eye on the approaching wall. Our one chance would be gone in seconds. Wind whipped tears from my eyes as I did a sharp one-eighty, signaling them to follow. Seconds later, Talon dismounted and prodded at the fake rocks.

"Yes," he mumbled. "These are holograms designed to hide something – but what? More things live underground than dwarves – and not all are friendly."

The roar of the wall increased. Trees creaked and complained as they sprang back behind the contracting sphere. There was no time for debate. I shoved Talon out of the way and dove head first into the fake rocks.

I felt descending soil, yelled that there was a tunnel and continued to scramble on all fours. After my head slammed into a tree root, I stopped to grope into the darkness. When I couldn't feel anything, I assumed the tunnel made a turn and was shocked to find as I slid forward that it did – downward! I was on a toboggan slide in the darkness, expecting at any moment to be slammed against a wall or dropped into a bottomless pit.

The floor disappeared and I was airborne trying to suppress a scream (I imagine unsuccessfully). Perhaps this was a trap for anyone without a magic password! I rolled into a ball and cringed, pretty sure that whatever was coming up was going to hurt.

Whomp! I landed on something soft. At the sound of skidding, I rolled to the side in time to avoid being squashed by Dorian.

"Raven? Raven, are you okay?" He gave an unmanly yelp at my touch.

"It's me, Dorian. Relax!"

"You could've warned me! Who knows what's down here?"

There was a rustle of clothing as his wand lit to reveal a cavern fifty feet across. Roots dangled from the ceiling and grew along the walls into which were carved three tunnels that led into more darkness. We turned our attention to the opening in the ceiling above. Where was our companion?

Nothing.

"What happened to Talon?"

"He was taking some kind of measurement with one of his gadgets so who knows. I had to go. The wall was almost there." I could feel the guilt oozing. I've noticed Dorian has a powerful protective streak, an almost palpable need to shield others. Maybe it was part of his leadership genetics.

A loud groan filled the cavern, roots strained upward, and I prayed the hedge was flexible enough to bend instead of being uprooted. Interminable seconds later, the strain released but the groaning continued as the hedge re-settled. I swear it grumbled.

Then there was a different sound. The sound of sliding! Talon sailed through the air to land in a heap. I ducked to avoid the broom that followed and scrambled to his side. His eyes were closed and even his toes were still. I touched where I imagined a carotid artery might be and heaved a sigh of relief at a strong pulse. He did have a heart!

I retrieved the small canteen at my waist, lifted his head into my lap, and poured a trickle between his lips. Nothing happened. I poured more. With a wheezing gasp, he erupted, coughing and choking, rolled onto his side and coughed some more. The look he sent me seemed to lack gratitude.

I straightened my spine. "I'm just trying to help! It's not like I'm a nurse!"

"That's obvious," he said when he could breathe.

The hedge was still settling. We heard a distant "thump" after which dirt rolled from the entrance. Dorian raised his wand, peered upward.

"The tunnel's blocked," he said. "We can't go back."

I looked at Talon leaned against the wall. "Are you alright?"

"Fine."

"Can I do anything to help?"

"You've already tried to drown me. That's quite enough. Shall we move on?"

Talon was a hard creature to like. I sent him a scowl as we floundered to the edge of the straw that had cushioned our landing and contemplated our three choices.

"What makes that glow?" I asked when my eyes had adjusted enough to perceive it.

"Luminous fungi," said Talon. "These tunnels are lined with it."

"Why wasn't it in the tunnel we came down?"

"It won't grow so long as there's even a hint of daylight."

Dorian extinguished his wand. "Any ideas?" he asked of no one in particular.

All the tunnels looked the same. "Too bad we don't have a dwarf guide," I said. "Even that cranky waiter probably knows where these go."

Talon held his wand on the flat of his hand. It began a slow revolution, stopped when it pointed at the right hand tunnel. He floated without hesitation to the right.

"Speaking of cranky," I muttered. Dorian's suppressed chuckle followed me.

The tunnel was tall enough for me to walk without stooping but I soon felt sorry for Dorian who had to hunch over. I'd hear him curse once in a while as his head connected with a stone or root hanging from the clay ceiling. Talon must've had some kind of radar that warned him of upcoming dangers. Of course, he floated in his little meditative position in the centre of the tunnel. Although side tunnels branched off, he continued at a steady pace, one that I found difficult to match.

After the tenth time I'd smacked my head on a root, I came up with my own curses. "Could you slow down a little?"

"Let's take a rest," said Dorian. "My back is killing me being stooped over like this!" He settled to his heels and leaned against a wall.

Talon spun. "We should push on!"

"What's a few minutes going to hurt? We're not in that big a hurry," growled Dorian.

"You won't worry about your back if we encounter one of the creatures that live in these gnome tunnels!"

Dorian's gaze shifted along the tunnel. "What creatures?"

"They're like giant slimy salamanders," said Talon. "And they eat anything."

Dorian leaped to his feet. "My back feels better. Let's go."

After a half hour, the tunnel acquired a sharp incline. I was huffing along when, without warning, Talon's long ears shot towards the ceiling which gave him the appearance of a startled jack rabbit. He glanced once over his shoulder. "We've only got a few seconds! Hurry!" He darted ahead.

I didn't need coaxing as I envisioned giant salamanders. Dorian was on my heels when Talon shot upwards into a jagged crevasse where he turned with frantic gestures. Of course I couldn't levitate under such stressful conditions so Dorian grabbed my wrist and hauled me upwards at an awkward angle. As we reached the narrow opening, Talon jammed me into it followed by Dorian.

"Keep quiet if you want to live," hissed Talon. Then he formed a translucent bubble over the entrance.

"What's that for?" My heart pounded as I tried to catch my breath.

Talon continued to watch below. "To hide your noise! Keep quiet!"

I ground my teeth (quietly) and subsided as I heard scrabbling sounds. As they intensified, I held my breath – quite a feat when I was still puffing from running. Talon watched through the shield he'd erected but I wasn't the least bit tempted to see a salamander big enough to eat me. I huddled in silence as far into the crevasse as I could push myself.

"Ack!" I squeezed my nostrils. "What a stink!" My stomach at a boil, I was worried I'd be adding to the slime on the floor.

Dorian knew the signs. "Is it safe to move? I'd rather Raven didn't throw up on me."

I shot him a glare.

"Be quiet!" growled Talon. "It hasn't gone far enough!"

Goose bumps raced up my back. I believe my face may have turned green as Dorian sent me a worried glance. "Are you alright?"

"Will be in a moment," I said. "Just need to swallow my lunch ... again."

If Talon had been anyone else, he'd have rolled his eyes. "Shall we proceed?"

He turned with a toss of the head that swung his long ears and floated into the tunnel now slippery with something gross. I discovered this, of course, by having my feet go out from under me the instant they touched. I was revolted to discover strings of slime stretched from my hands to the floor. Efforts at scrubbing it off spread it until I realized only copious amounts of strong soap would do the job. Cursing under my breath, I staggered to my feet to follow the purple fuzz ball who wasn't waiting.

The pungent aroma of salamander mixed with the scent of damp earth was tiresome. I wanted sunshine but stopped my mouth from asking the "are we there yet?" question, not being brave enough to invite more of Talon's scathing comments – or worse.

The tunnel darkened as we struggled up a steepening incline which made keeping my feet even harder. It seemed Dorian had the same difficulty from the occasional curse I heard from behind. When he hit his head now, he got slime in his hair. I figured by the time we emerged from the tunnels (if we ever did) we'd look like we'd rolled in the stuff. A hot shower would be heaven. I glared at our leader who floated in comfort, oblivious to my ire.

Talon lit his wand as the tunnel light faded and, minutes later, I rejoiced at the unmistakable glow of natural light at the end of a narrowing tunnel which reduced us to all fours. Talon stuck his head out the opening and growled in a barely audible curse.

"What's the matter?" I hissed in a half-whisper.

"A giant roc's nest. Complete with chicks. And all chicks have one thing in common."

"What's that?"

"They're hungry!"

"So are these roc things bigger than chickens?"

"Try bigger than horses!" he snapped.

Oh crap! "And I suppose they eat meat?"

"It's gratifying to discover you can figure a few things out for yourself."

His little butt was right in front of me and it took all my willpower not to kick it out the hole. I'd like to think innate humanity stopped me but, to be honest, it was more likely the thought that we might need him.

"Can the two of you pull magic from the tunnel and get us back to Cumulos?"

I was scared, exhausted, and my temper was short. "What part of our conversation about emergency transporting did you not understand, Talon? I've told you repeatedly that we could only be sure of transporting to Denver. And then we've only done it from outside! I've no idea if it'll work from in here. We could re-materialize inside a mountain, for god's sake!"

"If those birds hear us, we'll be materializing inside their gullets! I don't care where you take us, just do it! Now!"

I was unable, in the tight circumstances, to turn my head to Dorian. "What do you think?" I whispered over my shoulder. "Try it from in here?"

"I wouldn't count on it. It only takes a few seconds to cast the spell. How much time would we have after landing in a roc's nest?"

"No more than three seconds," said Talon. "Enough for the parents to recognize us as food for the little ones. In fact, the little ones are big enough to spot their own food."

I craned my neck in an effort to see past Talon. "How many are there?"

"Three chicks. One of the parents just left. If we wait a bit, maybe the other will go too. We won't escape an adult roc."

We waited in silence.

"Stinks in here." Crap! Did I just say that?

I was thankful they ignored my comment. "I think we should translocate to Denver if we have such a short time," whispered Dorian.

I rolled my eyes over my shoulder although I couldn't see him. "What if we materialize on a busy street? People may be unobservant but it'd be hard to miss a dog-sized purple alien."

"It'll just be for a few seconds and it's not like anyone would believe it."

True.

"If you two are finished your pointless blathering, perhaps we could agree on a plan to get out of this stink-hole! Has it occurred to you the roc nest may be here *because* it's a salamander hole? Perhaps because salamanders are known to come out of this entrance?"

"They wouldn't fit." I thought that was logical.

Talon sighed. "Salamanders don't hatch the size of the one we encountered. They come in all sizes. Young ones crawl all over the place."

My skin squirmed, panic rose, and I had to fight the urge (again) to shove Talon out the end of the tunnel which had suddenly shrunk in size – at least to my claustrophobic perception.

There was a great flapping of wings and Talon whispered, "The other adult just left. We won't have long. The chicks are facing away waiting for the parents to bring food. I'll dive out first, you two follow as fast as you can. Ready?"

I was ready for anything that would get me out of that hole. Talon's fuzzy butt lunged forward and daylight blasted me in the eyes. Nevertheless I charged forward and tumbled into an enormous nest lined with (yuck!) bird poo and feathers.

As I rolled to give Dorian room, the wall I leaned against shifted. It was also covered in feathers. Enormous clawed feet turned to face us and I was frozen with terror at the sight of an eight-foot chick, its enormous beak wide open. It tipped its head to peer from one eye, stretched its mouth wider and . . .

"Dorian!" I grabbed his hand in a death grip as he latched onto Talon's arm. The vicious maw descended . . .

Traffic was light. A bicycler cursed at our sudden appearance, steered around us and never looked back. Must not have gotten a good look – or whiff. We were crouched on a bike path covered in slime, feathers, and bird poop. A mother and daughter walked by, the mother in a hurry. The little girl watched us struggle to our feet.

"Mommy, can I have a purple dog?"

"Don't be silly, Amanda! There are no such things as purple dogs! What have I told you about making things up? Now come along; we're late!"

As the child cast a long look over her shoulder, I gave her a finger wave. Other pedestrians closed in and she was gone. People held their noses and screwed their faces into expressions of disgust as they neared us. At least the stench kept them too distracted to notice Talon.

"Your apartment?" asked Dorian.

I nodded.

"On three."

My living room congealed around us. I was almost naked by the time I got to the bedroom where I dropped my underwear, went straight to the shower, cranked it to high, and stepped into heaven.

By the time I emerged, I was the hue of a boiled lobster but every inch had been scrubbed until it stung. Feeling selfish, it occurred to me that Dorian would want to clean up too so I stepped into the living room wrapped in a towel. He and Talon were perched on stools sipping Earl Grey. After one deep inhale, I charged to the balcony doors and threw them open.

"Towels are on the sink, Dorian. Help yourself. Talon, park yourself out here."

Dorian headed for the shower as Talon floated off the stool and out to the balcony where he sipped tea in injured silence.

"You have to sit on a chair, Talon. We don't have purple floating aliens in Denver."

He scowled and drifted to a plastic recliner.

I'd changed into tights and sleeveless top and was pouring myself a tea when I noticed movement beneath the door. A small tube inched its way into the room. Feeling a growl in my chest, I raced to the balcony.

"Talon! Can you turn into a dog?"

He blinked like an owl. "Is that a hypothetical question?"

I pointed to the object under the door. "No! And now would be a good time!"

"I've seen pictures but I don't know much about dogs. Which breed would you like?"

"I don't care! Just do it!" I flung open the door. "Reg, you weasel! What are you doing sneaking around?"

He was crouched on the floor peering through an eyepiece attached to the tube. I snatched it away. "What's this Reg!" He scrambled to his feet and jumped for the item which I held out of reach. "You know spying on people's against the law? I could have you sent to juvie for this!"

Instead of answering, Reg charged into my living room.

"You've got an alien in here! I saw it drinking tea!" He struggled with something in his pocket and came up with a small camera. Just as I was about to grab him by the collar, he ducked away and onto the balcony where he stopped, wide-eyed. I could only hope Talon was as good as he thought he was.

"It's a dog now!" he gaped. "It wasn't a dog before and, anyway, you can't have pets in the building!"

"It's visiting," I said. "The dog belongs to Dorian."

"Why's it purple?"

"He used to be white but Dorian washed him with that shampoo for blue-haired old ladies. It hasn't come out yet."

Talon looked something like an Irish Setter in purple – that watched Reg with a less than friendly expression.

"Does he bite?"

"Yes. Don't touch him."

Reg stepped closer. "I'd like a dog."

"Not this one. He's cranky."

Reg squatted in front of Talon and reached to touch his fur. The dog raised its lips exposing Talon's impressive array of shark teeth. Guess he hadn't gotten it quite right.

There was a scream followed by a scrambling on all fours. Reg bounced off the couch, careened into the counter, and yanked open the door. "It's not a dog! It's an alien! I'm gonna report you! The gov'ment will come and take you all away!" He charged down the corridor. "Mooooooom!"

I closed and locked the door then tossed Reg's spying equipment in the garbage. "I swear that kid's even more offensive than you are, Talon." I held up the pot. "More tea?"

Talon, returned to his normal form, floated into the room with a sour expression. "If it had touched me, I might've been unable to refrain from ripping its arms off."

"Come now, Talon. He's just a kid, after all. Harmless." I maintained a bland expression.

"Don't you cull your offspring?" he snapped with a scowl of disapproval.

I blinked at the suggestion; disturbed a similar thought had occurred to me more than once with regards to Reg.

"No, Talon, we don't kill our children. We teach them." I glanced at the door. "At least some of us do."

At that moment, an incredible vision entered from the vicinity of my bedroom – Dorian clad in a towel slung low around his hips drying his hair with another.

"What'd I miss?"

It took a couple of tries to unstick my tongue from the roof of my mouth but I managed. "Uh … umm . . . ." I couldn't remove my eyes from his chest and … everything.

"Raven?"

"Um … just Reg looking for aliens." *Oh … my … god!*

Humour swirled behind his eyes before they slid toward Talon. "Did he find one?"

"Just a dog – with shark teeth and purple fur," I blurted, still mesmerized.

It took Talon's stench enveloping me to jerk my attention from Dorian. I couldn't bear to let him use my shower. There wasn't enough disinfectant in the world …

"Talon, do you think you could go back to Cumulos without us? Leave us a transporter disk and we'll be along. You're going to need some serious magic to get the smell of salamander out of your fur, and I don't have anything like that. Besides, that kid might come back looking for an alien and sometimes he brings his mother."

"I hope she's not planning more offspring." Talon's lip curled.

"I imagine Reg has cured her of that notion."

A few moments later, Talon disappeared in a blast of purple.

Silence settled. I was afraid to turn around. An almost naked Dorian was behind me smelling of soap and looking like … I think a whimper slipped out.

The silence lengthened as neither of us moved. Then I heard a sigh and Dorian's footsteps going to the bedroom. "Thanks for the shower, Raven." The door closed behind him.

Chapter 14

After three long baths at Cumulos, I felt like a new woman, although it could take days for my skin to recover and some of my hair might've been lost in trying to remove the odour. My fears were confirmed when Dorian and I met Cash at the main entrance before supper.

He took a sniff and his craggy face bunched. "Best be careful in the gnome tunnels. Magic doesn't work so well on giant salamanders."

I grimaced. "We know. Took us two hours to get out. It was a good thing we had Talon with us."

"For such a little guy, he can be scary. Knows his stuff."

If somebody as terrifying as Cash thought Talon was scary, I should be more cautious around the little alien.

I sniffed my hands. "How long does it take to get rid of the smell?"

"A mixture of herbs ought to do the trick. Basia will have something. Might want to talk to her before supper," he suggested, clearing his throat with the sound of a volcano erupting. "She's in the atrium feeding the grouse."

We took the hint and went to find her. Twenty minutes later, the odour of salamander had been swapped for the scent of camphor and mint.

We entered the dining room where my attention was jerked to a new person.

Hell-ooo… An attractive woman gave Dorian a covetous once-over. In fact, attractive didn't begin to cover it. She was gorgeous. Thick dark hair was topped by a witch's hat and she wore a glittering blue gown. It seemed the seamstress must've run out of fabric when it came to her chest. I glanced at Dorian whose attention had, of course, been snared like a rabbit in a trap. Expose a couple of generous mammary glands and men's brains fall right out of their heads. It was clear he needed my help.

Then I remembered Angus had sent for outside assistance. I'd even heard her name … something about flowers – bad flowers. That was it. Nightshade – a poisonous plant. To my jaundiced eye the name was perfect for her. I might be a wee bit possessive of Dorian but, after all, he was my best friend.

I took a seat and stabbed some fried chicken that promptly leaped to the floor.

"Something wrong?" asked Dorian, jerking his attention back to me.

I shook my head. "It's nothing." I jabbed a potato with my fork, stuffed it into my mouth and burned my tongue.

In Angus' study that evening, Frost and Talon were already in easy chairs. As I settled onto my favourite cushion next to a roaring fire, the door opened and in floated Nightshade in a smoky, flowing, silvery gown with yet another low neckline. A broad smile revealed perfect teeth as she made a bee-line for a vacant spot near Dorian. I could've kicked myself for leaving him exposed to such danger.

She placed a little hand on his arm and bestowed an intimate smile, unaware or uncaring of my presence. Fingernails caused stabbing pains in my palms.

Angus introduced Nightshade and informed us she'd be assisting for a few weeks. *A few weeks?* I started making plans to return home – and to take Dorian with me.

Trust Talon to see everything. Pale purple eyes swung between Nightshade, Dorian and me. His lips curved, probably the first time I'd amused him. I shot him a dark look and tipped my nose another direction.

Two hours of discussion failed to provide a workable solution so Angus suggested we reconvene after breakfast. By then my head spun with confusion and exhaustion. As I headed for the door, Dorian angled to join me but, with lightning speed, Nightshade slipped her arm through his, *accidentally* pressed a generous breast against his arm, and emitted a thousand-watt smile.

The dumb schmuck was a trout to a fly. I wanted to throw up. She was one of *those* women! At least that's what I told myself. Otherwise he'd be leaving with me, right? Sigh.

I gave up trying to sleep at sunrise. With a growl of frustration, I jammed into a pair of jeans and went for a walk. When I returned an hour later, Dorian was leaned against a pillar near the main door with arms crossed. I thought he looked relieved when he saw me but all he asked was if I'd eaten yet.

As we entered the gathering room, Angus arrived and, as I settled next to Dorian, couldn't resist a glance at Nightshade who gave me a dark look. Seems she noticed me now. It's possible I looked smug. That's certainly how I felt.

The next two days were spent working with the energy pyramid until I thought my arms would fall off. It took quite a bit of adjustment to get the magic of Cumulos to accommodate Dorian and me but the resultant pyramid was stunning to behold. Made of swirling, multi-coloured energies like soap bubbles in the sun, it reached far above our heads, gave off a slight hum, and intimidated the hell out of me. Eighty feet square at the base; it stretched a hundred feet to a glittering apex. It was hard to believe I was partly responsible for creating it.

Talon, Angus, Dorian and I met in the courtyard before lunch on the third day. Gloomy clouds threatened rain as we huddled beneath an overhang wrapped in cloaks to avoid a blustering north wind. Talon handed is each a baseball-sized blue orb and I was grateful for its warmth.

When Nightshade emerged from a side door, I felt a sense of disappointment that the wind didn't dislodge her hat. Of course she was ravishing in a navy-and-silver cloak. Her role was to ensure the safe arrival of the unicorns but I didn't think that was all she had in mind as her acquisitive gaze scanned Dorian.

Talon grasped the broom that hovered next to him. This was a surprise because I didn't know he ever used one. "Shall we go?" He made a sweeping gesture and I had time to grab mine before there was a loud "pop."

The courtyard was replaced by a grassy canyon bathed in sunshine. A thin stream splashed over rocks and collected in places to fill small pools. Dozens of unicorns grazed along the hillsides, thick tails swishing at insects.

We shot to the heaviest concentration of animals, got into position, held our orbs aloft, and a thin blue light shot from each to create a glowing blue triangle the centre of which rose to produce the multi-coloured pyramid. In seconds, we had twenty-three unicorns enclosed. We pronounced the incantation in unison, I experienced a nauseating sideways sensation and … the unicorns were gone.

The pyramid collapsed and, using hand signals to coordinate, we moved to the next group. Thirty-one were clustered at the stream. We got into position and raised our orbs. The pyramid materialized and expanded and, in moments, a second group was on its way.

The rest of the animals were scattered so batches were smaller. Checking my chronometer some time later, I realized we'd collected seventy-nine animals in fourteen minutes. My nerves were frayed and I looked over my shoulder a lot.

We got into position around six animals, four on one side of the stream, two on the other, a deep pool in the middle of the triangle. I noticed a frown cross Talon's face but, as that wasn't unusual, I readied my orb for activation. Talon was slow to place his and I wondered if he sensed something.

With a shift of my focus, I felt a cool, predator-like presence but saw nothing. I'd tell Talon after we sent this group. As we activated the spell and the pyramid rose, I thought I saw several small objects get sucked from the water as the unicorns disappeared.

Dorian cast a sharp look towards the stream then at Talon and me. "Did you see that?"

Talon lowered his orb and the pyramid collapsed into sparkles of light. "We should go back. Something may have transported along with the unicorns."

We materialized in the midst of a fiery maelstrom, ducked behind a wide stone column as flames roared on either side.

"What the hell's going on?" I bellowed to Talon over the furor.

"Water dragons! We picked them up with the last transport. Once their spell's been neutralized, they expand to natural size."

I chanced a quick look at the muddy sky and couldn't believe my eyes as five silver-blue dragons with huge webbed feet soared overhead. Nearly thirty feet long, their serpentine tails ended in fish fins. Membranous bluish skin stretched over long, thin wing bones. I was more worried though, about the flames that jetted from their mouths – and the long, sharp teeth. I shuddered. Were Angus and Frost alright? I tried to conjure sympathy for Nightshade but am ashamed to admit defeat.

"Can you two throw an umbrella spell?" As Talon ducked another blast, I caught the acrid odour of singed fur.

"I think so . . ." I hoped he could hear me over the noise.

"I'll conjure the main umbrella; you two support mine!" he snapped. "Angus will know what I'm doing. Once we have the dragons encircled, we'll send them back to the stream." At our nods, Talon stepped into the open, wand raised.

A half-circle appeared above him. Dorian and I sprang to either side and did the same. I tried not to focus on the dragons as they turned towards us. I could see them suck in air in preparation for blasting us to cinders. *Focus on the spell!*

Dorian's umbrella formed; after an aeon of watching a dragon grow in my sight, mine congealed as well. Together they shielded us from the flames. More umbrellas formed at different spots throughout the courtyard. Blue lights shot from one wand to another until a sphere of blue light formed within which the dragons were trapped.

Although they roared and shot walls of flames, the spell held. They were squeezed into a shrinking orb until the sphere was just large enough to contain them. They looked like a teeming ball of snakes moving like lightning. Sympathetic claustrophobia closed in as I recalled my own experience within a similar shrink trap.

I hoped we had them all…but I had a bad feeling. A bright yellow flash came from Angus' position across the courtyard, the sphere blazed, and the dragons disappeared.

As I allowed my umbrella to dissolve, I noticed it was pouring rain and ducked beneath a covered walkway. "Did we get them all?"

"We got four," said Talon.

"I thought there were five."

"There were . . ."

Sometimes I hate being right.

The fifth dragon was nowhere to be seen and, as we wandered wet and bedraggled into the castle, I was disgruntled to notice some people looked even better in wet clothing. I however wasn't one of them. I ground my teeth and pushed dripping hair from my face.

Nightshade slithered against Dorian, wet bosom heaving and, with a possessive hand on his arm, slid me a look of triumph as she led him away. Frost moved beside me, eyes on the witch.

"Her name's Nightshade for a reason," she murmured.

"I don't think Dorian's noticed that," I grumbled.

Frost placed a hand on my shoulder. "If he has any perception at all, he will before long."

That's what I found worrisome. He was around me all the time and had no idea how I felt. I thought he had the emotional perception of a rock.

"So what do we do about the fifth dragon?" I asked, by way of changing the subject.

"First we get warm and dry," said Frost. She removed her hat and wrung water from it. "Angus will call for more mages if needed."

"I hope they're not all like Nightshade," I growled.

Frost glanced my way and said nothing. She didn't need to. I realized it was a childish comment. "Sorry," I said on an outbreath. "Dorian's a free man." I made a personal promise to keep my comments to myself in future.

We rounded a corner to Frost's chambers, the door opened, and the warmth of a roaring fire met my chilled body. I shed soggy clothing before I was halfway across the room

Since the unicorns were the priority, we returned to collect the remaining thirty-two from the canyon. With over two hundred, the grounds were crowded but we had enough to stall Mydryth.

Time to search for the fifth dragon. The theory was that it would return to one of the lochs in Scotland where this type of dragon had originated. When I asked about their history, Angus related the story of how, hundreds of years ago, swarms of dragons had preyed upon humans and farm animals; set cottages and crops aflame.

A group of powerful mages had tired of people complaining about the latest damage and got together (which is unusual as mages can be a solitary lot) to create a potent spell to shrink the dragons so they'd never be a threat to mankind again – unless they were released by magic, of course. All the dragons needed to be enchanted at the same time as a free one could free the others. I began to understand how important it was that the dragon be returned.

Dorian and I would accompany Angus while others spent the day scouring Cumulos.

"Been a day or two since I've used this," said Angus, examining a broom scarred and black with age. But his touch was almost tender, as if ghosts of the past swirled through it.

"Will we be able to send the dragon back to the stream?" I asked as I straddled my own pristine model.

"Three or four mages should do it but first we need te find the beastie."

"Can we outfly it?" asked Dorian.

"Hard te say. They're verra quick."

In seconds, Cumulos had dropped away. The sky was a beautiful deep blue dotted with puffy clouds. Angus performed a time compression and we soon skimmed over an undulating landscape. Here and there amongst heather-clad hills the ocean sent searching fingers far into the land. Long, narrow, and deep, the lochs were home to mysterious creatures. No wonder Angus thought the dragon would go there. We crossed a couple of small waterways but our destination was King's Loch.

As we crested a tall ridge, an enormous body of water came into view. It was at least a mile across, its choppy surface dotted with whitecaps that continued as far as the eye could see.

"Wow!" I said to no one in particular. "This could take a while!"

We hovered over the ridge that sloped to the loch as a breeze, fresh with cool dampness, whipped our cloaks.

Angus scanned the water. "If I were a water dragon," he said, "tis where I'd hide." He reached into a deep pocket and handed us each a round flat crystal set into a carved solid silver frame. Each was four inches across. I couldn't tell if the blue fire in its depths was a reflection of the sky or part of the crystal. It was mesmerizing and I found myself staring into it.

"The crystal will turn green in the presence of a dragon, but don't look into it for any length o' time," said Angus. "It'll empty your mind – forever."

I jumped and looked away.

"We'll cover half the width o' the loch at a time. If tis down there, these crystals should pick it up."

We started down the waterway with Dorian nearest the shore, me next, Angus at the centre where the water was deepest. Our proximity to the surface ensured we were splashed by energetic whitecaps once in a while but we moved along at a fast pace.

As I stared into the water, the motion of the waves became hypnotic and, at times, I thought I caught flashes of monstrous sinuous grey shapes moving in the depths. My imagination, having nothing better to do, conjured images of giant dinosaur-like creatures. They had long snake-like necks and mouths filled with shark teeth. Perhaps they could leap from the water or reach out and snap me from the air ...

Yikes! I gave an involuntary shriek and darted upwards. Angus looked over with a raised brow. Feeling foolish, I gave him a "thumbs up" and returned to my position. What was wrong with me? As if I didn't have enough real problems, I was inventing more! With a firm grasp on my slippery imagination, I went back to watching for the dragon.

It was half-an-hour before I caught a flash of green. I slowed and waited for it to happen again. When Angus and Dorian noticed me lag, they swooped around and we hung suspended over the choppy water.

"I saw something! I know I did."

"Are ye sure?" asked Angus. "I don't see anything."

About to admit to a mistake, I caught a glimpse of movement. All the crystals flashed green as a grey shadow expanded.

"Go!" shouted Dorian and jerked his broom straight up. I hesitated as Angus shot by in front of me. The water boiled and a glistening scaled head emerged followed by reptilian wings beating against the water. Before I could get out of the way, it slammed into me and I lost hold of my broom.

Arms wind-milling, I fell backward, landed on something solid and, when I opened my eyes, discovered I was wedged between two vertical rows of thick plates that ran down a scaly back. A fish-like fin at the end of the tail waved from side to side. Powerful leathery wings lifted me higher with each stroke. If I hadn't been so terrified, I'd have fallen off but I couldn't have unclenched my fingers if my life depended on it … which it seemed it did.

Dorian and Angus dwindled. Guess dragons could out-fly brooms.

Would the thing turn around a blast me? I peered along the sinewy body. What was going to happen when the dragon landed? Was I to die as a lunch snack? I couldn't think of a more gruesome or embarrassing end.

"Put me down!" I screamed, just to be doing something.

There was a heart-stopping lurch as the dragon rolled a surprised eye in my direction. It must've been so intent on getting away, it hadn't noticed me.

"What are you doing there?" asked a deep telepathic voice. "You don't feel like the usual mage."

My fingernails dug holes in its stiff plates. *Dragons could talk?* Why hadn't Angus told me that? Kind of important information to leave out!

"I ... uh ... I'm a powerful mage from a far-away land."

"Which far-away land?"

A creature that lived in a stream would never have heard of America. "A continent far over a great water to the west."

"You mean the Americas?"

I've gotta say that was a surprise. "What do you know about the Americas?"

"We're telepathic, and there are dragons in North American streams too. I've always dreamed of going there."

I was confused. This sophisticated creature couldn't be the same dragon who'd scorched us two days ago!

My ride continued. "If you paid attention to history, you'd know dragons are associated with pearls of wisdom. How do you think that happened? With telepathy, everything anybody knows is shared with everyone all the time. It's an efficient system."

"If you're so knowledgeable, why do your kind eat humans and farm animals?"

He turned his head and lifted his lips. "See these babies?" Sunlight reflected from ten-inch canines. "These are for ripping and tearing meat! What do you suggest we eat? Porridge?"

Good point. I swallowed. "I ... guess not."

"It's fun being able to fly and shoot flames but life in a stream isn't so bad. Size is relative. There are all sorts of insects and water animals to eat so we never go hungry; there are tons of places to explore. Weather is never a problem; water is always water. Creatures don't run screaming whenever they see us."

He rolled the eye I could see. "Tough to expel fire in water but it's safer than living as full-sized dragons trying to evade magical spells and people armed with swords. Though I understand we'd now have to dodge projectile weapons."

His lips lifted in what I thought might be a dragon grin. "Was kind of fun though, watching you mages scatter when we blasted you! I can see why we got into so much trouble when we were air dwellers. So intoxicating!"

I didn't know how to respond to that so peeked over the front edge of a wing to see a patchwork of farms dozing in the warm summer sunshine far below. "So ... where are we going?"

"Thought I'd have lunch. It's a full-time job at this size to get enough to eat; took me two hours to catch enough fish for breakfast. Don't want to take that long for lunch."

I figured I'd make … what … ten or so fish? "So … again, where are we going?"

"I hear there's a new invention. It's called a slaughter house. A big pile of insides!" He licked his lips. "Major smorgasbord!"

My stomach roiled at the thought but, to be fair, both mages and humans eat animal protein so who was I to say a steak tasted better than intestines? My own intestines however didn't agree.

The emerald eye rolled backwards again. "Figured you were gonna be lunch didn't you?"

I tried not to look relieved. "Well … not … really … well …. yea. I did."

As a low rumble of laughter threatened my grip, I got a clear view of his enormous teeth. "The look on your face was priceless!" he chortled. "Why, you wouldn't even make a decent snack! And it's not worth all the hassle. People are *so* unforgiving! And it's not like they're unable to make more children or breed more livestock. There's a built-in renewal system, after all. There wasn't any shortage then and there isn't now. I don't get what all the fuss is about."

So says an immortal being. I could see we weren't going to agree on this one. Scotland was slipping beneath and I didn't want to watch the dragon filling up on cow insides. Logical or not, the very thought made me ill.

"My friends won't give up on me, and they won't quit until you're back in the stream."

"The two with you?" He snorted. "They can't catch me!"

"Don't count on it. Let's stop and talk to them. I promise they won't hurt you."

"Why would I believe that?"

"Because I'd like to survive the day and lying to you is not conducive to that end."

"I'm not going back to the stream. After lunch, I'm on my way to the Americas. I've heard you can travel thousands of miles up and down the rivers. There are giant freshwater lakes that make King's Loch look like a puddle. I want to explore everywhere! Imagine! A whole continent in which to play! No point living for thousands of years if you're stuck on an island."

"My friends can help you get there."

He heaved a deep dragon sigh and banked to the left. "I might regret this but I think I may need help. It's a long flight."

"Maybe we could make a deal. We're trying to protect a herd of unicorns and you'd be a great asset."

"I tried unicorn once when I was a youngster. Threw up for three days. Won't be doing that again."

Thank heaven for small favours.

As two small dots enlarged into Angus and Dorian, I was relieved they hadn't abandoned me to my fate. I waved to let them know I was unharmed. As the dragon rolled an eye in their direction, I noticed black smoke begin to pour from his nostrils.

"No!" I said as if I was talking to Reg. "Those are my friends! Don't flame anyone!"

He gave a giant dragon sigh and the smoke stopped. "I can see why dragons and mages had communications problems. You're no fun at all."

"Speaking of communication, you seem to be telepathic."

"Of course. I will say though, it's rare for a mage to communicate this way. Shocked me when I heard your voice in my head."

Goose bumps flew up my back as I realized I hadn't been speaking aloud. I was conversing telepathically with a dragon!

"Why don't I drop you here and your friends can pick you up? This should be about right." He peered down and closed one eye as if measuring the drop.

My fingers cramped. "I can't fly!"

"I can make you fly, but you may not know how to land."

"That's called falling!"

He shrugged a massive shoulder. "Tomato, tomahto."

"Look," I said, before he decided to do an aerial roll, "I promise no one will hurt you or send you back to your stream as long as you promise not to attack."

Massive lips pressed in disappointment. "How about one or two small shots for fun? Make them jump?" His eye had a hopeful gleam.

"No! You'll make them defensive! If you behave, I'll talk to Angus about getting you to the Americas without being seen."

"Why would I be seen?"

"Ever heard of aircraft?"

"No human would ever report seeing a dragon flying alongside. I hear they lock people up for that."

"You'll get no argument from me but the military monitor mysterious aerial phenomenon no matter what it looks like. And they have serious projectile weapons. Now would you please land without dropping me? By the way, I can't call you "dragon." Do you have a name?"

"My friends call me Bluescale. If they could see me now, they'd call me Blue *flame!* They're all excited about flying. Too bad about the mages. They'd cause a big fuss if more of us left the streams."

"I imagine," I said with a smidgeon of sarcasm. I remembered what Angus had said about one dragon being able to release others and wondered if Bluescale knew how. Not wanting to give him any ideas, I refrained from commenting and smothered the thought. *Could he read my mind?*

Angus and Dorian pulled to a stop, wands out, eyes on Bluescale whose circles tightened until a left wing scraped the ground. Claws on his hind legs brushed against stone followed by a gentle touchdown of front talons. Great leathery wings folded to his sides with a soft, slippery sigh.

He turned to me. "Need help?"

I thought his idea of help might be to shake me to the ground so declined and clambered down his side, over an enormous foreleg and into the heather. Angus and Dorian floated nearby.

"It's okay," I said. "He's … somewhat friendly. I promised he could leave if he wanted to."

"You promised he could leave? Why?" asked Dorian with a look that said my recent ride must've shaken something loose in my head.

"He's not evil. Just a dragon doing what dragons do. He'd like to live in the rivers in the Americas but needs to fly to get there. Unless there's another way . . ." I looked at Angus who watched the dragon's iridescent scales shimmer in the sunlight.

He didn't answer but began to speak in a strange language. Bluescale jerked to attention and peered down a long snout at Angus. Even more shocking, he responded in a rusty, deep voice with a hissing overtone that sounded like it issued from a cavern.

Dorian and I did a double-take. The strange sounds continued for several minutes before Angus turned to us.

"He's o' the ancient line o' Syth, a descendant o' the Old Ones. Before the Isles were formed and mankind wandered the land in small groups, the Old Ones existed. Humans were easy prey so they were hunted. One day, six young men in white robes and with long white hair appeared at an annual dragon gathering. A protective iridescent bubble formed around the men each time the dragons tried te flame them nor could the bubble be broken.

"When they realized they could nae hurt the visitors, a giant Red made the first attempt te communicate with man. The strangers spoke the ancient tongue o' the dragon and told them they'd need te find other prey. The humans were te be left alone te multiply in the land or the dragons would be destroyed. After one o' the herd erupted into flames and died on the spot, the dragons agreed te the request and thereafter hunted wild animals.

"After many thousands o' years and the White Headed Ones had been forgotten, the dragons again began te hunt mankind but, by then, the population had expanded and magic had been established. Having gained a sense o' their power, the mages enchanted the dragons and deposited them into the waterways o' the world."

"They're everywhere in the world?" asked Dorian.

"Pretty much. Ye see every river spills sooner or later into the ocean. Since the dragons can live in both salt and fresh water, they move along the seashore and up rivers. When the world was warmer, they moved along the north and from there into all the continents. Most of the waterways in the world have dragons."

"I gather they can't cross an ocean."

"They could but it would be dangerous. Not only is the food they need scarce at the ocean surface, they're likely te become prey themselves."

"Do we help him?" asked Dorian with an uneasy glance at the giant reptile.

"We're bound by Raven's word as a mage so canna force it back te its stream until we fulfill her promise."

I suggested Bluescale could be useful in protecting the unicorns.

With a hopeful gleam in his eyes, he turned my direction. "Can I flame something?"

"Mmm … maybe." I glanced at Angus for confirmation.

"Would ye be willing te help us fight a dark mage?" asked Angus. "He's dangerous."

Now the blue iridescent head shot towards Angus. "Can I flame him?"

"If tis in self-defence."

Bluescale's lips curled in what I took to be a smile. "I can make anyone want to kill me!"

I was not surprised.

Chapter 15

When the dragon was a shrinking dot in the sky, Angus transported us to his study. By then I wanted to curl up in a comfortable chair in front of the fire with a good book and perhaps have a nap and a snack, not necessarily in that order.

For once Dorian was thinking like me. "Let's see if we can scrounge up some lunch in the kitchen. I need to recover from seeing you carried off by a fire-breathing dragon!"

"Me too." I sighed and leaned against him. His arms came around me as Nightshade glided by the open doorway. As she shot me a poisonous glare, I bared my teeth.

"Nightshade!" called Dorian with a broad smile. "How goes the hunt for the mysterious invader?" He released me and trotted after her.

Her expression underwent a miraculous change and, with a triumphant sneer at me, she took his arm. "I'd like your advice," she said with a glowing smile. "Walk with me?"

"Of course." He glanced at me. "Meet you in the kitchen."

Yeah, right. Like that was going to happen! Ask a man for advice and he'll follow you anywhere. I swallowed an acid remark, sent the dark witch a glare of my own, and flounced away, stubborn chin leading the way.

A spoon of chocolate ice cream was awaiting its turn when a movement morphed into one of the young dwarves who worked in the kitchen.

"Hello, Darvana," I said, cramming the ice cream into my mouth.

"Is something wrong?" Her raspy voice was irritating in my present state of mind. "Do you need another carton of ice cream?"

"If I eat any more ice cream, my heart will explode!" She looked confused. "Never mind, Darvana. I'm just cranky because of that b…witch…Nightshade. How does somebody that evil get to be beautiful? Tell me that! It isn't fair!"

Darvana's squished face worked. "She has a dark aura and doesn't like dwarves."

I frowned. "How so?"

"I like working in the kitchen. I should not talk . . ."

"I'm not angry, Darvana. Everyone should be treated well here at Cumulos. If they're not, I want to know about it."

"She treats us like we have no intelligence; like we don't matter."

"Let's agree she's a bitch!" I dug out a huge scoop. "Would you like some?"

Darvana gave me a shy smile and presented a tiny bowl. I heaved a deep sigh, scooped some for her, ate more, and watched the doorway through which Dorian did not walk. Not that I expected him to. The black-hearted witch would keep him busy with something oh-so-important!

I imagined Nightshade as a target for Bluescale's flaming enthusiasm. *But I probably couldn't get away with that.* I hurled the empty container into a trash barrel and stalked outside. Maybe Cash and Basia could cheer me up – or I could ruin their day.

Okay! I admit it! I was jealous! What did she have that I didn't? She was a gorgeous, powerful witch who knew what she wanted and was willing to do what it took to get it. I turned a corner, flicked a look at one of the few mirrors in the castle and stopped short.

The face in the mirror was mutinous; its hair was straggly, clothing torn and dirty. And I smelled of dragon.

Hard to blame Dorian if he looked elsewhere. It occurred to me I'd never had real competition as I was his sole magical friend. His dalliances with human females were not a threat because I knew nothing would come of them, and I'd never indicated to Dorian that I had a romantic interest in him. How would he even know? It wasn't like he was remotely perceptive.

Time to get on the playing field if I didn't want to be flying home solo. I sprinted to my room.

Why did castles need so many bloody stairs? I knew a great electrician who could wire up a couple of elevators. There had to be a way! My thighs burned as I wound my way to the main floor. Could've been the high heels I wasn't used to.

Ebony hair was tucked into a faultless chignon; green streak gleamed with cleanliness, makeup perfect. The floor-length dress was ice-blue and form-fitted; sapphires and diamonds glittered at my ears and throat. I looked magnificent! Take that, Nightshade!

Frost had instructed me in the magical creation of clothing. No wonder Nightshade looked gorgeous! A mage or witch could create whatever she imagined. I smoothed the dress over my thighs and took another careful step. A sprawl down the stairs could ruin the effect I was going for.

I was halfway down the final flight when Dorian emerged from a side hallway, Nightshade still attached to his arm. He smiled down at her but something made him look up. He stopped dead. I watched him watch me as I continued my graceful descent, sparing a single triumphant glance for Nightshade.

Glory be! Her complexion was a few shades darker and her green eyes nasty slits. My smile broadened as I looked again at Dorian. I'd gotten his attention. What was I going to do with it? One thing at a time. Get to the main hall in one piece!

I breathed a sigh of relief when I reached the flagstones. Two vertical grooves appeared between her brows when Nightshade was unsuccessful at reclaiming Dorian's attention.

BLAM! The hall shook and billows of black smoke poured through a gaping hole where the massive front doors had blown open. My heart pounded as self-defence instincts went into over-drive. I twisted an ankle as I dove behind one of the hall's massive pillars. The smell of cordite filled the room. Gunpowder? If gunpowder worked here, why the hell didn't electricity?

Boiling black smoke caused my throat to close. Tears streamed down my face, and I spared a rueful thought for my perfect makeup. Was there some kind of a spell that kept me from looking good in front of Dorian?

As shadows flitted through the blackness, a hand grasped my arm. I tried to jerk away but Dorian's soot-blackened eyes appeared over a bandana that covered his nose. "It's me!" he coughed. "Here!" He tied a handkerchief over my nose and mouth. I didn't see Nightshade.

"I don't know where she went," he gasped. "When the door blew, she said something about Angus and took off. Let's go!" He grasped my wrist and took off at a jog.

I kicked off the stupid heels and ran down twisting hallways in bare feet, sparing a thought to wonder how he'd learned his way around the back passages of the castle so fast.

In short order we arrived at the same dead end passage Angus had used to transport us to the village. Dorian passed a hand in front of the dark crystal wall, it wavered – and we were on a street corner in wonderful fresh air.

I pulled the handkerchief from my face. "Where'd you learn that?"

He seemed to have difficulty with an answer. In fact, it looked like he was making a valiant effort to choke back a laugh.

My eyes narrowed. "Dorian! Are you laughing because I don't know how to transport?"

With obvious effort to control the tremulous muscles at the corners of his mouth, he said, "I'm thinking how you've changed in the past few minutes." His voice had a suspicious waver.

"What do you mean, changed?" Then I noticed how the whites of his eyes gleamed in the blackness of his face which was streaked with tears. If he looked that bad, I could only imagine what streaked makeup would look like.

I grimaced. "Oh. I imagine I look a sight." I heaved a deep sigh and looked at the ground. "I just wanted to look good for once. How can everyone else look gorgeous while I look like I've been in a dog fight?"

I rubbed my cheeks with the handkerchief and it came away black. I didn't want to look in a mirror; didn't want to know.

Dorian removed his bandana, spit on it and swabbed my face. I felt like a kitten getting a bath from its mother. "It's going to take more than this," he said, giving up. "Let's go. Somebody will know Angus." As we started down the street, I resisted eye-contact with startled pedestrians.

We'd gone a block when Dorian took my hand and tucked it under his arm. "You know, of course, how gorgeous you are," he said, eyes ahead.

My mouth opened but nothing came out. We walked further. "You … you think I'm gorgeous? Are you serious?" I stared up at him.

He glanced down, humour dancing in his eyes. "Well, perhaps not at this precise moment . . ." then ducked as I took a half-hearted swing at him. We fell silent; again stopped short of venturing further onto shaky ground. *So much to lose.*

We entered a narrow lane lined with tall thin houses topped by crooked brass stovepipes. Where had all my bravery gone? When was I going to tell him? What was wrong with now? Nothing. Except it was *now*. Not *some-other-time*.

I sighed and kicked a pebble with a bare toe.

"What's the matter?"

"I'm a coward."

His lips quirked into a half smile. "I doubt that." We walked on. "What makes you think you're a coward?"

I looked into his eyes. "You."

His eyebrows rose. "Me?" I nodded. "What do you mean?"

I turned to face him. Struggling for words, I looked deep into his eyes. "I think it's time we talked . . ."

"There you are!" An angular, impossibly thin man with spectacles perched on a hooked nose hurried up, shoulder-length grey hair trailing in the breeze. "Tommy Longstraw at your service! Angus hoped you'd escaped. Asked me to watch for you."

"Is Angus okay?" I blurted. "Do you know what happened at Cumulos?"

His head bobbed. "He's alright, but the dark mage attacked! No one in or out!"

My stomach tightened. "What about Frost and the others?"

He held up a hand. "Perhaps I should first ask if you are alright." He scanned our soot-covered clothes.

Dorian gestured in dismissal. "Nothing a little soap and water won't cure. Tell us about Cumulos."

Our companion cast an uneasy glance over a shoulder. "We should retire to my home." He flicked another look at our clothing. "I'll find you something to wear."

As Longstraw poured water from a gleaming kettle into three earthenware cups, Dorian and I perched on leggy stools before a tall wooden table. The tea smelled heavenly. I surveyed the room as our host prepared a plate of honey cakes.

The floor was made of smooth stone blocks; wooden walls were discolored with age, and a high ceiling was covered with what looked like live mushrooms. Copper pots and pans hung from an iron ring near a wood-burning stove and the room was scented by a pleasant earthy aroma that drifted from bunches of herbs hung from the ceiling.

Dorian looked delicious in borrowed attire of loose white shirt tucked into dark pants while I felt like a child in grownup's clothing. A voluminous tunic was cinched with a leather belt that encircled me twice and the sleeves were rolled several times.

Longstraw slid onto a matching stool and dumped cream into his tea.

"Do you know what happened?" Dorian spread gooseberry preserves onto honey cake and took a bite.

"Talon was closing on a dark-ghost before the explosion. He said the alarms had begun to get agitated soon after you scryed Mydryth so maybe the dark mage saw it; at least knew where it came from."

"What would such a creature look like?" asked Dorian.

"They can be semi-solid," he tipped his hand from side to side, "kind of human-ish or smoke-like."

"That would explain the proximity alarms. When it became more solid, it'd set them off." Dorian looked at me. "And now we know what was on the tower stairs."

I shivered. "Why would it want to kill me?"

Longstraw shrugged. "Why do they kill anyone?" He raised his hands palms up and dropped them into his lap. "Perhaps Mydryth's afraid of the two of you.

"Afraid of us?" I aked. "How could that be?"

"He'll be afraid of any magic he doesn't control."

Dorian was still focussed on the attack. "How did the explosion happen?"

"Not sure yet. Must've found a weakness somewhere. Would only take a second or two for Mydryth to transfer a message." Tommy pushed round spectacles back into the dent on his arched nose. "A dark-ghost can't do much on its own. It can only appear solid for a few seconds at most. For instance, it couldn't move a keg of gun powder by itself but it could pass on instructions."

"How did the gun powder get there?" asked Dorian. "Nobody in Cumulos would've done it."

"Mydryth could've used a spell to explode the gun power," I said, "but you're right; who would move it into position in the first place?"

I took a bite of honey cake drizzled with nasturtium sauce. Delicious! I cursed under my breath when the sauce dripped onto my borrowed trousers. As I tried to remove it without anyone noticing, it smeared. Dorian's lips acquired a suspicious quirk but he continued to converse with our host.

"Just so." Longstraw mumbled and pulled at his lower lip. "Or a delay spell could've caused the explosion."

"Any idea what's going on now?" asked Dorian.

Longstraw shook his head. "Angus managed to get a message to me before the second level of the magic shield closed. Said if I was to see you to remind you of a blue scale." He looked at us. "So, what's a blue scale?"

Dorian and I stared at one another. How could the dragon help?

Since we couldn't return to Cumulos, Longstraw offered to put us up. We'd finished tea when he peered at a complicated arrangement of concentric brass rings which spun at different rates. "Two o'clock," he announced. "Gotta run. Be back in a couple of hours. Make yourselves at home. Bedroom's in the back."

He slipped off the stool, pulled a long red scarf from amongst other long scarves hanging on a peg, and wrapped it around his neck. Since the day was warm, I didn't see the need but I was beginning to feel somewhat stupid considering I couldn't understand his clock either.

After the door slammed, Dorian and I cleaned the dishes and set them on the drain board. The silence thickened to become uncomfortable. We'd rarely been alone since our arrival at Cumulos.

I cleared my throat. "Shall we check out our rooms?" Longstraw had waved towards the back of the house in a vague manner when he'd invited us to stay.

The first bedroom was Tommy's. Next to that was a largish bathroom followed by a second bedroom – *one*. My heart sank when I peeked in and saw a long bed covered with a multi-coloured patchwork quilt. Heavy curtains were attached to six-foot-tall hand-hewn bed posts. Perhaps his relatives were also tall.

"This should be interesting," murmured Dorian in my ear. A shiver swept through me and I stepped into the room to get some distance. To my mortification, my cheeks burned, and a set of gingham curtains became fascinating. Dorian watched with something like amusement. Did he find this funny? Where did all my newfound bravado go? Confident one second and shaking in my boots the next? What was wrong with me?

"Let's go for a walk," said Dorian. "See if we can figure out how Bluescale can help – if we can find him."

I shot out of the room and flew down the hallway. "Where's the fire?" asked Dorian, catching the door I slammed in his face.

"Sorry. I … uhh … we need to figure this out fast."

"Not *that* fast … Why are you running?"

"I'm not running. I just … you know … walk fast."

"Sure you do." He grabbed my hand. "Let's walk. We're not going anywhere special. Take a deep breath," he said. "Relax. I'm capable of sleeping in the same bed and keeping my hands off you."

Speak for yourself. "I know. After all, Nightshade's available."

He stopped, pulled me to face him. "What's this got to do with Nightshade?"

I should learn to shut up. "Nothing. I just noticed she seems to ... like you ... a lot."

"Is that a problem?"

"Of course not. Our relationship has always been based on friendship. I don't care what you do with her." It's a good thing lying wasn't punishable by lightning bolts.

His mouth acquired a sardonic twist. "Thanks for your permission."

"I didn't mean . . ."

"Never mind," he said and, keeping my hand in his, walked on down the street. I remained silent. Anything I could say at this point would make matters worse ... if that were possible.

The winding street sloped to a stream crossed by an arched stone bridge where we rested our elbows on the railing to gaze into the gurgling water. Green-headed ducks swam about, bobbed below the surface to reappear downstream. Red-winged blackbirds chirped as they clutched cattail stalks that lined the stream bank.

"It's beautiful here," I said.

"Hmmm," murmured Dorian as he stared into the water. "Feels different to be so ... accepted."

We watched the stream for a while, my hand loose in his, the sun warm on my back as I tried to imagine what it would be like to spend more time like this with Dorian.

A sudden cool breeze lifted the green of my hair and brought with it the scent of a forest thick with wildflowers. I glanced around, looking for the source. We were in a village surrounded by meadows in which most of the spring flowers had already turned to seed. I flashed back to the imagined scent in my apartment. Hmmm. I was about to ask Dorian if he'd noticed it when a voice crashed into my thoughts.

"My wings are getting tired!"

"What . . .?"

"I said my wings are getting tired. Would like to land sometime. Mind letting me in?"

"Bluescale?"

"Expecting someone else? Got a lot of dragon friends?"

"I. . . of course not. You surprised me."

Dorian stared. "Who are you talking to?"

"Did I say that out loud? Sorry. Bluescale's waiting for me to let him through the shield."

"Tell him to meet us at King's Loch."

I sent the thought to Bluescale. Dorian flicked his wand and our brooms appeared.

"If I didn't know better," he said, straddling his, "I'd have said you'd arranged this to avoid the bed thing."

Before I could find a suitable retort, he'd grinned and shot into the air.

Chapter 16

A chill breeze whipped whitecaps from the grey waters of King's Loch. I pulled further into my cloak as we hovered along the south ridge wishing Bluescale would hurry the hell up. I was chilled to the bone. Just as I believed he wasn't going to show, a gigantic blue form erupted from the loch, a fish in his mouth. With a flip of the head, the dragon tossed it in the air and caught it head first. One swallow and it was gone. I swallowed too when I realized the fish would weigh as much as I did.

Bluescale sailed over, made a smooth circle and a graceful landing on the grass, iridescent blue-green scales gleaming in the sun.

"Did you find the ... smorgasbord you were seeking?" I didn't want to know but hoped to appear friendly. Standing beside him reminded me of how enormous he was. Half a dozen people could stand beneath one wing with room to spare.

The sinewy neck bent and Bluescale's enormous emerald eyes fastened on me. "I did! It was glorious!" His scales shivered with pleasure. "I'll be full for a week!"

His belly *was* round. Mine was queasy. "So what's with the fish? Dessert?"

"It practically swam into my mouth. How could I refuse?"

Time for a change of subject. "The dark mage we told you about has attacked Cumulos."

Bluescale looked like he was waiting for me to say something important.

I gritted my teeth. "I'm guessing you don't care?"

He pressed rubbery lips together and shrugged massive shoulders. "Why would I? Mages have been fighting for centuries and it's not like I have any great reason to get involved. My kind have been victimized by them all." Heavy scaled brows rose. "You're not naive enough to expect them to stop, are you?"

That was exactly what I'd been thinking ... after Angus was back in charge. Bluescale's laughter rolled along the valley and echoed off the steep-sided loch.

Annoyance and embarrassment vied for position, and a crunching sound encouraged me to relax my jaw before I lost bits of enamel. "Is that necessary?"

Bluescale's guffaws diminished to the occasional chuckle. "You are funny. Best laugh I've had in centuries!"

Dorian was wise enough to remain silent. After all, I didn't need help to make a fool of myself.

"Alright then," I ground out, "how about you help us put Angus back in charge, and we'll transport you to the Americas?"

Small stretchy ears perked forward. "Anywhere I want to go?"

"As long as it's Denver."

"What's a denver?"

"A city near mountains – real mountains, not like these. We'll put you into a stream there and you can explore the entire network."

He looked speculative. "When?"

"After Mydryth is removed from Cumulos."

His head came up. "Mydryth?! *That's* who's taken over Cumulos?"

"Yes. Why?"

"He killed my brother!" Vertical pupils narrowed, I heard a deep rumble, and black smoke boiled from his nostrils. Before he got carried away, I suggested he save the flames for the mage.

His eyes glinted. "I can flame him?"

"Be my guest. Just don't harm Cumulos residents in the process." I'm ashamed to say I was tempted to exempt Talon and Nightshade.

"How long have you known Mydryth?" asked Dorian.

Bluescale stared into the distance. "Must be a couple of thousand years, I suppose."

A couple of thousand years? How long did these beings live?

Over the afternoon we discussed a number of ideas but nothing sounded too … well … sound. In light of Dorian's insistence on making an attempt to penetrate the shield and my determination to try something else, I'm afraid our conversation got heated. I've found Dorian can be unreasonable at times.

I worried there was no way to tell what modifications Mydryth may have made to Cumulos, and Dorian was convinced the dark mage hadn't had time to change anything. I pointed out with perfect logic that it may not take long to adjust the shield to kill.

The horizon had flattened the bottom of the sun and I shivered as we settled onto our brooms to head back. Bluescale would remain in the loch until he heard from us.

We skimmed grass-covered hills in brittle silence until it occurred to me that Mydryth may not know about the gnome tunnels beneath Cumulos and that some of them ran to the cloud village. Rarely used, their intricacies weren't common knowledge. If the shields didn't penetrate the ground, we could use them to sneak into the castle.

Dorian mulled it over. "Might work. The tunnels are deep and we still have our invisibility talismans. If we can get as far as Angus' study, we could knock out the shield and let Bluescale in. He'd be a fantastic distraction!"

I was so relieved at the release of the tension between us, I agreed and decided now would be a good time to stop talking.

The golden glow in the west had diminished and purple fingers of night stretched from the east to contrast with the flickering lanterns of Cumulos. We'd agreed to keep spells to a minimum in hopes of sneaking by the castle without being spotted so I pulled my cloak tighter and entertained a fond but futile hope that visualizing a hot fire and warm cider would stop my teeth from chattering.

We skimmed close to the ground, ducked around trees, and worked our way toward the quiet collection of stone huts. Evening swans in the pond below the village set up a short ruckus as we passed. Of course, the only swans in the world that could make any sound at all had to be on our route.

Dorian thought he knew where one of the tunnels emerged in the village and, as we touched down near an herbal shop, I glanced in to see a short, bent old man with a long nose sweep the floor with a ratty broom. At the rate he was moving, this might've been his entire job for the day. The village was calm considering the confusion that must be going on at the castle though it was possible the take-over had been so fast, the villagers didn't know of it yet.

I messaged Bluescale that we'd arrived and he could begin his journey but he wasn't to show himself until I gave the okay. As I disconnected from the dragon, an insistent growl from my stomach reminded me it'd been hours since breakfast. Even though time was short, there was no telling how long it would be before we got the opportunity to eat, and hunger was a weapon I didn't plan on handing Mydryth.

As I pointed out it would take Bluescale at least a couple of hours to get there, Dorian agreed to stop for supper. I suspected it might also have something to do with his crazy belief I get cranky when I go without food. I don't think it's true – well, not all the time.

I wobbled along the cobblestones in the deepening shadows trying not to trip or twist an ankle while we looked for an eating establishment. I hoped it was a sign of good fortune that we found a diminutive restaurant situated across from our goal. A faded sign pointed to a spiral stone staircase set below street level, and I stepped on the first smoothly-worn stair with considerable trepidation, uncertain as to what we'd find. Cauldrons boiling and bubbling in the shadows presided over by ancient crones in black hats and robes? Who knew?

I pushed against the door at the foot of the stairs, peeked around its edge – and blinked in surprise as strong light flooded the stairwell. It took a few seconds for my eyes to adjust as I stepped into a busy plant-filled room.

Aromatic and colorful flowers hung from the ceiling and spilled from tubs scattered throughout. The back wall was occupied by a few small tables decorated with clay pots containing a miniature rose each. During the day, the room would be flooded with sunlight from ten-foot-tall windows inset into the opposite wall. At the moment, numerous glass spheres six inches in diameter, each encircled by a brass ring, floated at the ceiling and gave off a bright but not dazzling light – an astonishing change from the usual dark buildings of the village. Not surprisingly, this beautiful oasis was filled with customers.

A slender woman with masses of red hair twisted into a thick plait appeared from amongst the plants to guide us to an unoccupied table near the windows. Voices lifted and fell in muted tones, and the gentle trickling of water came from somewhere in the foliage. It seemed we were correct in suspecting the attack was not public knowledge. The woman held a chair for me and set two clean, leather-bound menus on the polished table. I began to look forward to the meal. This was almost a date!

As Dorian cast a quick glance at the retreating form of the shapely woman, I felt a scowl imprint itself on my forehead. I smoothed it away with my fingers and jerked the menu towards me hoping they sold gigantic steaks. I flipped through eight pages of parchment that were somehow spotless – flipped through them again.

Where was the meat? A horrifying thought flitted through my brain. Don't tell me this was a vegetarian restaurant! I needed meat! Lots of it! I scrabbled through the pages once more and groaned. I'd be a huddled bundle of low blood sugar by morning.

Dorian pointed to an entree of bean stew accompanied by heavy black bread. Butter and cream along with fresh goat milk were available. Perhaps I'd live after all. The addition of a bowl of fresh nuts should help.

As it turned out, the stew was all I could eat. By the time I waddled from the restaurant, I entertained visions of collapsing into bed for several hours, the challenge of sneaking into Cumulos far beyond my capacity.

I rubbed my stomach, leaned against a brick wall opposite the darkened alley that housed the tunnel entrance. "Whose idea was it for me to eat so much?" I whined.

"Nobody twisted your arm," mumbled Dorian as he peered with narrowed eyes at the darkened alley.

I may have mentioned before that perfect friends are … well … perfect. Don't you hate that? I don't think Dorian has overeaten in his entire life. Where's the fairness in that?

I sent him a sour look that he never saw. Men can be so obtuse.

"Let's go." Without waiting, Dorian strode into the darkening alley as night settled in. The low glow of his wand revealed a narrow door which opened in silence. I spared a glance along the alley and hustled after.

As the door eased closed behind us, Dorian increased the light enough to enable us to find our way to a stairway. At one point, a deafening squeak of the wooden floor caused the hair to lift on the back of my neck and my breath to catch in my throat. We'd reached the rickety banister and Dorian had taken two steps down when there was a soft thump. I sank my nails into his arm.

"There's someone here!!" My horrified whisper was loud in the silence.

Dorian grasped my wrist and squeezed until I gasped and released my hold on his elbow. "You're making me bleed," he whispered, then interrupted my apology. "Hush!"

The darkness, thanks to my active imagination, contained monsters of all kinds – beasts that made thumping noises as they stalked their prey. I snuggled close to Dorian and searched for movement.

My heart lurched as something brushed my leg and tentacles slid around my ankles. At my screech of terror, Dorian jerked me behind him and amplified the light.

I gaped at the absence of tentacles. "But … I felt it! Something was winding around my ankles!"

One side of Dorian's mouth went up. "Is this what's so frightening?"

I peeked under his arm to see two bejeweled eyes.

"Meow?" A sleek calico cat stretched its back for a pat and pushed against Dorian's legs as it erupted with purring.

The wand light diminished. "Shall we continue?" asked Dorian, "– or is there someone in the village still asleep?"

I hunched my shoulders and inched down the stairs after him. We were almost to the bottom when a half-dozen glow bulbs burst to life. A gnome, who'd had his head on a desk, jerked erect. I don't know who was more startled, us or him.

He blinked sleep from his eyes and stumbled erect. "Who goes there?"

Really? That was his question? Most of the villagers knew who we were by now.

"We're the mages from below," said Dorian. "We need to access the castle through the gnome tunnels." He gestured to a heavy door set into a wall next to the desk.

The gnome blinked. "Why?"

"The castle was attacked and taken over. We're helping Angus get it back."

After swiping at his nose, the gnome twisted his face into a grimace. "Cumulos has never been attacked. What are you trying to do?"

"I take it you're responsible for guarding the tunnels?" I asked. He straightened and nodded. "Then your primary role is to protect the castle, right?" He nodded again. "The only way we can get into the castle is through the gnome tunnels. All other entrances are blocked."

The little guy shook his head. "Haven't heard of any disturbance at the castle."

"Could that be because you're in a basement?"

"Somebody would tell me."

A sense of victory washed through me. "We're the ones telling you. Now, you can let us pass or we can force our entry. Which would you prefer?"

"Well … I have to get permission. Spyders have been seen lately."

"Do we look like spyers to you?"

He looked from one to the other of us. "Guess not."

Dorian gave a grunt of impatience, directed his wand towards the door, and it swung inward. "We don't have time for this." He grabbed my hand and I stumbled after him into utter darkness. I froze and sucked in a breath of terror.

As Dorian lit his wand, I saw a grin. "A little claustrophobic, are we? Don't worry. We have enough light, but we need to turn it off at the other end. If I remember from touring the castle with Nightshade, there's another heavy door on the Cumulos side." He frowned. "Come to think of it, how did she know about the tunnels? Thought she was new to Cumulos." He shrugged. "Maybe she's a fast learner."

Fast learner, my ass! I bit my tongue and adjusted my wand to full power. As Dorian gestured for me to proceed, I stopped dead. "*I'm* not going first. I don't like dark places!"

After he'd slammed and locked the door behind us, Dorian moved to my side.

The tunnel was eight feet wide, brick-lined and curved to a point – tall enough we didn't need to walk single file, and the light from both wands should make it feel less like a dungeon. I shuddered as skittering noises in the darkness reminded me that rats frequented such places. I came from an area that seldom had to deal with them and had never seen one except for Cyril although I suspected he was unusual in the world of rats.

We hustled along, ducked cobwebs and jumped small rivulets. I kept fingers of awareness searching for dark-ghosts, all the while hoping we wouldn't encounter any because, of course, I couldn't remember Talon's counter-spell.

Things progressed well for twenty minutes after which I discovered my thighs burned and I was panting like a dog.

Of course the village was a mile down the mountain from Cumulos so we climbed ever upwards. Dorian never drew a deep breath.

"Dim your light," he said. "We're not far from the end." I fought rising panic at the encroaching darkness. Dark-ghosts functioned perfectly well in the dark. "Let's use the invisibility talisman," he said. "Dark-ghosts shouldn't be able to sense us." As my body disappeared, I was grateful to feel a strong hand searching for mine. I was conflicted. On the one hand, I like to think of myself as having a certain amount of courage. On the other, I'd be happy to have someone do the hard stuff for me. Too bad I can't let that happen without a significant loss of self-respect. I heaved a sigh of resignation, grasped his hand, and followed along in the darkness.

After I'd stumbled over yet another stone, Dorian's whisper drifted from the darkness. "Raven?"

"What?"

"We're invisible, not inaudible. Try not to make so much noise!"

I bit my lip. The hard heels of my oversized borrowed boots were not quiet, and the dimness of our wands kept me from seeing the pebbles. I thought Dorian must have the eyes of a cat. "I'm trying but it's dark in here. Maybe we should strengthen the light."

"I'd rather not. Follow in my footsteps. The tunnel was a good idea, by the way. We'd have encountered the shield by now if we were going to. "

I experienced a warm response to the offhand compliment. Perhaps I was turning into a big old dog. Pretty soon a pat on the head would have me rolling over to have my tummy scratched.

"The door's just around the next bend." A few steps further, a thin line of light glowed near the floor. Dorian extinguished his wand and, with a sense of doom, I followed suit. My skin crawled at the thought of dark-ghosts skulking in the shadows. Dorian squeezed my fingers. "It's alright Raven. You've done more dangerous things than this."

Too bad I couldn't remember when. My fingers were cramped around my wand and I still couldn't remember Talon's spell to immobilize a dark-ghost. It'd seemed complicated at the time. Still did. Something about webbing at the correct angle and it needed some kind of … impulsion … I was too nervous to remember. Why couldn't things be easy? Who designed this system anyway? I seemed to be losing focus.

With shallow breaths, I inched along behind Dorian. My hand said it was safe in his warm grip but my eyes said I was alone in a dark tunnel. We'd reached the door when the light flickered. Someone was on the other side. We flattened against the bricks, a latch scraped, and a shoulder slammed against solid wood. As the door swung toward us with an ear-splitting screech, I realized I was getting light-headed from not breathing.

Two gigantic trolls, twins to the ones we'd met in Mydryth's dungeon, lurched into the tunnel four feet from us. I hoped they couldn't hear dripping sweat.

A nasally voice followed them. "Out of the way!" A wand attached to a silk-clad arm reached in, scribed a swirling motion, and sconces along the walls burst into flame. Mydryth, dressed in what I think of as his mage robes, stepped into sight. As flickering light illuminated the tunnel, I gave silent thanks for the invisibility talisman.

After ordering the trolls to check the length of the tunnel, Mydryth grumbled something that sounded like "stupid imbeciles" before the door slammed and quick footsteps receded.

The creatures sneered at one another (could've been the troll equivalent of a smile – or maybe not) and tromped down the tunnel. Personal hygiene didn't seem to be high on their priority list and I covered my nose to keep from gagging.

Dorian and I waited until the great lumpy shadows disappeared and the sounds of their lumbering passage had faded. Then he gave my hand a squeeze and moved to the door. A flick of his wand and it swung open.

We peered to the right in time to see Mydryth and two scarecrow man-beings in dark rags disappear around a corner. Dark stringy hair sprouted from skeletal heads. The stuff of horror movies … I didn't want to get any closer to those things. Must be some of the creatures in Mydryth's army. The dark-ghosts could get in anywhere to spy but they'd need physical beings like the trolls and these scarecrow men to carry out the actual attack.

I remembered Longstraw's explanation that Mydryth had performed some kind of super-translocation spell and, after the shields had failed, trolls and scarecrow men had materialized all over the castle. Even seemed to know who to target. Frost and Talon were unconscious before they could move a muscle, but Angus managed to get a message to Longstraw before the transmission was terminated. The attack had been flawless and fast. I made a mental note to remember Mydryth was not a stupid man.

I leaned against Dorian to whisper. "Angus once told me there were null-magic cells in the dungeon. That's where they'll be held as it'd be the only way to control them." I wanted to believe they were still alive. Dorian pulled a folded parchment from his robe. "What's that?" I whispered.

"A map of the castle I borrowed from Talon to learn my way around."

As Dorian re-folded the map into a different configuration in what appeared in my heightened state of awareness to be slow motion, I cast an edgy glance down the hall.

"There!" Dorian pointed to a row of square shapes on the map. After we'd managed to figure out where they were, Dorian refolded the parchment and tucked it into his robe. "We're not that far away so let's see if we can manage a rescue. That way Angus can worry about the shield."

I took my boots off, tied the laces and hung them on my belt so I could run without making a racket. Dorian waited while I fumbled with my footwear but, since he was invisible, I couldn't tell if he was impatient or not. As I straightened, a warm hand grasped my left breast. In the moments it took for him to jerk his hand away, a warm sensation flooded my belly.

I heard a mumbled apology. "Grab my arm!" he growled. *Dorian doesn't handle embarrassment well either.*

We jogged to the top of a stone staircase, paused to check the way ahead then sprinted down the first flight. I almost lost my footing at the next turn but we didn't slow until after three more. Hard to believe the dungeons were deeper than the tunnel. A narrow flight curved to a landing lit by flickering sconces that illuminated the entrances to four hallways.

"The map says we go straight," whispered Dorian. "There'll be guards if our mages are here."

We tiptoed and flattened against a nearby wall. In less than a minute, the rumble of harsh voices drifted from the dimness. We peeked around a corner to see two hairy, loose lipped trolls at a rickety table rolling dice. Broadswords leaned against the wall and curved knives filled scarred leather scabbards.

I felt of stab of frustration that I'd left a can of pepper spray on my key chain at home. I'd have to talk to Cash about getting some kind of weaponry that I could use without risk to myself (or unintended others). Knives make me nervous. Besides, I couldn't imagine using one against another human being. All that bleeding and stuff. Yuck!

I peered past the guards to the cells. The locking mechanisms seemed simple – heavy iron bolts in solid frames that slid into deep sockets. But how to get past the guards? They filled the corridor and we were no match for even one of them. We withdrew to craft a battle plan in sibilant whispers.

I tried to create a small glow on the tip of my wand beneath my robe – nothing. This was definitely a null-magic area. We'd have to perform a rescue the old fashioned way. As I pondered our situation, it occurred to me that our invisibility talismans worked. When I pointed it out to Dorian, he thought maybe it was because their power came from space. Who knew, but this was not the time to ponder the question.

After minutes of fruitless brainstorming, Dorian mused, "Remember how we used to use magic to make us run faster?"

I nodded. "Haven't done that in a day or two."

"We could use it now."

"You have a plan?" I was happy about that because I'd drawn a blank.

"One of us acts as a decoy while the other opens the cells." Silence.

I made a long, slow grimace. "I'm guessing *I'd* be the decoy in this scenario?"

"I'm stronger. Those old latches might be tough to open."

As I peeked around the corner again, the guards seemed to have grown. "What if they're faster than they look?"

"The null-magic area shouldn't be much larger than the dungeon. Run back up the stairs but make sure to get a good head start. As soon as you're far enough away, you should be able to use magic to outrun them."

"I'm supposed to do it on my own until then?"

"You're in … decent shape. I'm pretty sure you can do it."

"Pretty sure . . ."

"Well. . . yeah."

"That would mean you're not sure."

He played his trump card. "You've got a better plan?"

I ground my teeth and hissed. "Alright Dorian, but make it fast!" I stepped into the corridor.

"Hey!" I yelled. "Hey! You pair of morons, you missed one! Come and get me!"

They cast startled looks my direction then, with a unified roar, grabbed their broadswords and sprang to their feet. I gulped, turned and ran faster than I ever have without the help of magic. I charged straight to the stairs, took them two at a time, and skidded around the sharp turn at the next flight. I was half-way up the second set when my thighs began to burn. I tried magic. Nothing!

The two guards were closing fast without any signs of tiring. Funny, they'd looked slow. My lungs laboured as I strove for the top where I hoped the null-magic area would end. The guards weren't ten feet behind when, on trembling legs, I reached the top stair. I grasped the banister, pulled myself to the right, and staggered along the hallway.

Monstrous dirty fingernails clamped onto my shoulder and a shaft of pain pierced clear through my body. Somehow I managed to slip from its grasp but was knocked almost sense-less when I was swatted like an insect. I skidded across the corridor into a stone wall. Something sticky ran down the side of my face and the world tilted at an alarming angle.

As I lurched to my feet, a massive wall of odoriferous flesh and the leer of jagged, black teeth loomed into my fuzzy vision. Filthy hands reached. I staggered away and – wonder of wonders – felt a familiar tingle.

I ducked a grasping paw and engaged a magic-enhanced burst. A glance behind showed the two trolls come to a confused halt. I skidded to a stop at a safe distance, pushed my hair back in a habitual gesture, and was appalled to see my hand come away red and slippery. My head swam. I've never been good with blood. *Pull it together, Raven! Don't pass out at the sight of a little blood even if it is yours! Focus!!*

I waved and trotted back a few steps, my head pounding so hard my vision fluttered like a scorched moth. My instinct was to run away but Dorian might need more time. They lowered shaggy heads and scowled; confusion in red-rimmed eyes. One curled his lip to reveal the remains of teeth in need of dental attention (Are there no dentists in magic land?).

I moved closer … taunting. *Stupid, I know.* They growled but refused to take the bait, paced in frustration and swung maces and broadswords. I discovered they had extra-long arms as I scrambled back from a slice that came too close.

How long had it been? I wasn't crazy about this game of chicken.

Could there be more guards further down the corridor? I slipped around a corner, activated the invisibility talisman, and crept back. My pursuers tramped back down the stairs. Guess they'd given up. I needed to get ahead to squeeze past the guard post. Since there wasn't any room to pass undetected on the narrow lower stairs, I'd have to overtake them on the first flight. I bit my lip, sucked in a breath to make myself smaller and, heart in mouth, slid by the larger of the two.

Whew! I didn't think anything living could smell that bad! I held my nose to keep from gagging.

The guard stopped and sniffed the air. Maybe he thought the same about me. I froze like the proverbial deer in headlights. His pig eyes narrowed to almost disappear into his face. I don't know how long we stood there, probably not as long as the hour it felt. Then he shook his great greasy head and resumed a ponderous descent. I was less than two feet from the gigantic broadsword he held like a toy.

I scurried to catch the other guard who'd reached the next landing. Before he got to the narrow stairs, I made a wide swing around his bulk and spooned my way in front as his monstrous appendage hit the first stair. It was a good thing too. He used the entire width of the stairwell.

Praying I wouldn't trip, I scampered as fast as I could but, when I hit the flagstones, the heavy tread of the guards was still too close. I scuttled to their station, slipped past, and plunged into the gloomy dungeon where I found … empty cells.

Dorian must've been successful. I wondered if there was a back door and wished I'd paid more attention to the map. A quick glance showed the guards had returned to their abused chairs and resumed their game of dice. They hadn't even checked the cells. I guessed they didn't come from the top echelon of the Mydryth military.

I felt stupid. Here I'd rushed to help Dorian and instead had gotten myself trapped! I hugged the cloak I'd gotten from Longstraw in a weak effort to lessen the chill and hoped Dorian remembered I was still here.

I couldn't go back so continued down the dank hallway. These old castles were filled with secret passageways. Maybe I'd run across one. Unfortunately the operative word here was "secret."

A rat skittered across my foot and I bit a knuckle to smother a scream. *I'm really not a screamer but there are limits and mine are rats.* I stopped long enough to tug on my over-sized boots.

Scurrying shadows got busier as the darkness deepened. Perhaps I was far enough away not to need the invisibility spell. It interfered with vision; made everything look like it was underwater. I neutralized the talisman and flicked my wand, praying for a glimmer – and a glimmer was all I got… I could eke miniscule bits of magic from the surroundings. The good news was the edge of the null-magic field was close; the bad news was, in order to get out of it, I had to go deeper into rat-infested darkness.

I could've sworn at one point a black shadow slid along my spine, and the hair on my arms and the back of my neck flew up like a Halloween cat's. After I'd resumed breathing, only an innate stubborn streak kept me tramping over ancient debris and forging ahead. I distracted myself by muttering threats about what I'd do to Dorian when I found him. As I recall, this had been his idea . . .

Chapter 17

Curved stones were slippery underfoot and water trickled down the sides of the mildewed and malodorous tunnel. Tiny red eyes reflected weak wand illumination, and squirming things brushed my ankles and squiggled beneath my feet. The last burning sconce far behind, blackness sucked the feeble light of my wand with a force of its own. How long had I been down here? An hour? Two? Forever?

In time, the tunnel intersected another at a ninety-degree angle and ended in a blank wall. Black liquid I hoped was water inched in a sluggish manner along a shallow channel intended for the purpose. I tried to see further along the raised brick shelves that ran along either side. Which way?

Would Dorian and the others have taken this route? Or was there another way?

The wand's meagre glow intensified shadows. Although I must be outside the null-magic area, perhaps the spell followed the tunnel. Path of least resistance?

Maybe Talon's trick would work. Worth a try. I held the wand on the flat of my palm and asked it which way to go. It spun to the right – in the direction of water flow. It was a pleasant surprise. I'd have to remember that one. The brick shelves were each two feet wide and, as I soon found, crumbled in places so I worked my way back and forth between the shelves, depending on which was sounder. Where both shelves had collapsed, I waded in the icy, ankle-deep channel, jaw cramped with the effort to stop my teeth from chattering.

I heard a rumble in the distance … surely not …

I thought my senses had deceived me but soon I recognized the glow of natural sunlight. I broke into an uneven run, stumbling over rocks and rat carcasses in various states of decomposition. I rounded a jagged corner; skidded to a halt before an enormous grotto into which water burst from a huge angled slash in the back wall, its foaming torrent assimilating my small trickle into a deep swirling pool. The roar was deafening. The water spun in a dizzying vortex before it shot into space through a gap in the outer wall.

My heart sank. Even if I'd had my broom, the opening was too narrow and impossible to get to. I wondered how far from Cumulos I'd come and if Dorian and the others were okay. On the one hand, I hoped the battle was over but, on the other, I was miffed at feeling so useless. Humiliating.

The hair on my arms lifted at the deep chill of a *presence*. Had something followed me from the dungeon? At the same time, a familiar tingle made my head spin with relief that my magical abilities had returned – not that they'd get me out of there.

As the deep chill came again, I flexed my knees and brought my wand to a defensive position. At the sound of an eerie supernatural hiss I could hear above the thunderous roar, I spun around to see black smoke coalescing into a solid shape. A bony hand slammed my chest and, a moment of disbelief later; I tumbled towards the boiling torrent. I managed to suck in a deep lungful of air before the raging waters closed over my head and I was out of control.

Slammed against rocks, I scrabbled to find something to grab onto but there was nothing, only the choking reality of frigid water. Twice I was able to take a quick breath before being sucked beneath the surface into the terrifying spin yet again

As my lungs screamed for air, the pressure ceased and I was thrown from the torrent. My gratitude lasted long enough to spy the distant base of a gigantic waterfall down which I tumbled. My broom couldn't get here in time, and previous attempts at levitation hadn't gone well. Ground and sky rotated and a curious calmness settled over me in the face of certain death.

A teeth-rattling jar broke into my serenity as I slammed onto something rough and slid off. Must've been a rocky outcropping. It hadn't hurt as much as one would've expected. As I slammed onto the rough surface again, a voice boomed. "For Pete's sake, hang on! I can't do everything!"

In disbelief, I realized I was jammed between Bluescale's vertical rows of plates. I grabbed one and squirmed until I was flat against his heated back. As realization hit that we were in a vertical dive with the base of the waterfall looming, I wrapped my arms in a death grip around a plate.

"Go!" I screamed.

Great leathery wings spread as we dropped into boiling mist where powerful centrifugal force crushed my lungs – and we were soaring into a clear blue sky.

Bluescale looked back. "You don't look so good . . .even for a human."

"I don't feel so good." I struggled to a sitting position and shivered. "Wow," I said in a flat tone. I hadn't yet caught up to this reversal in my fortunes.

"Don't be too grateful," he said, narrowing an eye.

"Sorry. I'm still a little shook up about not dying. Might take a few minutes to re-group … how did you know?"

"Dorian managed a telepathic contact. He's not as good as you are, by the way. His message was garbled but it sounded like he wanted me to find you. Seems he couldn't get back to the dungeon. Knew you were in the mountain but that was all."

"He was probably stressed. He's in a battle to reclaim Cumulos from Mydryth."

"That would explain it. I knew the waterfall came from one of the tunnels so I hung around hoping to hear from you." He eyed me. "Seems Dorian was right to be concerned. Since humans cannot fly, imagine my surprise to find you sailing through the air."

"Had a little help from a dark-ghost," I said, resentful at being made to look a fool – again. "And I'm not fully human! My father is magical."

I peered in front of Bluescale's wings at toy-sized farms and the shadows from puffy white clouds that slid along the ground. Considering he'd just saved my life, I decided to let the slight go. "Where are we going?"

"Mydryth's made Angus' study his base of operations. He figures he's safe there but we've got a surprise for him."

"What surprise?" My clothes were drying in the rush of warm air and I was relieved to stop shivering.

"Angus' study is in one of the towers."

I nodded. "It is."

"Solid stone ceiling?"

"Yes."

"No."

"What do you mean?"

"It's a hologram."

My mouth dropped open. "Would a holographic ceiling keep out the rain?"

"There are different densities of holograms." His eye examined me again. "You really ought to study more, Raven."

Don't you hate it when people – or dragons – are right?

"Anyone who's been around a long time collects enemies," he continued. "And Angus is a mage who likes to think ahead. In fact," he said, with surprise, "he'd make a great dragon. We think in terms of thousands of years. Hmmm … never would've thought it of a human."

"Well, he is a mage. Could we get back to the plan?" I was still grouchy from his comment about my lack of education. I knew I was clueless about magic but he seemed to insinuate I knew nothing about anything. A disturbing thought but it was beginning to seem so.

"Hmmm? Oh, yes. Once Angus dissolves the hologram, I swoop in and nab Mydryth from his hidey hole."

"Umm … do you plan to kill him?"

"Of course! Why else would I agree to this? I want my revenge!"

"Does Angus know your plan?"

"We never discussed the details but I don't see why he'd have a problem with it. Gets rid of his enemy and my brother's murderer."

"Maybe Angus has his own plan."

Bluescale's eye got a stubborn gleam. "I don't care!"

I swallowed. "Mydryth's a powerful magician."

"And I'm a powerful dragon!" As his eye narrowed, I detected a hint of red in its depths. "This has been a long time coming!"

I didn't care for his change in tone and cleared my throat. "How did he kill your brother?"

Dragon lips flattened. "We'd already changed to eating animals but Mydryth liked to kill for fun – anything would do. One day my brother and I were hunting deer when Frederick froze in midair. I couldn't see what was wrong until I noticed a magic arrow had pierced his underside, letting out the acid we use to make us buoyant and create flames. I still remember the shock in his eyes as he fell."

His lip curled. "Mydryth floated on his broom behind us laughing. It's one thing to hunt for food or defend yourself but it's something else to murder a dragon for fun. I went after my brother but it was too late. The fall had killed him. After that, I made it my business to hunt Mydryth. Sooner or later, I'd have succeeded but it wasn't long afterwards the mages got together and sent us all to the streams. "I swore if I ever found him again, I'd kill him. And I intend to."

Bluescale looked savage. I swallowed. "Did Dorian say how much help Mydryth has?"

"Lots of dark-ghosts, dozens of trolls, and some skinny guys who look like they're already dead. At least three mages."

We rounded an outcropping of the mountain, the village in a wide meadow ahead. The castle beyond billowed with smoke which we could only see because we were high in the air. No one in the village would be aware of it.

"Would you like me to drop you in the village? Not literally, of course. I've had recent evidence you really can't fly." He raised his lips in what I took to be a dragon grin that exposed a lot of teeth.

"Drop me off? I'm not getting off! They might need my help!"

"Going to get hot!"

"I don't care! Besides, you'll need me to get you through the first shields. Angus won't drop more than the second level. If he dropped them all, Cumulos would be visible to humans and he'd never do that."

"Don't blame me if you get singed."

"Leave me on one of the towers. I can find my way from there … and Bluescale?"

"Hmmm?"

"Thanks for saving my life. I was a goner."

"No problem. It won't be the last fun thing I do today."

We curved along the mountainous slope towards the castle in the distance. I needed to see the shields so I gave my wand a quick flick and two half-spheres, one inside the other, shimmered into view, arched over the castle. Disturbing black columns of smoke rose from deep within. I chaffed at the sight. Come on, Dorian! Get that shield down!

We circled high above the castle so we could see without being seen. When at last the outer shield flickered and faded, I grabbed a tight hold of Bluescale's plates; he folded his wings flat to his sides, and we went into a vertical dive, the wind whipping my eyes so hard I had to close them. It occurred to me if I was going to keep doing this I should devise a seatbelt and conjure some goggles. I peeked from one eye, waited until the last possible second, and cast the spell to let us through the inner shield.

I felt like an insect on a windshield as powerful leathery wings shot out. A couple of seconds later, the dragon skidded onto a rampart, reached back with those huge teeth, grabbed my cloak, and dumped me onto the stones. One powerful downward flap and he was over the wall, smoke pouring from flared nostrils.

I tried to suck air into my lungs but for some reason they wouldn't work. Eons later and only after immense effort, I managed to squeak in miniscule amounts and roll to hands and knees. All I could think about as I wobbled about was that even one decent inhale would make me happy. I *HATE* getting the wind knocked out of me! Not only do you look like a gaping fish, you've no control as to when or even if you'll ever breathe again. My ribs hurt but I didn't care. I was in a panic. This should be done by now! Breathe! Dammit, breathe!

I managed to squeak in some shallow breaths, pushed to my feet by grasping the low wall and peeked over it. The courtyard was filled with malevolent smoky shapes that swarmed through the air like flocks of starlings. The unicorns were protected by a covered walkway enclosed behind sealed magical walls. Bolts of blue energy shot from behind stone pillars but the dark-ghosts were quick – and I was appalled by their number.

At a deafening roar from above, I looked up to see Bluescale dive into the fray. A gigantic jet of flame blasted from his mouth and dark-ghosts in his way drifted to ash. The dragon twisted and spun; his speed awe-inspiring as he pursued elusive wisps of shadow. Searing flames added to the heat and smoke that rose from the courtyard but the distraction provided by the new ally enabled the blue spheres to connect with more dark-ghosts. In short order, the shadows were fewer.

It occurred to me I wasn't much help. I called my broom, activated the talisman, and headed to a position from which I could watch, careful to keep out of Bluescale's way. Fire wasn't stopped by invisibility. I hovered over a balcony and watched the holo-roof. Maybe I could delay Mydryth long enough for Angus to get to him. The thought of what Bluescale would do to the dark mage made my stomach roil.

The occasional dark-ghost that dared to emerge lasted only seconds as Bluescale patrolled the courtyard. It seemed most of the scarecrow men and trolls must be in the castle but they'd soon have to challenge the dragon – or maybe it would be the mages who offered the challenge.

A movement at the corner of my eye was the stone roof of the study as it flickered twice then dissolved. As I turned to look for Bluescale, I was blown into the wall by his passage. More bruises. I righted myself and shot after him though I'd no idea what I was going to do.

The dragon climbed down into the study using the book-shelves as a ladder. Smoke from his nostrils formed thick, black clouds as books tumbled in an avalanche. The flexible; snake-like neck whipped from side to side as his deafening roar reverberated in the small space.

Bluescale's power to engender absolute terror was stunning to behold. I was behind him and shaking in my boots so couldn't imagine how Mydryth felt. I peeked in to see the dark mage cowered against the fireplace transfixed by the fire-breathing monster coming at him.

The dragon sucked in a deep breath – as Angus popped in front of Mydryth, arms spread in a protective gesture. I didn't know if he was protecting Mydryth or his precious books.

Bluescale's massive head reared back and green eyes reddened. Angus spun blue swirls of energy to encircle the giant snout and, as the dragon lunged from side to side in fury, books tumbled by the hundreds into a dusty pile.

It seemed Bluescale didn't understand Angus' actions any more than I did.

In the midst of the maelstrom, Dorian burst through a side door and skidded to a stop next to the fireplace. Mydryth was plastered against a shelf of books out of his line of sight, fixated on the infuriated dragon. His eyes shifted but I saw his intention a second too late. Although I threw a rigidity spell, he diverted it, swiped his wand at the wall, and a red vortex appeared. With a vicious sneer, he threw a lightning bolt at me and disappeared.

I ducked, shot past the writhing Bluescale to sprawl in a heap next to Dorian who was mesmerized by the struggle between dragon and mage. There was nothing either of us could do. I staggered to my feet. When a bolt of blue energy melted the rock next to us, Dorian formed a shield and pulled me against him.

Angus barked short, intense sentences in the ancient dragon tongue as he maintained the crackling swirls of energy that enveloped Bluescale, one of which remained curled around his snout to prevent blasts of flame.

As I watched from the safety of the fireplace, I got the oddest sensation that Angus and Bluescale were spinning. My knees buckled. As I slipped from his grasp, Dorian dragged his gaze from the altercation, his expression of awe switching to one of fear. He crouched beside me and brushed my hair back, swallowed and paled a couple of shades.

"My god, Raven! You're bleeding! And … how did you get here?"

I touched the wound. "One of the guards was faster than I'd hoped but I imagine if I was going to die, it would've happened by now. I think the bleeding's slowed. How does it look? Will I need stitches?" I turned my face so he could see.

Dorian swallowed. "It's … possible." He produced a square of cloth and pressed it against the wound with a light touch. "Here. Keep pressure on it. How'd it happen?"

I winced as the swelling beneath my fingers complained. "One of the guards slammed me into a wall at the top of the second flight of stairs."

He expelled a breath. "I'm sorry, Raven. I should've been the one to act as decoy. The locks weren't that hard to open after all. Umm … how did you get away?"

While keeping a wary eye on the odd blast of power and the writhing, roaring dragon, I gave Dorian a condensed version.

"If it wasn't for Bluescale," I ended, "I'd never have survived. How did you escape the dungeon?"

His face went bland. "You aren't going to like it."

"Why not?"

"There's a secret passageway a few yards down the tunnel."

I stopped short of slamming the heel of my hand into my forehead. "I knew it! There's *always* a secret passageway!"

"It wasn't long before we were out of the null-magic area," he continued. "Talon and the others went hunting dark-ghosts and whatever else they could find, and Angus and I headed for his Plan B control room." He smiled. "Angus always has a back-up plan.

I wanted to go back for you but dark-ghosts kept after us and then some kind of scarecrow things and giant trolls attacked. I tried messaging Bluescale in the midst of it all and I must've succeeded from what you tell me. I wasn't sure he heard."

"I was lost in those tunnels for *two hours*, Dorian!"

"I … It took that long to get to the control room. Mydryth has a considerable army."

I didn't have the heart to blame him. "I know." I put my arms around his neck and snuggled against his chest.

His arms tightened. "Are you okay?"

"You saved my life – you and Bluescale. We can talk later." I glanced at the enraged dragon. "Once he calms down."

Chapter 18

In a soporific stupor, I gazed into a flickering fire, a carafe of strong black coffee on a nearby table. The dark-ghosts were gone, ceiling back in place, and Bluescale, still exhaling puffs of dark smoke, was sprawled around Angus' desk, taking up most of the available space. Although to my astonishment he could reduce his size by deflating his interior airbags, he was still a good-sized creature.

It'd taken a half-hour for Angus to calm him to the point where he'd listen long enough for the mage to explain that evil entities were trapped in objects around the room, sometimes in old books by mages of old. Even Angus didn't know how many there were. If the books and objects were burned, not only would Angus lose his library, all the entities would be released.

Losing Mydryth could not compare to the consequences of allowing that to happen.

The stare Bluescale bestowed down his long nose led me to suspect we'd lost even more respect in his eyes. If we'd learn to communicate by telepathy, there'd be no need for books. They were ancient technology as far as he was concerned.

The main doors had been repaired; the castle once again secure. I smothered a yawn, poured viscous coffee with an unsteady hand, and chomped on a stale biscuit in an attempt to get sugar into my brain. After two days of hyper-vigilance, my thought processes had seized and I longed to join the fat black cat that snoozed next to the fireplace.

Nightshade had vanished and, as signs of her involvement mounted, concern for her welfare dwindled. Although she'd been close to the blast, no one had seen her leave. A tour of the castle with Dorian would've been a perfect cover for locating the gunpowder storage rooms.

It would've made more sense to set the explosion at night to take the castle occupants by even greater surprise but, seeing me on the stairway might've caused a spontaneous change-up to her schedule. Temper tantrum maybe? I hoped so.

Dorian winced. No man appreciates being used. From the set of his jaw as he stared into the fire, I wouldn't want to be Nightshade when they met again.

I didn't wince at the news. My spirit burst into song! It couldn't have worked out better if I'd planned it myself. I knew there was a reason I hadn't liked the tramp! Now her intent was clear to everyone, I soared with vindication. I felt I could do anything. . . except stay awake. A great, jaw-cracking yawn burst forth.

"Ye and Dorian get some sleep," said Angus, brushing soot from a knee-high argyle sock, "and we'll finish this discussion in the morning. Ye needn't worry; the castle will be monitored through the night. A half-dozen giant bats are patrolling the perimeter along with Cash's soldiers so the castle will be safe enough."

There was a scrape of stone and Cash filled the doorway. He ducked and turned cornerwise to slide into the room (I couldn't see that he was any smaller sideways than front on). He greeted Bluescale with a wide grin and patted the broad snout. After they exchanged pleasantries, Cash stepped over the enormous tail and worked his way to the oversized bench near the fire. Wood creaked as he settled and I wondered what a giant weighed.

"Sorry I'm late. Basia thought she saw dark-ghosts near our cabin."

"Have ye news o' Mydryth?"

"Bits here and there. Seems to have returned to the Highlands. Has an old castle on the ocean to the northeast. Wickness, it's called. The land is barren thereabouts and they say a cold wind always blows from the North Sea."

"Sounds like the place for him," I grumbled. "Why doesn't he stay there?" I lurched to my feet. "I need to sleep. Sorry to rush off, Cash, but I'm about to collapse. "

"I'm surprised ye've lasted as long as ye have, lass," said Angus. "I'll see ye in the morning."

"Late in the morning." As I stepped over the end of Bluescale's tail, I felt Dorian's hand on my waist to steady me.

"A moment." Angus waved his wand … and I was in Frost's quarters. I gave a sigh of relief. Thank you, Angus!

Two days later, Dorian and I lounged on a second-floor balustrade with an eye on the unicorns, a sight that never ceased to move me. "How long can we keep them?" I asked. "The grounds are getting crowded."

Dorian had one knee drawn up, back against a pillar, an arm rested across a bent knee, fingers relaxed. "I heard Angus say we have to return them soon. Without the influence of the unicorns, evil grows."

"Mydryth will just take them again."

"Not if we bind his magic."

Brows met my hair. "We do we do that?"

"Angus thinks he can – with our help."

I shuddered at the idea that the two of us might be all that prevented a worldwide disaster. "What's his plan?"

"We need to dig Mydryth out of his hidey-hole and, since Wickness is guarded by a horde of dark-ghosts, that could be problematic."

"That would be one word for it."

As a silver foal kicked up its heels and raced around its mother, Dorian's serious expression softened. What is it about baby animals that delight us? A playmate joined in and they chased each other around the common area, tossing their heads and bucking. The small nub that would grow into a horn by the second year must've been nature's way of ensuring the little guys would grow up without poking each other's eyes out.

"Aren't they gorgeous?" A silly smile plastered on my face. Somehow they aroused my miniscule maternal instinct. I wanted to keep them safe.

Dorian's lips quirked as he slanted a look at me. "Careful Raven; next thing you know you'll be kissing babies."

I sent him a mock glare. "Don't even joke!" I liked children … sort of … as long as they belonged to other people. Sometimes they were even cute in a messy sort of way.

He tipped his head back and laughed. "I've never met anyone more afraid of children than you, Raven! It's like you grew up on a desert island!"

I scowled and looked away. "I think it'll rain this afternoon."

"Why *are* you so uncomfortable with children?"

"I'm not uncomfortable with children. They're fine."

He gave me a measured look. "One of these days you're going to tell me about it."

"There's nothing to tell." I broke off at movement to the side. "Talon!" I snapped, trying to hide my initial reaction behind a forced smile. "How nice to see you!"

He glared in response, his customary expression. He glanced at Dorian. "Angus, Frost and I have been strategizing while the two of you . . ." he observed our relaxed positions, "waste the morning in idle stupor." Guess our heroic deeds had been relegated to the annals of history.

"I don't recall being invited to a council of war!" I was stung at his attitude in spite of personal promises to ignore it.

"I would suggest," said Dorian in a deceptively mild tone, "that if you want our help, Talon, you might be more gracious in asking for it. I remind you our assistance is voluntary."

Talon re-directed his glare at Dorian who held his ground. "Perhaps you would care to accompany me … please."

That was all we were going to get. Dorian, after holding Talon's stare long enough for the message to sink in, dropped his feet to the walkway. "Lead on."

Talon, floating ahead, reminded me of an indignant purple Buddhist.

A frigid wind crashed huge waves onto a jagged shoreline. I tucked my travelling cloak close and tightened the leather sash. Eyes tearing from the cold, I adjusted the hood and attempted to stuff my entire self into it. My jaws cramped with the effort to keep my teeth from crashing into each other, and I decided to procure long underwear the instant I got back to Cumulos. Grumbling at the lack of a heat spell, I reminded myself the use of unnecessary magic was to be avoided. If you ask me, heat is necessary.

Angus' red hair blew about as clear blue eyes rested on the forbidding castle in the distance. The cold wind that blew his kilt around thick legs covered only by knee-high socks didn't seem to bother him at all. A plaid throw, tied around his shoulders, whipped in the wind. Maybe I didn't have enough Scots blood in my veins. Squashing an envious impulse, I returned my attention to our goal.

Wickness squatted on a savage spit of stone that overlooked a steep cliff beneath which a frothing ocean pounded. A narrow road became a tunnel that pierced the near edge of the spit and emerged onto a flat area on which half-a-dozen stone outbuildings perched behind the castle. In place of windows, the castle walls had tall narrow slits which would've made it an impregnable fortress before the invention of heavier-than-air flight. Even now, it was forbidding.

As Dorian moved to break the wind for me, I gave him a grateful glance and tucked chilled fingers into voluminous sleeves.

"How long do you think this'll take?" I glanced at Angus. Talon hovered, grey cloak snapping in the wind. Without a broom, he looked like a shapeless blob.

"Nae long. Just studying the castle defenses."

Minutes later, Angus sank from view over the edge of the cliff. We followed and I was grateful when the wind lessened though occasional bits of spray from the thundering surf splashed high enough to wet our feet. We hugged the granite face, worked north along it towards the castle as Angus scanned the rock, stopping now and again to frown before moving on.

My shivers had reached epic proportions and I was starting to get a wee bit cranky when the wall swallowed him. Dorian and I peeked around a bulge in the rock … where we spied a long narrow crack wide enough for a person to slip through. A thin ledge ran along its base and the idea of standing on it gave me the willies … but Angus must've gone that way.

"I'll go first," said Dorian, moving forward.

"No," I countered. "I'm going to drop off my broom of frost-bite if I don't get out of this wind. I'll go first. Besides then you can catch me if I fall."

He backed away and gestured for me to proceed. The ledge didn't look any wider as I approached. I glanced down at jagged rocks. "Can you catch me?"

He surveyed the pounding surf and pursed his lips. "Most likely."

"You two hurry up or get out of the way!" snapped Talon.

I shot him a dark look and edged to the opening. I'd have to dismount, get onto a ledge barely wide enough for my feet, turn sideways, and slide into the narrow opening. The world lurched and my knuckles turned white where they gripped my broom. Talon glared at the helpless female.

To be honest, I hadn't been much help so far other than to introduce Bluescale who lounged in King's Loch at the moment. He'd wanted to come but there was no way he could approach the castle without being spotted. He'd agreed to wait so long as I promised to inform him the minute we had Mydryth.

I maneuvered parallel to the wall above the tiny ledge, reached with my left toe, and shifted my weight. As the broom moved to the side, my heart stopped. At least I'm sure it must've. My toe slid off the ledge. The broom moved back under me until I was balanced.

Brooms maintained a sense of their rider's position so when I shifted my weight to get off, it had assumed there was a flat surface beneath and moved to get out of the way. It had no way of knowing there was nothing to stand on. As Dorian sank beneath, I didn't know whether to be comforted, terrified or insulted.

Talon waited twenty feet away, beak nose tucked into his cloak, goggles splattered with water droplets. "Perhaps today?"

Stubbornness replaced a smidgeon of terror. As wind gusts slammed me against the stone, I realized I'd need to time my dismount. I swallowed, took a death-defying grip on my broom, and lowered next to the ledge again. I spared a quick glance at Dorian who returned my look with a "thumbs-up."

Heart in mouth, I took a mighty leap and flattened against the wall. As a pebble slipped beneath my foot, I closed my eyes and searched for more secure footing. My toes were unsupported and the opening to my left might as well have been in Canada. Further movement was out of the question as every muscle in my body decided it was time to override my stupidity at getting into this situation in the first place. I was frozen in more ways than one.

My upper arm was seized in a vice and I was dragged through the opening before I could scream (not that I ever scream). Angus, his face spooky by the light of his wand, pushed me onto a nearby rock and shoved my head forward.

"Keep your head down." *I'm sure it was just a precaution. I never faint.*

Dorian and Talon slipped through the narrow opening. "You know, Raven, with your vertigo, I don't know how you can ride this." Dorian handed over my broom.

I narrowed my eyes at him. "That's different!"

He shrugged. "Apparently."

He held his wand aloft to flood the area with a light blue light save for a large triangular gap in the back wall. Visions of rats scuttled through my mind and I peered into the shadows.

"This passage is an old escape route," said Angus. "Since the entrance is'na visible unless you're right in front o' it, I thought it might nae be guarded."

As my shaking lessened, I sat up. Angus handed me a packet of foul-smelling paste. "Eat this." At the revolted expression I must've made, he pushed it closer. "Twill help."

A wave of dizziness washed over me. "All of it?"

It looked enormous but was not more than a tablespoon. My head swam again but it could've been from the idea of putting something so abhorrent into my mouth. It smelled like … moldy pig weed mixed with pine tar. Perhaps it was.

I took a deep breath, scraped it off the packet with a forefinger, shoved it into my mouth, and forced myself to swallow several times. As my eyes watered from gagging, I held a hand over my mouth in a useless attempt to hold it down. Although I'd never had occasion to feel resentment towards Angus, this might do it.

"The gag reflex will only last a minute or so," he said with an encouraging grin. At that moment he looked positively evil.

As I peered at him through blurry eyes, I wondered if I could get away with throwing up on his shoes and saying it was an accident. I sucked in cold air hoping to calm my insides, dropped my head into my hands and waited for the sensation to pass.

A high-pitched whine like the granddaddy of all mosquitoes emerged from the depths of the tunnel. Right up there with rats, mosquitoes are my least favourite life form, their sole function that I could see being that of spreading disease and crazed frustration. The whine emanated from the black triangle and was getting louder.

I fumbled for my wand. Had we been detected? Would we be sucked dry by giant bugs? Angus mimed for us to stay put. His wand winked out and we were left with thin grey light from the narrow opening.

As the evil paste continued to churn my stomach, I focused on keeping it down; doubtful I could vomit in silence. Curse you, Angus … and then to my stunned disbelief, the nausea faded. In fact, I felt stronger than ever. A wave of warmth swept from my core to the tips of my extremities and I tingled from head to toe with well-being. Who'd have thought? Perhaps I owed Angus a mental apology. *I'd no intention of offering him a real one.*

The shadows moved and a glowing orange light the size of a baseball emerged from the black triangle. The shape of the tunnel must've magnified its sound because it wasn't as big or loud as I'd expected. After a brilliant flash, the ball dropped to the floor, its glow extinguished. Angus picked it up.

"What is it?" I asked.

"A lightning ball. Made o' gold, transmits small amounts o' lightning. Used for gathering information. It sends what it views back te a scrying mirror but I think I was able te disable it in time." He turned it some more. "I wonder . . ." He glanced at Talon.

"You're thinking a reversal spell might make it work for us." Talon dug into a pocket. "I've a scrying mirror right here and, as long as no one tries to access this particular ball, it might go undetected."

"Wouldn't Mydryth monitor his security measures?" I asked.

"He'll check low risk areas less often." As Angus pried at a thin slit in the ball, a hatch snapped open. He held the object in his hand, palm up, and chanted. A yellow triangle of light formed, shot into the gold sphere, and the door snicked closed. In seconds, it began to glow and float upward. The buzzing whine didn't sound so terrible any more.

"I imagine you're sure this will work," I said. Talon gave me a withering stare which I ignored.

Angus smiled. "Twill work."

We watched the orange ball disappear into the black tri-angle. Too bad we had to follow it. Talon handed his scrying mirror to Angus who passed a hand over the surface and gazed into it. In the minutes that passed, I itched to take a peek.

"Tis coming te the shaft now. We should be safe enough te follow the tunnel that far." He brightened his wand. "Are ye ready, Raven?"

At my nod, we strode into the darkness between narrow walls. All four of us held our wands high to avoid low-hanging rocks. Although the darkness was oppressive, I was relieved to be warm and dry, not to mention, pleasantly surprised at the absence of life forms. No rats, no snakes, not even spiders – at least that I could see.

Ten minutes later, we came to a shaft fifty feet in diameter that was hewn from solid rock. The walls were cylindrical and smooth with a curved stairway that hugged the wall in a spiral from top to bottom. It had to have been formed by magic. If I hadn't had a stomach full of Angus' potion, I'd have experienced a return of vertigo.

The curved walls emitted a faint blue-green light; tunnels intersected the stairway at intervals and, as a glowing orange ball disappeared into one across from us, I wondered if it was "ours."

As Dorian's body pressed against mine in the narrow space, my focus snapped back. Wow! He felt really…good. I chewed my lip and tried to focus on the shaft.

Angus stared into the mirror. "I've sent our spy upward te see what's at the top o' the well as Mydryth will have guards there."

As I glanced up, I thought I saw a grey shadow flutter against the wall. I blinked. Had it been a trick of the imagination? It was gone now.

Angus chanted an invisibility incantation and I got an odd sense of disorientation as we faded from view. "We'll float straight up. There's a lot o' magic here so we may not be noticed."

A hand grasped mine and I heard Dorian whisper, "So you don't get lost."

Again I didn't know whether to be insulted or comforted so refrained from comment as we lifted in silence. The stairwell seemed to go on forever (I was thankful not to have to climb all those stairs) and, as we drifted, I watched for dark-ghosts or other life forms.

It was going well until Angus hissed, "Stop!"

A red sphere trailed by a thin sparkling streamer sizzled down from above. In a flash, Angus had formed a glowing blue shield over us; there was a blinding red flash, a sharp retort, and an explosion shook the shaft. Rocks plunged past, the stairway now missing a few chunks. Red streaks of lightning flashed everywhere and, each time a bolt struck our shield, it left the scent of ozone.

"So much for the element of surprise," growled Dorian.

"We must've triggered something," shouted Angus above the din.

We shot up, barely avoided two more explosive devices which trailed streamers of sparkles. As red lightning bounced around the shaft, it left black smoking holes. With a death grip on my wand, I jumped each time our shield was impacted. Talon, surrounded by a purple sphere, rose like a bubble in a caldron. Dorian grabbed my broom to hold us together so we could maintain a shield big enough for us both.

"Ready?"

I nodded.

The walls blurred as we darted towards an arched stone ceiling. Angus and Talon were just ahead, the channel below a hellish maelstrom of reverberating energies. I felt a return of queasiness as I looked down. No escape that way.

We were at the top of the cylinder where a ten-foot walkway encircled the shaft. Two corridors with identical stairwells led upwards from opposite sides. As we moved to the right some instinct made me look up – to see a sparkling net descend.

I shouted a warning and shot towards the nearest stairs (*which, of course, Dorian later described as a scream. I don't know why men can't remember clearly when they're under stress*).

A sharp pain ripped through my leg as the netting grazed it and I spun to see the others convulse in agony before floating motionless. Through my horror, I realized an automated defense would alert defenders and I probably had only seconds to save my companions.

What affected lightning? Water. It conducted electricity but could also short it out. Rain! Talon had described how to make rain just last week. How had he done that? My mind was a blank. Sometimes I don't think well under pressure.

At the sound of footsteps pounding down the stairwell, the formula sprang to mind. Maybe the pressure needed to be life-threatening to make me think. I intoned the incantation.

Nothing happened. Not surprising. It hadn't worked last week either. Try again! Louder and with more conviction! Talon always said. "Don't ask! Demand!"

As I screamed the incantation, a bluish-grey cloud formed over the net to be followed in seconds by a mini cloudburst. *Well, I'll be.* The first raindrops caused sparks followed by a brilliant flash as the net dissolved into tendrils of grey ash. As my companions began to fall, I shouted a levitation spell (that also seldom worked) but, to my great surprise, they stopped falling and floated. At my spell of attraction, they drifted closer. I was on a roll!

A clank from behind sounded a lot like armor. The only upside was that I'd rather deal with warriors than with dark-ghosts.

As my unconscious companions floated towards me at a snail's pace, the clank of metal and heavy footfalls approached with the speed of light. A broadsword grasped by a hairy paw appeared around the curve of one of the staircases. Tiny eyes overshadowed by a heavy brow and sloped forehead glanced around before fixing on us. With a bellow, the creature raised its sword and clomped down the remaining stairs.

I doubled the attractor spell and raced up the opposite flight in hopes it went somewhere the guards weren't. At a landing from which two corridors branched, I took the one to the right, my companions trailing along like balloons. As coarse bellows and the clang of metal grew louder, I raced down the hallway, praying at least one of my friends would awaken. It was clear evidence of my level of desperation that I'd even have welcomed Talon's help.

I rounded a corner and slammed flat into a brick wall. I staggered back, head ringing from the impact. Who on earth would brick up a corridor? Then I remembered a similar wall in Cumulos. Of course! The wall required a spell to get through. But what was it? I'd no idea.

Dorian's feet nudged my shoulder as he floated to a stop. None of them had so much as quivered but I had to believe they'd be okay. The shouting grew louder and, as the first two guards rounded the corner, a knife glanced off the bricks next to my head. In panic, I shouted the first incantation that came to mind.

A hairy hand the size of a dinner plate reached for Dorian's shoulder as a vortex began to spin. I'd no idea what I'd done or where we were going but it had to be better than where we were. Colours flashed and I lost all sense of direction.

Pain stabbed through my shoulder as I slammed onto a hard surface. I lay flat, trying to catch my breath, grateful I'd landed on grass and not the concrete sidewalk a few feet away. Four loud thumps followed.

Four?

I scrambled to my feet as a dazed guard sprang to his feet. He'd never seen a human neighbourhood – and a human neighbourhood had never seen him!

We were next to the enormous oak in which lived the chatty squirrel. It peeked from between the leaves and set up a tirade, fuzzy tail jerking in agitation. A man next to the post box stared and a woman with a ten-year-old boy backed away. As I attempted to wave, a stabbing pain shot up my arm. I winced and pasted on a smile.

"Just practicing for a movie!" I called. "Nothing to worry about!"

Their faces relaxed.

The guard's attention turned to me and, with a bellow, he raised a broadsword. Would be tough to explain a lot of real blood. Not that I'd be doing the explaining. As I dove behind a lilac hedge redolent with the scent of flowers, I tripped over an errant root and sprawled on my face. With a panicked look over my shoulder, I saw the man mountain's slack lips curl in a sneer of anticipation as he lifted the weapon high above his head.

I couldn't stop staring at the terrifying apparition as I felt around in the grass for my wand. As the monstrous sword descended, I braced myself for the impact.

In mid-stroke, his expression changed to one of surprise. As he froze, I scrambled out of there like a rabbit, scooped up my wand, and spun to see Dorian on his knees with wand pointed at the guard. His eyes were glazed. I mumbled a return incantation and the guard vanished.

Dorian sank forward, head bent. As I rushed to him, I heard moans from the others. At least they were alive. I lifted Dorian's head onto my lap and brushed the silver locks from his face. His eyes were closed, face pale.

The man and the woman with the boy peeked around the hedge, curious about the movie.

"Where's the guy who played the guard?" asked the man. "That guy was enormous!"

"Yes, wasn't he?" I agreed.

The man's brow furrowed as he peered at Dorian. "He alright?"

"He … fell kind of hard. Needs practice I guess."

"Should use a stunt man!" he said as though he was an expert. "That guard actor coming back? I'd like his autograph!"

I gritted my teeth. The idiot wanted an autograph from a Neanderthal? "He … had to leave … dental appointment."

The boy pointed at Dorian. "Is he dead?"

"No, dear," replied his mother. "He's an actor. He's pretending to be hurt. It's not real."

The freckled face, deep in thought, stared at Dorian. "Looks hurt to me."

Angus and Talon staggered to their feet. "He'll be fine," I said, hoping it was the truth. Angus and Talon slipped their wands into their pockets.

"Great costumes!" enthused the boy. "What's he," he asked, pointing at Talon, "some kind of alien?"

Angus looked down at the kid. "Aye … some kind o' . . .alien."

"What's the movie going to be called? I want to see it!"

"It'll be an adult film. Too much violence for a child," said Angus, rolling a shoulder and checking for damage.

With no cameras in evidence and no more action, the humans lost interest and wandered away. I'd begun to worry about Dorian when a pair of chocolate eyes opened.

His grin was weak. "You were worried about me."

I inhaled a deep shaky breath of relief. "I was worried about all of you."

"Of course." He looked like he didn't believe me.

"I … we need to get moving. Can you stand?"

"I think so." I helped him sit then lurched to my feet, adding my strength to help him up.

"We need to get off this street before any more humans see us," said Talon. He waved his wand and the street vanished.

Chapter 19

I sipped cider and enjoyed the warmth of the fire along with being congratulated on how I'd dissolved the lightning net, rescued my companions, and transported us all to safety. With what I thought was a suitable level of humility in accepting accolades, I bowed twice.

The fat black cat next to the fire almost dislocated its jaws with a tremendous yawn, stretched, then lurched to its feet to contemplate the plethora of laps. Mine won the competition which I hoped wasn't a comment on its softness.

It strolled over and summoned enough energy to leap up. Well, almost enough. As it slipped, it sank a lot of claws into my leg. I yelped, grabbed it around the middle, and settled it on my thighs. It felt solid as it searched for the perfect spot then flopped down, heaved a deep sigh, and surveyed the room. I stroked its sleek fur and understood why it had moved. Much longer in front of the fire and I believe it would've burst into flame.

A rolling rumble emerged and its eyes slit in contentment. Perhaps it could teach me a lesson. It wasn't afraid to ask for what it wanted.

I observed Dorian from beneath my lashes as he talked with Frost. Did I want to disturb what we had? Was it worth the risk? I continued stroking the cat who sounded like a mini lawn mower. I didn't have to decide tonight.

As Frost rose to refresh her drink, Dorian sensed my gaze. Although there was no change in facial expression, subliminal messages flew between us. Too bad I couldn't understand them.

"If Raven would stop making moon eyes at Dorian, perhaps he could focus!"

I resisted the impulse to turn Talon into a toad as it seemed we needed him. "I wasn't making moon eyes!" I snarled. "I was thinking!" One corner of Dorian's mouth curled upward but he made no comment.

"That kind of thinking isn't going to neutralize Mydryth! If you have other things in mind, perhaps you'd like to return to ... Dunver, is it?"

"It's Denver! And no! We promised Angus we'd help – in spite of you if necessary!"

"Perhaps we could stick te the subject," interjected Angus. "After all, time's short. We need te return the unicorns soon and, in order te do that, we need te deal with Mydryth."

A thought popped into my head. Could it be that simple? I raised my hand. "I have an idea." I ignored how Talon rolled his eyes. "Could Mydryth be confined to the streams the way the dragons were? After all, they're magical beings too."

Angus fingered his chin. Talon for once, made no comment. Crackling flames and my purring lap rug were all that broke the silence.

"Ye may have something," said Angus. "The spell would need te be changed verra little te capture a mage. There'd be no room for error though. If Mydryth got the slightest inkling o' what we were trying te do, it'd be all over. What do ye think, Talon?"

Talon seemed disgruntled at the thought I could have any idea at all let alone a good one. "We should've considered it before. If we use a direct attack, Mydryth's automatic counter spells would protect him but, if we had a big enough distraction…" he glanced at me, "such as a dragon . . ."

"If Mydryth and Bluescale were close together," said Angus, "our people could cast a reducer sphere big enough to encapsulate them both. We'd need something as big as a dragon to get solid contact.

My stomach tightened. "I promised Bluescale I'd take him to the Americas."

"What difference does it make? Streams are streams," snapped Talon.

"And a promise is a promise," I retorted. "I won't go back on my word! I'll agree to help on condition Bluescale is released afterwards."

She's correct," broke in Angus. "If a person's word is of nae value, then o' what value is the person?" He turned to me. "I give ye my word te release Bluescale from the stream after the mage is trapped."

"What'll happen to Mydryth?"

"He'll be transformed into something like a salamander. The only magic he'll retain is the ability te re-grow damaged body parts."

"Will he remember being a mage?"

"At first te some extent but, as time passes, he'll forget."

"What if he were to be released by magic?"

"Like the dragons, he'd regain his full abilities and memories. Let's hope that does nae happen." He clasped hands behind his back and scanned the rows of dusty books. "I seem te remember . . ."

Since I had nothing better to do than pet the cat, I watched him. After ten minutes of pacing, he pointed to a thick volume on the top shelf which shifted then descended in a shower of dust to float before him. A wave of his hand and the book opened. He turned pages, frowned, and opened it to the back cover where he retrieved a folded parchment.

"Ahhh . . ," he said with a satisfied smile. The book closed and levitated to its place.

"What's that?" I asked.

"Years ago when the mages worked together, we built all the magic castles te be used by all o' us. Over time, differences o' opinion caused a separation and we each took a castle for ourselves. Since I never like te discard information, I kept maps o' all the mage castles, including Wickness. It's been here for so long, I'd almost forgotten I had it."

He unfolded the parchment, muttered something, and hand-drawn blueprints appeared. Each time Angus turned the parchment over, it showed a different level, an amazing number, many deep in the earth.

"I expect we'll find Nightshade in residence at Wickness," said Angus.

I thought the cat had growled but it was Dorian. "Traitorous little . . ." He refrained from finishing the statement but his jaw flexed.

"She's not worth getting worked up over," I said, with perhaps a smidgeon of satisfaction.

"You knew what she was like. You saw through her. I thought you were just . . ."

My eyes narrowed. "Thought I was just *what?*"

"Umm . . . nothing. You saw something the rest of us didn't."

I continued to glare but the man has an extraordinary ability to ignore me when it suits him.

Talon cast us a long-suffering glance before turning to Angus. "We'll need a way to circumvent his army and protective spells."

"Aye, we will. Perhaps ye'll assist me, Talon." And the two of them, mumbling together, returned to the bookshelves.

Frost announced she had security to see to and swept from the room. That left Dorian, me, and the cat. Of the three of us, only the cat was relaxed. Dorian cleared his throat, avoided eye contact, and got half-way to his feet. I clamped a hand onto his wrist.

"Stay!" He resumed his seat and gave me a sheepish look.

"Coward!" I lashed. "We need to talk!" It always amazes me how anger gives me such courage. Too bad it's … well … anger. Not often productive in a positive sense.

He glanced toward Angus and Talon. "This is not the place."

"Anywhere you like."

"Fine!" He snapped his wand and a second later we were on a balcony high above the rest of the castle.

I spun to face him. "What's going on with us?"

I could almost see the cogs turning as he stared into my eyes. He leaned against a pillar, folded his arms, and crossed one leg over the other. As the silence lengthened, I grew impatient.

"Well?"

His brows drew together. "I'm thinking."

"Then think louder! Did you assume I was jealous of Nightshade? Answer me that!" I was proud of my even tone as I suppressed what might've been construed as a burst of temper.

"Don't yell at me!"

"I'm not yelling!"

"I think I've suffered hearing damage and you're red as a beet!"

"My face is perfectly normal!"

Dorian looked like he was reining in his temper. His lips thinned, eyes narrowed, and he huffed out a deep breath.

"I didn't come up here to fight," he said. "I value our friendship. It's just that sometimes . . ." He trailed off.

My stomach tightened. "Sometimes, what?" Sometimes he'd had too much of my company? Sometimes wished I was a better mage? My heart thudded at my feet. Even though I had no idea what I'd been hoping for, this wasn't it.

"We've known each other for more than a year," he continued, choosing his words. "We've been comfortable . . ." His eyes flicked and he corrected himself. "I've *believed* we've been comfortable with each other."

My head swam and I realized I needed to breathe.

"This past year has made me feel as if I have a real life. You've been so much of my world."

I couldn't wait any longer. "Are you saying now we've found other magical folk, you want more space from me?"

He looked surprised. "No! That's not it! The people here aren't us!"

"Then what are you saying? Spit it out so we can get this over with!"

He looked puzzled and frustrated. "You wanted to talk; now you're in a hurry to leave?!"

I bit my lip. Now I wanted it over. I'd initiated some of these discussions myself. They usually started with, "You're a great guy, but . . ." or "It's not you, it's me . . ."

"If you want something else, Dorian, just say so. I won't get in your way. Just because it's always been us doesn't mean it has to continue. Things are different now. I understand."

He tipped his head to the side. "I'm not sure you do."

With lamentable timing, a message ball materialized, its tinny voice informing us Angus requested our presence. With a determined set to his jaw, Dorian said, "We'll finish this later."

I didn't know whether to be relieved, frustrated, or scared.

Bluescale stared down his long snout with a stubborn gleam. "I said I was going to the Americas and that's where I'm going!"

"We'll recover you from the stream after Mydryth is captured," I said. "Angus gave his word and we need your help for this to work."

"My friends in the stream won't thank me for bringing him there."

"He'll be one more salamander swimming around. You won't even notice him."

"If I spend any time with him, he'll be a snack and the problem will be resolved forever. There'll be no need for him to take up space anywhere."

"I understand the mages could've killed all the dragons years ago but let them live."

He snorted. "As bugs!"

"That's true," I said, "but you're alive, and one day you'll be free to fly the skies again. You may be in a different form but you're all still dragons deep down. You can be returned to your true form and, since you're immortal, what difference does even a few hundred years make? There are entire worlds to explore in the streams. You'll have experiences you'd never get as a dragon."

I must've been making progress as he looked thoughtful.

"You'd take me out?"

"I promise. I told Angus I wouldn't have anything to do with the plan until he agreed."

"Mydryth knows I hate him. He'd never trust me."

"Tell him Angus has hinted at sending you back to the stream. He'll believe that. After all, he was part of doing it in the first place."

Black smoke puffed from Bluescale's nostrils. "Why all the fuss? I could kill him and be done with it!"

I had to think of something fast. "But killing is so quick! Won't it give you greater satisfaction to put him in the same trap he set for you? Perhaps forever? Angus plans on sealing it with a forget spell so he'll be the only one with the ability to release Mydryth."

Bluescale's massive lips compressed as he weighed the pros and cons. He rolled his eyes towards me. "If this doesn't work, I'm going to kill him. Also," he held up a sharp claw. "I want four others to come to America with me."

Funny, I'd never thought of Bluescale as having friends. "I'll check with Angus. I'm sure we can work something out." I took the point of his claw and we shook on it.

Angus, Dorian and I peered into dense forest below, Bluescale's body hot beneath my palms as he dipped a wing into a wide, graceful turn which caused a warm breeze to ruffle the green strip in my hair. I was reluctant to exchange the gorgeous day for a life-threatening tramp through a dingy forest but we were on a trek to find a rare plant. Angus had claimed it would produce an elixir that would nullify Mydryth's powers.

A specially-sealed pouch was strapped across his chest to contain the bulbs we hunted. Angus had frightened us (at least me) when he pointed out that any leakage from the bulbs would cause a broom to crash so we'd taken advantage of Bluescale's offer to fly us to the forest.

The dragon's considerable bulk needed a small meadow or clearing in which to land safely – safely for us, that is. He flew in circles around a steep incline at the bottom of which were ideal growing conditions for the plant. "That ridge is big enough," he said, and tipped at right angles to the ground.

I jammed my knees under his vertical spinal plates and dug in my nails.

"Hey! Easy on the uprights!" He glanced over his shoulder.

A powerful arm slipped around me as Dorian pulled me against him, warm breath close to my ear. I tried to ignore the tremor that lanced through me at the unfamiliar touch. Typically male, he misread it and responded in an insulted tone, "I'm keeping you from falling."

"What else would it be?" I snapped. He could be so dense! I must've touched a nerve because he sucked in a breath and eased away although his grip remained firm.

A hand from behind pointed to a level area near the end of the ridge. "That spot will do, Bluescale, and thank ye for the ride."

The dragon folded enormous leathery wings against his sides, gave a great roar of pure fun, and dove for the ridge. I sucked in a breath and pushed against Dorian's chest. I thought I heard a masculine chuckle but it might've been the wind. I was going with that.

Perhaps you never develop the concept of falling if you're born with wings. I gritted my teeth and promised myself I'd master that emergency levitation spell Talon had so far been less than successful at teaching me (probably his fault, right?). The wind whipped tears from my eyes. Only a few more seconds…

As Bluescale's wings shot out, all three of us collapsed onto his back.

"Sorry about that," he said with a glance back. "Not used to passengers."

I mumbled something rude.

"What?" His green eye regarded me as he made a gentle landing on the grass.

"Nothing," I said, feeling green myself. The solid earth looked wonderful. We scrambled down Bluescale's side, along a front leg, and dropped to the ground where I tottered around in circles.

"Are you alright?" asked Dorian.

A large granite rock was nearby. I held up a forefinger. "Give me a minute." I staggered behind it where my stomach evacuated its contents.

When I was finished, I leaned my forehead against the cool rock and cursed. There are few things less attractive than being physically sick. If I was Dorian, I wouldn't want anything to do with me either. When I got back to Cumulos, I was going to ask if there was some kind of herbal concoction I could take (other than Angus' vile remedy which just wasn't worth it).

As I wobbled back to the group, Bluescale peered at me, leathery brow ridges raised.

"What was that noise? Sounded like you were strangling a cat!"

I shot him a nasty look "Never mind!"

Dorian suppressed a grin as he raised a hand to the dragon. "She gets vertigo." When the dragon looked blank, he added, "She's afraid of heights."

Bluescale's eyes rounded. "How can anyone be afraid of heights?"

I held my stomach and growled up at him. "I'm not afraid of heights, you ninny! I'm afraid of falling!" I caught the hint of a surreptitious hand motion by Dorian meant to silence Bluescale but the dragon was on a roll.

He lowered his huge head close to me. "You're a funny colour," he said. "Why is that?"

I cast a furious look at Dorian. "If somebody doesn't shut him up, I swear I'll turn him into something I can stomp on!"

At Bluescale's look of bewilderment, Dorian, shoulders shaking with suppressed mirth, turned away and gestured for Bluescale to follow. The dragon, listening to Dorian, glanced back with an expression of disbelief. I swear, sometimes it's a toss-up as to which of them is more annoying.

Minutes later, there was a mighty whoosh and Bluescale lifted into the sky. I was still amazed something that big could fly but dragons have hollow bones like birds and large cavities mixed chemicals to create the fire they shot from their mouths. Big bags of wind, I thought.

I sucked in a deep breath and straightened; thankful I was at least on the ground and the sooner we got started on the next leg of our journey, the faster we'd be done. I tried not to notice how incredible Dorian looked in a soft deerskin jerkin and leather leggings as he strode amongst scattered stones.

"He'll be back in two hours," he said. "You okay to travel?"

I shot a look at Bluescale who disappeared into the distance. Give me my broom any day. I took a deep steadying breath and nodded. "I'm fine. Let's go."

Angus was already descending along a faint trail that led to a forbidding darkness into which we were about to plunge. I grasped my wand, grateful for the familiar tingle that assured me there was magic at my disposal – at least for now.

In minutes we'd exchanged a bright cheerful day for a heavy, ominous black canopy interspersed from time-to-time with flashes of blue sky to tease our senses. Nothing green grew on the forest floor. Grotesque mushrooms, some taller than I, pushed out of black rot next to roots six feet thick that crept along the ground before plunging out of sight. Old mouldy logs strewn about caused us to detour on a regular basis. Angus insisted we not use magic as evil creatures would be drawn to it. But I could tell the forest had noted we were there – and didn't like it.

It'd get no argument from me; I'd rather we were somewhere else too. But maybe we'd be lucky enough to sneak in and out without mishap.

Right.

We'd completed a detour around yet another mammoth, moss-covered log when we came to a steep ravine through which a sluggish stream oozed. Mostly hidden by mist, I estimated the stream to be fifty feet below. Angus started down the sharp incline.

"Maybe we should look for a way around," I said, peering into the gloomy depths. "We can't see what's down there."

Angus pointed. "See those black spiky plants next to the water?" He parted the mist with a gesture.

I nodded.

"Those are indigo warts. You two keep watch here while I collect them. I won't be able to use magic while I'm there."

"Any idea what we're watching for?"

"Anything that approaches will be dangerous no matter how small. I'll be a few minutes."

After three steps, the mist, like a living thing, swallowed him whole. The air acquired a distinct chill and the stench of rotting vegetation was nauseating. It was a good thing my stomach was already empty.

I reviewed defensive spells as Dorian and I moved back-to-back to survey the menacing darkness. Scrabbling sounds made me jump and I had a sense of being watched. A movement caught my eye and my heart thumped as a grey snake slithered a pace from my foot. It was longer than I was. I shuddered but it appeared disinterested and, with graceful movements, disappeared over the lip of the ravine. I hoped Angus was watching.

As a branch dropped at my feet, I jumped against Dorian's broad back causing him to spin to see what was wrong.

"S … sorry. It's just a branch."

He picked it up then peered up into the blackness. "It's green so it didn't fall on its own."

Why hadn't I noticed that? My fear was magnifying events and I needed to get it under control. Although I knew my sense of loyalty would override any impulse to flee, a shiver swept through me. What I'd heretofore considered a strong personality trait looked at with a critical eye could appear anti-survival oriented.

Another branch dropped along with some mouldy and blackened leaves. My scalp crawled. Considering where I was, I didn't want to think about whether it was goose bumps or something more mobile. I resisted the urge to scratch, pressed close to Dorian and focused on our surroundings. Now was not the time to be distracted. I estimated how long Angus had been gone. Surely he'd be done soon … if the snake hadn't gotten him … or any number of dangerous life forms hadn't been attracted to his movement.

The mist thickened until it filled the ravine with an ominous grey sludge that wrapped around trees, slithered beneath logs, and deepened the darkness. I thought I was seeing things when a black shadow flickered. I blinked; stared. It happened again.

"Dorian?" I said on a rising note. "Did you see that?"

"Something's flying over us – something big. Maybe a few somethings."

My stomach cramped. "Shouldn't Angus be back? How long are we supposed to wait?" My voice was reaching new heights.

Dorian was calm, his voice level. "We wait until he returns. Angus is a powerful mage. Nothing will get the best of him."

"What about us? Probably *everything* can get the best of us! We don't even know the half of what's in here!"

"Relax, Raven; we'll be alright. Stand your ground and keep your wand ready."

"What do you mean? I'm relaxed! Don't I sound relaxed?" Something like a smothered laugh came from behind and I felt the shudder of his shoulders. "You're laughing at me! This isn't funny, Dorian! We could be killed in here!"

"That's unlikely with Angus less than fifty feet away."

"Have you seen how thick this fog is? He might as well be on another planet! We could be carried off and he'd never know."

I heard a groan but it wasn't an evil foe. "I'm beginning to think even an attack is going to be better than listening to you complain, Raven. I know you're scared. I get that. You should be. We're in danger here but take a deep breath and relax. We'll be gone in no time."

Precisely what I was afraid of.

"What did you say?" he asked.

"Never mind."

I sucked in a deep breath and huffed it out, pushed fear to the back of my mind where it wouldn't distract me. "You're right. I'm sorry. I'm fine now."

"I know you are. You've got more courage than anyone I know. You just forget it now and again."

As the words ignited a warm glow in my chest, I was disgusted with myself that I could be so vulnerable to a compliment.

My newfound confidence was doomed to a brief existence as black shadows dropped from the trees without warning. We ducked and rolled to the side – opposite sides as it turned out. A bolt of blue light shot from my wand to light a strange combination of bat and human – at least somewhat human.

Where did these things come from? A magical experiment gone wrong hundreds of years ago? Old lessons in mythology flashed into my brain. Harpies! Human/bat crosses. I did not want to know how that had happened.

As I sprang to my feet, I caught a glimpse of sharp talons designed to slash and gut prey attached to ankle tendons above large dirty feet equipped with prehensile toes. Needle-sharp teeth were bared in hairless thin faces, and hands equipped with ten fully-extended retractable claws groped towards me.

As I turned the nearest creature to dust, raucous screaming erupted and rock-hard wings knocked me to the ground.

I rolled to my feet while taking aim at the next shadow. The flash to my left confirmed Dorian had connected with his target but unfortunately it damaged my night vision. I shot a bolt of energy in the vicinity of another creature dropping toward me, got lucky as it crumbled to dust. I'd spun to target the next when I was slammed from the side and again knocked from my feet. I tasted blood.

By the flash of Dorian's wand, I saw another oncoming. There was no telling how many creatures there were but one thing was for certain – there were a lot more of them than of us. If we didn't get back-to-back again fast, we were done.

I targeted a creature whose claws pointed straight at me and gave a satisfied grunt as it dissolved with an enraged scream. Another dark shadow flashed toward my companion.

"Dorian!" I screamed across the deafening melee.

He spun and blasted a harpie from the air – which left him exposed to another attacking from behind. As I shot it, something dug into my shoulders and my feet left the ground. Another came at me with gutting talons extended. Ignoring the screaming pain, I blasted it and was about to aim blindly above when I was dropped like a sack of refuse. I caught a glimpse of Dorian's white face above his still-glowing wand.

I rolled to transfer some of the vertical energy to horizontal (falls from horses in childhood came in handy). At the same time, Dorian dove into a shoulder roll and slammed into me. Back-to-back we blasted harpies as if we were in a shooting gallery (one in which targets got to fight back). A part of my brain recorded the fact that Dorian bled from a head wound and blood soaked his right arm.

We'd killed a dozen of the creatures but the darkness was still filled with enraged screams and flashing claws. Where was Bluescale when we needed him? Probably filling his gullet with fish! We drew energy from the ground to supplement our magic but it was sluggish and sour.

A minute passed … two. I didn't know how much longer I could continue. My shirt was soaked with what I hoped was sweat. Where was Angus? Had the mist held him down there?

Without warning, the blackness was lit by a bright flash followed by a roaring jet of flame, the crash of branches and the arrival of a huge raging body. Vicious teeth snapped a harpy from the air, gave a quick crunch, tossed it aside; snapped up another. In seconds, the stench of scorched fur and flesh filled my nostrils. Fading screams of fleeing wounded drifted throughout the forest as an eerie silence descended upon us.

Smoke poured from Bluescale's nostrils, blood dripped from his fangs, and battle lust morphed green eyes to red. I shuddered; glad he was on our side.

I dropped my head against Dorian's back as I looked up at Bluescale and caught my breath. "Thanks for that. How did you know we needed help?"

He paused in searching the singed foliage and tipped his head to look at me. "You called. Well … screamed."

"I did?"

"By the way, I wasn't fishing. I was surveying the area."

"I recall thinking a dragon would be helpful, and I remember trying not to die. Anyway, I owe you one, Bluescale."

"Actually," he said with a dragon grin (which looked creepy considering his mouth dripped blood) "you owe me two!"

"And you're counting, of course."

"Until I get to the Americas."

"Fair enough."

I groaned and staggered a few feet, got a good look at Dorian, and my heart froze. "Oh … my god!"

He swiped at blood that poured down his face with a blood-soaked sleeve. The result was a crimson smear.

"Dorian! You're hurt!" I spun to Bluescale. "We've got to get him to Cumulos!"

Dorian raised a palm. "I'm okay, Raven. Most of it's not mine and a head wound bleeds a lot. I'll be fine." He swallowed. "But I don't think you are."

"What?" Still anaesthetized by the energies of the battle, I hadn't considered my condition. But now I thought about it, I hurt … a lot.

Dorian blanched as he stared at my chest – and it wasn't lust. I looked down. The little that was left of my shirt was soaked in blood that ran from my shoulders at an alarming rate. I had the odd sensation of being sucked into a whirlpool and a dim awareness of Dorian reaching for me.

"I … think we should go back now," I mumbled. As we sank to the ground, an apparition appeared from the mist. With a giddy laugh, I managed, "Great timing, oh powerful mage!"

Angus, not a hair out of place, stared at the ruinous state of the area and the copious amounts of blood that leaked from Dorian and me. It seemed sounds of the battle hadn't carried into the indigo wart ravine.

Dorian whipped off the remains of his shirt and pressed it against my wounds to slow the bleeding then swept me into his arms and strode to the dragon who nudged us between his back-plates. The snapping and crashing of branches fell behind as we swept from the depths of the forest into the welcome warmth of sunshine.

Chapter 20

"She'll be up and about in a few days." I tried to ignore the voice which intruded into my slumber. "She needs to wake up to eat though. It's been long enough."

"How do I do that?" Sounded like Dorian.

"Whatever you think will work as long as it's not violent. I need to get some supplies. I'll be right back." Quiet footsteps retreated.

Someone held my hand in a warm grip but I was too groggy to open my eyes. I drifted instead into a pleasant dream where warm lips pressed against mine. If I'd been more aware, I might've questioned the owner of those lips but it felt so wonderful, I enjoyed it for a while – even participated. I wished Dorian would kiss me that way.

I was disappointed when they withdrew. With a vague sense of frustration and the dream no longer so attractive, I struggled to the surface of consciousness. I opened my eyes and slammed them closed again as bright sunlight slanted through tall windows.

Fire had taken possession of my shoulders and I couldn't swallow. As I licked dry lips, a straw was inserted between them and I revelled in the sensation of cool water running down my throat.

I turned my head to see Dorian set an empty cup on a nightstand. "Hello," he said. "Nice to have you back." He looked, it seemed, kind of smug.

"How long . . ?" My throat was scratchy.

"A couple of days."

"Why so long?"

"The physician wanted you to stay asleep so your body could concentrate on healing."

As memory flashed of the harpies, I moved a shoulder and sucked in a sharp breath at the stabbing pain. "Doesn't seem to have worked."

"Your injuries were deep and harpies are filthy creatures that could cause all kinds of infection. Scared me half to death when I realized they could pick you off the ground."

Exhausted as I was, I narrowed my eyes. "Why was it such a surprise?"

He grinned and his eyes twinkled. "That healthy, corn-fed metabolism of yours has its advantages. You're solid as a rock!"

I had the vague impression there'd been an insult in there somewhere but gave it up. Too tired to figure it out. I scanned the white bandage above Dorian's left eye. "Is that going to leave a sexy scar?"

"Probably. Do you like scars?" Our gazes locked.

What was he saying? I remembered the dream kiss. Could it have been … no. He'd never do that. Then again … I touched my lips. "Dorian, did you . . ." I stalled.

"Did I what?" His eyes were mysterious and the corners of his mouth curved up.

"I seem to remember . . ." Did I remember something? or had it been a dream? "I … never mind. I'm confused."

His smile grew. He leaned over and gave me a quick, impersonal kiss on the lips. "The nurse is coming back. She said I had to leave after you woke up. I'll talk to you later." Whistling a tune, he strode away. Now what had made him so happy all of a sudden?

Downgraded to office employee! I stomped around Angus' desk and flexed my shoulders. It'd been over a week but even powerful healing potions hadn't completed the job. I itched to do something outdoors – anything. Maybe not combat harpies but there had to be a job I could do. I passed a scrying mirror balanced on a marble pedestal, its mysterious surface two feet in diameter, glanced in to see what was happening with the others.

Another attempt to pry Mydryth from his lair was in progress. This plan, unlike our earlier one, involved Bluescale. Our people would appear to attack Wickness while Bluescale charged to the rescue in hopes of convincing Mydryth they had the same interests. The mage might be so ready to gloat over taking something as valuable as a dragon away from Angus, he wouldn't ask many questions – and his ego would never suspect a mere dragon could manipulate him.

As the image cleared, I saw robes flap in the wind as they hugged a rolling landscape and raced towards forbidding grey towers on the horizon. With thin, vertical eyes, Wickness stared over an angry grey sea dotted with whitecaps, the tips of icebergs visible in the distance.

"*Are they there yet?*" I jumped at the voice in my head and couldn't resist a chuckle. "*What's so funny?*"

"Nothing, Bluescale. They're approaching Wickness. Should arrive in the next ten minutes. Where are you?"

"*In the ocean.*"

I shuddered. "Aren't you freezing?"

There was a pause while I'm sure he questioned my intelligence yet again. Patiently he explained, "*Raven. I … am … a … dragon. I'm filled with fire and smoulder on a continual basis. What about that would make you think I could get cold?*"

"Sorry. I forget. I don't have bar-b-que insides."

"*What?*"

"Never mind. Angus and the others are spreading out as they approach Wickness." I sucked in a breath. "Dozens of dark-ghosts are pouring from the castle! Mydryth knows they're coming! How can we defend against so many?"

"They won't need to. If dark-ghosts try to suck the life out of me, they get a bad case of indigestion. I however, can burn them to a crisp." He paused. *"Should I go now? Is it time?"* He sounded like he was primed in the starting gates.

"Wait a bit. If you interfere too soon, Mydryth will suspect something. You have to save the day at the last moment."

"That's me," he crowed, *"a hero!"*

"Of course. We're counting on it." I was glad he couldn't see my eye roll.

Dorian, Talon and Frost skimmed a steep ridge, wands out. Blue balls of fire shot towards the approaching hoard causing one dark-ghost after another to flare and disappear. Another … and another! It was working! Angus had supplemented the spells with indigo wart, each of which now contained a distillation which caused the target to drain of magic. The dark-ghosts became cautious and flew around the three of them.

Three? Where was Angus?

I enlarged the focus until I saw him slip over the edge of a cliff where he hugged the rock wall until he was below Wickness then shot straight up and hurled a blue fire-bolt at the tallest tower. There was a blinding flash followed by raining debris. A figure shot from amidst the dust and smoke, a twisted line of red running from the end of his wand toward Angus.

As angry red lightning searched for its target, Angus twisted out of the way and met it with a clear blue bolt. Where the energies melded, a glowing ball of hellish purple expanded, inched towards Mydryth as Angus maintained pressure.

Once more, I enlarged the view. Mydryth's face was a study in concentration and perhaps desperation.

"*Now?*"

"I'll let you know when!" I snapped. "Angus and Mydryth are above the castle shooting fire bolts and lightning at each other!"

"*Those two don't even know what a fire-bolt is!*"

Probably true compared to a dragon's blast. "They seem to be evenly matched, Bluescale, so we should give them a few more minutes. The others are holding their own with the dark-ghosts. Is your story clear?"

"*Of course, it's clear. It's not complicated! I think I should come now.*"

"A little longer . . ."

Mydryth flashed through the courtyard pursued by Angus. As they neared the wall, Mydryth shot straight up as a volley of arrows flew from the shadows. At the last second, Angus veered to the right and most of the arrows bounced off stone. The rest deflected from a hastily-formed shield – all but one. That one embedded itself in his thigh. I winced in sympathy.

"Go, Go, Go!" I bellowed. "Angus has been hit! Distract Mydryth!" I heard something that sounded like, "*about bloody time!*" after which Bluescale went silent.

I shifted the view to see a glistening blue-green monster create a gigantic fountain as it erupted from a frothing ocean.

A few powerful strokes brought Bluescale above the castle where he made a tight circle while belching black smoke.

Then he folded his wings and shot straight down. Just above the castle, he sent a stream of flame as long as his body and made a lightning pass over the ramparts. It appeared he was targeting Angus but I could tell the aim was off.

Mydryth seemed confused. He would recognize Bluescale. The dragon made another convincing feint towards Angus who grabbed his leg, appeared to think better of the whole attack strategy, ducked over the outer wall, and disappeared as his pursuer flew in circles blasting the dark-ghosts which threatened him. The obvious message to Mydryth was, "I want to talk."

The dark-ghosts turned as one from their attack and drifted back to Wickness giving Bluescale a wide berth. Our guys (I thought of them as our guys – like it was some kind of hockey game) waited at the top of a knoll which must've been a muster point.

I knew Mydryth had seen Angus get injured and, though it was good for the present scenario, recent personal injuries generated a surge of empathy. Behind that sympathy was a slight sense of disappointment. Considering Angus' reputa-tion, I would've expected a flawless ability to protect himself – and he'd been struck by an *arrow*? Really? That was right up there with being hit by a rock! I chewed a fingernail.

The others hovered and watched the castle. What the heck were they waiting for? The air in front of Talon shimmered and Angus materialized. He smiled as he reached down … and plucked the arrow from his leg! Something wasn't right! He wasn't bleeding and it didn't seem to hurt! He tossed it into the air where it dissolved into dust.

A ruse! Angus had taken advantage of the hail of arrows to pretend to be hit! He knew Mydryth had a standing army, knew he was being led into a trap! Misdirection is its own form of magic.

I reconsidered my assumption of his failure, replaced it with another notch of respect for his brilliance. I did a victory jig, careful not to jar my shoulders while the cat watched from the desk, no doubt wondering if I was suffering some kind of spasm.

Now, if only Bluescale could refrain from killing the mage. I didn't want that on my conscience. We'd soon be able to return the unicorns, the earth would be safe again (at least as safe as it ever got), Dorian and I could … what? Return to Denver? Would that be enough now? One part of me couldn't wait for it to be just the two of us again. Another relished what we'd found in Cumulos, valued our magical friends.

I'd have to think about it tomorrow. At the attack of a spontaneous yawn, I wandered to a divan next to the fire. I collapsed onto the soft cushions and was awake long enough to feel the cat snuggle against me. Contented purring was the last I remember.

The next day, Dorian and I decided to enjoy an evening that didn't included life-threatening events. Shafts of light from a setting sun created streaks of shadow as he ducked beneath a low doorway into the dim interior of one of the village inns.

Close on our heels was a man whose blonde-streaked hair brushed his shoulders. Tiny lines extended from the corners of green eyes that surveyed the room and his body, well over six feet tall and dressed in faded green tunic and leathers, was lean and strong. He didn't look more than thirty but was obviously an outdoorsman. As he brushed my shoulder, I caught the scent of summer flowers and dark forests, surprised by the oddest sensation of familiarity that I couldn't place.

Dorian and I selected a table against the back wall where a candle stuck into a lake of wax flickered in a stone holder. A plump barmaid with a lot of chest showing flicked a look at us then, hands on ample hips, wandered over to drop off stained menus. We ordered ginger beer and scanned the selections.

As she left to get our beer, my gaze was again drawn to the stranger seated across the room. "Wonder who that is?" I murmured.

Dorian glanced up from his perusal of the menu. "He's a Rider. Angus told me about them."

"What do they do?" I tried not to stare.

"They work for Gaia, travellers who look for irregularities in the flow of magic. Apparently there hasn't been one here for years. Maybe Gaia picked up on Mydryth's intentions towards the unicorns and his bid for control."

I stared at Dorian. "Where do you learn this stuff?"

His eyes held a touch of humour. "I ask questions."

"So do I, but nobody ever tells me this kind of thing!"

"Perhaps you pick up on different things." He took a sip from one of the glasses the barmaid slid onto the table. She gave Dorian a private smile and an excellent view of an acre of cleavage. Dorian grinned at me, knowing full well I'd noticed.

I chose not to comment. Instead I focussed on enjoying the muted murmur of contented conversations. The door opened again and the room fell silent. It was Angus and he seemed to be looking for someone.

I gave him a wave. He waved back but continued to survey the crowded room. As the Rider made a small motion, Angus made his way through the tables. The barmaid served drinks then left them with their heads together.

Curiosity stirred. What on earth could they be talking about? What did a Rider do when he found irregularities in magic?

Dorian shook his head at my questions. "Why don't you ask Angus, Raven? He'll know."

At that moment, the rider looked up, his eyes met mine, and communication flashed. I gasped at the sensation. If he tracked irregularities in magic, maybe he'd noticed ours was different. I remembered a fleeting glance as he'd entered the room. For some bizarre reason, my cheeks burned.

"Something wrong with the ginger beer, Raven?" Dorian was looking at me with a raised brow.

I suspect I flushed even more. "That . . that … Rider! He looked right at me!"

"I saw that," he said. "What was that about?"

"I've no idea. Why would he single me out? Do you think he can tell our magic is different?"

"He never once looked at me, Raven."

"I suppose if he wants to talk to me, Angus can let him know where I am." I took a gulp of ginger beer while staring at the Rider – a bad idea in retrospect since my lack of attention caused a good portion to slosh down my windpipe. When I'd finished choking and gasping, Angus and the Rider were gone. Dorian watched me with a bland expression.

"What?" I choked, wiping my mouth. "I nearly drowned!"

"I saw that." He shook his head.

"What?!"

A spontaneous smile worked its way to his mouth. "I don't know how you manage to stay alive from one day to the next, Raven. If that isn't magic, I don't know what is."

I drank my ginger beer in silence. Dorian watched the others in the room with a sharp eye. For a quiet person, he doesn't miss much and, I have to admit, I could wish for half his observational skills.

He dropped a few coins onto the table and rose. "Ready?"

I glanced at my half-finished ginger beer. "Now?"

"Got a feeling we should leave."

Dorian's instincts are never wrong. I took a final careful sip then followed him through the tables. As it was dark, Dorian touched my elbow to guide me through the narrow, winding street. I'd like to think I didn't need it but I have to admit to being clumsy at times. As we rounded a corner, I caught a movement to the side and stopped dead.

"Angus?" I peered into the shadows.

The mage stepped from a dark alley into the light of a gas lamp. He was followed by the Rider who looked directly at me. For some reason, I forgot what I'd been about to say. Visions of cool quiet forests came to mind and I couldn't tear my eyes from the man.

"I'm Valgren," he said in a heart-melting tone as he stretched out a hand. It was warm, dry, and calloused. Once again I swam in the sweet scent of a forest.

"I'm … I'm Raven." I cleared my throat to remove the squeak. "Nice to meet you." As his smile kindled something deep within me, it crossed my mind to wonder if he was human.

"Your magic has strange properties," he said. "Perhaps we can spend some time together while I'm here. I'd like to … explore it."

"I'm Dorian," said my companion, extending a hand.

Valgren took it briefly. "Good to meet you." Then he returned his attention to me.

The phrase, "rocked my world," didn't begin to convey his effect on my senses. "I'd like that," I blurted.

"Perhaps tomorrow?"

Dorian stiffened as I nodded.

"Seven o'clock?"

"In … in the *morning?*"

"Gaia is freshest then."

"Oh . . .um … of course. Seven it is."

"I'll meet you in the Cumulos courtyard." He bade farewell to the others and dissolved into the shadows.

"Well," said Angus, "tis a beautiful evening!" He clasped his hands behind his back and sauntered towards the castle.

I avoided looking at Dorian though I couldn't imagine why I felt guilty. After all, it wasn't as if we were dating or anything… Besides, it was about magic . . .

Chapter 21

I managed to brush my teeth and dress before seven o'clock then stumbled down the stairway as the sun cleared the horizon. The courtyard was empty except for Sin, my cat friend, who sat on the railing soaking in the morning warmth. I scratched under his chin which set his purring machinery in gear.

My purring machinery however wasn't even primed. This guy better show up! As I leaned against a dew-covered railing, the seat of my jeans soaked through in an instant. I groaned. The day hadn't even started!

I paced, shot a glance at the clock tower. Three minutes to seven. I'd give him five minutes then go back to bed.

A distant clopping sounded, the wrought iron gates swung open, and the most gorgeous stallion floated through. I say floated because, though his hooves touched the ground, he seemed to be doing a graceful dance. He was big – far bigger than the average horse with flowing silver mane and tail. Solid muscles flexed beneath a glistening silver coat, neck in an elegant arch.

The aptly-name Rider rode as if part of the animal, hands light on the reins. His eye caught mine as I smoothed the emerald streak in ebony hair that spilled down my back, noticed he noticed, and could've kicked myself. He approached and checked the horse with a slight flex of fingers.

His mount, though graceful, was enormous. Most horses this big weren't used for riding. They pulled plows and worked in fields but I'd bet this horse had never seen a harness. I realize I was focused on the horse because Valgren's smile was making my stomach quiver.

He wore a white, loose-sleeved shirt under a leather vest, carried a bow and quiver strapped to his back, and a hunting knife in a leather scabbard attached to a tooled belt. His green gaze flicked over my jeans and tank top under a jean jacket – the same clothing with which I'd arrived at Cumulos.

His smile widened. "You look … appealing." I could swear he knew exactly what I was feeling. And that made it worse.

He swung a leg over the pommel and slipped in one smooth movement to the ground. "Let me introduce you to Moonlight." As he moved to the horse's head, Moonlight turned to nuzzle the Rider, nickered low in his throat.

"He likes you," I said.

"We've been together a long time." Valgren patted the satin cheek.

I'd ridden horses a lot as a teenager but felt small beside the huge animal. "Hello, there," I murmured and stroked the silky neck. Rock-hard muscles rippled beneath my hand as he bent his head toward me and whuffed air through his nostrils.

Valgren rested an arm on the curved neck. "That's his way of saying hello."

I stroked the backs of my fingers against his velvety muzzle. "Hello, to you too," I said softly. I glanced at Valgren. "He's gorgeous!"

As the Rider slid his hand along Moonlight's neck, brushing mine as he did so, he didn't seem to notice the catch in my breath. His eyes revealed the trust he felt when he looked at Moonlight. I'd never trusted anyone or anything that much. I cleared my throat and stepped back.

"You wanted to know about my magic," I asked. "What did you have in mind?"

"Do you know what I do?"

"I've heard you look for irregularities in magic."

"That's some of it."

"That would likely include Dorian and me."

"It does."

"Are you some kind of … policeman or … enforcer?"

"More like an investigator. I keep track of what's going on; look for unusual energies that could impact Gaia."

My stomach clenched. "Are we a danger to Gaia?"

"Not even a little."

"Why isn't Dorian here too?"

"My ride is a two-seater and I'd rather take you."

"Two-seater? Where do you plan to take me?"

"I want to see how your magic interacts at ley points. Don't worry; it's not dangerous. We can cover everything in a day."

"A day?! I … I'm not prepared to leave for the day! I've got to tell Dorian, Angus …"

"Angus knows so he'll inform your … companion. There's food along the way." He moved into my space which caused every nerve to tingle. "You did offer to help."

Wildness swirled deep within tilted moss-green eyes, daring me to back out, challenging me to come along.

I don't often back down from a challenge. "Where are we going? And how?"

With no warning or effort, he grasped my waist, deposited me astride the saddle and, with a movement so fast and smooth I could barely take it in, he was seated behind me. A powerful arm curled around my waist, pulled me close.

"If we're going to ride," I said, shifting away, "I can sit behind. I've ridden horses before."

"Not like this," he said. As his lips brushed my ear, shock slammed through my body. It occurred to me that perhaps I'd been celibate too long – and maybe I should've clarified exactly what kind of magic he meant. His left hand flexed and the horse moved off in that smooth dancing motion.

As the wrought-iron gates closed behind, I took a deep breath, willed myself to relax. "You don't need to hold me so tight. I'm not going to fall off."

He pulled me even tighter, made a curious noise, and something impossible happened. Great silvery wings unfurled from Moonlight's sides, he moved into a slow gallop then added a burst of speed, spread those great wings – and we were airborne. As the ground dropped away, I grabbed the front of the saddle.

Valgren's arm flexed. "It's okay, Raven. Angus told me about your fear of heights. That's why I put you in front."

A corner of my mind began to simmer that Angus had been discussing my shortcomings with strangers. Wait until I got back!

"He expected telling me would make you angry but I wanted you to come and Moonlight is my ride. It isn't much different from riding a dragon – except here you have your own seatbelt." He tucked me closer. "I'll keep you safe."

I'll keep you safe. No one had ever said that to me before…not ever. I had no idea of how to respond, so I didn't.

Puffy clouds dotted the early morning sky and the air was warm. As Moonlight leveled out at about five hundred feet, I began to relax. It was a fantastic view. A flock of evening swans skimmed the surface of a small, clear lake and splashed into the water next to a thick stand of bull-rushes where they'd rest for the day.

As the lake fell behind, Moonlight banked to the left to follow a valley that wound between low mountains. An updraft would lift us now and again but Moonlight knew his business. Feathers spread wide at the tips of his wings and I could see minute adjustments to accommodate changes in wind conditions.

The valley ended at a level plain presided over by a huge flat-topped pyramid covered with soil and topped by megalithic stones balanced on end. They were arranged in three concentric circles reminiscent of Stonehenge without the lintels.

"Our first stop." Valgren's voice murmured in my ear.

I realized my hair must've been blowing in his face so I twisted it into a braid. "Sorry," I said. "I wasn't thinking."

"Don't worry about it," he said, and I could feel his smile. "It smells delicious!"

Before I could formulate a reply, Moonlight began a smooth descent, turning in a lazy circle. As his hooves touched the grass, he adjusted to a gallop then came to a graceful stop.

Valgren released his hold and slipped to the ground. "I'll catch you," he said, and reached for me.

I was about to refuse when I realized he was right. A sprained ankle would be embarrassing. Lifting a leg over the front of the saddle, I slid into the Rider's arms. The catch was timed beautifully and somehow I ended up against him, immersed in the scent of a forest.

Not trusting myself to look up into those green eyes, I disentangled myself and walked toward the stones, awed at their sheer size. How on earth had they gotten here? Who had set them up? And why? The monoliths of the outer ring were each over twenty feet in height.

"What are you expecting to find?"

He gave a foreign shrug. "I don't know. I feel Gaia's energy in you and her energy is strong here."

Gaia. The name of the earth. I touched a stone and flinched at the unexpected tingle. It felt like electricity but … thicker – sort of.

He noticed. "Would you walk to the centre of the circle and tell me what you feel?"

"You sure it's safe? There's a lot of energy here."

"It's Gaia's energy. She won't harm you."

I recalled quite a lot of harm coming from Gaia over the years – or perhaps that was Nature. Was there a difference? Nevertheless, my curiosity drove me on. A few steps further and energy swirled through the souls of my feet.

When I told him, he said, "Open the energy gate at the top of your head to allow the magic to flow through."

I glanced back. "How do I do that?"

"I'll help you." He took my hand. "Come." I followed, curious.

At the exact centre, he turned. "I need to be close to you." At my nod, he threaded his fingers through my hair until his left hand covered my crown and I was pressed against him. He gave a soft sigh and closed his eyes. My body threatened to burst with the sensuous energies that flowed through the man and into me.

"Imagine a portal opening at the top of your head. Feel the flow from Gaia going up your body, through your crown, and into the universe. You will modify the power of Gaia into magic that can be used."

Other than a tingling, all I was aware of was Valgren's energy and power, Valgren's body. . .

As I closed my eyes, the coolness of a forest filled me and I experienced the unusual sensation of belonging. Odd. I'd never felt like I belonged anywhere. I leaned into the Rider's chest where his heart beat with a calm rhythm as he held me in a gentle embrace.

"Trust Gaia," he whispered. "She'll take care of you."

The tingling grew until I felt I'd burst. I don't know how long we stood as surges of magic and emotion washed through my body. I felt like I was being cleansed on all levels.

"Open the portal," he whispered. "See it open and it will."

If I didn't do something soon, I was going to explode. I visualized an opening like the iris of an eye an inch above my head, mentally directed magic to flow through it.

Nothing.

I added emotion to direction. Caring and compassion. The world needed all it could get. I felt a loosening and the lightest motion at the top of my head, like the opening of a flower. Perhaps the Asians had it right – the opening of a lotus flower.

Chaotic magic became coherent as it burst through the top of my head and, in seconds, I was a fountain. Magic flowed from the ground through the souls of my feet, throughout my entire body and, with joyous abandon, showered around us. I experienced an indescribable sensation; my whole being resonated with the harmonics of a flow that felt like … living music.

I wanted more.

I don't know how long I'd have stood there if Valgren hadn't moved. His Rider's hands, contradictory in their calloused gentleness, stroked the sides of my face.

"White Raven," he whispered. "Raven, you need to move out of the circle now."

I didn't want to move … ever again. Gentle lips brushed mine. That was nice. I'd like some more of that. I enjoyed it for a while, leaned into it.

As the warm lips pulled way, I came back to earth with a thud. My eyes shot open and the cascade of magic dissolved.

What the hell was I doing? One minute I'm day-dreaming about Dorian and the next I'm kissing some stranger! His arms still around me, Valgren looked down, the wildness replaced by controlled desire.

"Are you alright?" he asked.

My cheeks must've flamed. I didn't know whether to be embarrassed or angry – but I felt like an idiot. When in doubt, go with what you know. I charged from the circle rubbing my arms to get some semblance of normalcy back, swung around as he approached.

"How dare you take advantage of me like that? I'd no idea what was happening in there! You ask me to trust you and this is my reward!"

His smile was easy. "I didn't want you to be frightened. It's a shock to the body to cut the magic off and I wanted to ease you out of it." He approached and looked down. "I don't need to take advantage of women, Raven, and I retreated after I'd gotten your attention."

My hands were clenched. "You couldn't have come up with some other way of getting my attention? How about, "Gee, Raven, maybe you should stop now. You're getting overloaded!""

"I did. You didn't hear me."

"You couldn't have tried again?"

He hooked his thumbs in his pockets and looked at me without a trace of guilt. "I think we both enjoyed this more."

"I think you took advantage of me!"

Warm hands on my shoulders caused me to look up into mysterious, moss-green. His voice was gentle but evaluating. "If you're going to use powerful magic, Raven, you need to be completely honest – especially with yourself. I didn't force you and I didn't take advantage. You don't want to admit your attraction to me because it confuses your feelings for … your companion."

I hate it when people argue when I'm attempting to dump a shitload of crap onto them! Why couldn't they just accept it and move on? Then I wouldn't have to do all this damn introspection! I hate introspection! As far as I'm concerned, understanding yourself is overrated. Who cares anyway? We're all crazy to one extent or another. I don't need to know the exact dimensions of my particular brand of insanity.

But I was stumped for words. The man made sense. I set my jaw like a mule and blurted. "I don't want to be honest!"

Humour swirled behind the moss-green and the corners of his mouth tilted up. "Ahh…you see? We're making progress. At least that's honest!"

The second site was hidden in a thicket. In a small clearing, Valgren caught me as I slid from Moonlight but set me aside with a quick motion. With a smooth overhead movement, he extracted a sword from a sheath next to the bow on his back. Sunlight reflected like blue fire from a blade I'd never noticed was there.

He motioned me back. "Stay with Moonlight."

He advanced toward the thicket with flexed knees, sword raised. At a muttered incantation, the thorns moved outward like a parting of the sea to reveal a flat stone six feet across and three feet high. Looking like he expected trouble, Valgren leapt onto the stone, did a slow revolution then squatted to draw a pentagram with a soft crystal without removing his gaze from the undergrowth. Then he stood erect and began to chant in a powerful voice.

Rustlings began in the thickets along with coughing roars which caused the hair on the back of my neck to prickle.

A pentacle made of light rose from the stone, glowed brighter by the second, expanded, turned on edge, and made slow revolutions. It grew to five feet from point to point, the centre a-glow with pure white light.

Growling grew to a roar. A shriek of rage made me leap against Moonlight who watched with placid interest. He'd seen it all before. Well, it was new to me and, frankly, it scared the hell out of me. I couldn't imagine what would make such terrible sounds.

Valgren raised both arms high, sword glinting in the sun. As the pentacle spun faster, the thickets leaned towards it as if drawn to a vacuum. More screams.

A dark shape shot from the shrubbery to be sucked into the pentacle. I had time to see fangs, claws, and red enraged eyes on a body with some resemblance to a dog – an enormous dog. Seconds later, another was drawn into the spinning vortex. In all, five monsters were swallowed before Valgren stopped chanting.

The energy in the clearing stilled. Then the thicket did something I've never seen a thicket do. Brambles and rough branches shortened until they pulled back into the soil to leave a smooth ring of grass around the centre stone.

Valgren sheathed the sword with a smooth motion then spread his hands on either side of the spinning pentacle. As he shouted a command, it disintegrated into a shower of sparkles that dissolved upon touching the earth.

He waved me forward.

I scanned the meadow. What if he'd missed some?

He gestured again. "They're gone. Let's see how you do here." He was relaxed now. Seeing my hesitation, he continued. "Those were werewolves. Must've been sent here to close the portal."

"Who would send them?" I edged closer. "And why? What does closing a portal do?"

"Gaia's magic can't flow if the portals are closed. Maybe this is connected to Mydryth's bid for power."

I found the stone to be warm though it'd been shaded by the thicket.

Valgren slipped to a sitting position, legs over the side of the stone. "Portals draw energy from the sun to mix with Gaia's. The thicket screened the sun from the stone and doubled as a hiding place. I haven't been in this realm for … well … a long time. Need to step up surveillance."

As I placed my hands on the rock to swing up beside him, I felt a deep hum that continued as I settled in. When I asked him about it, he said it was one of Gaia's notes, her song of life. Each portal was different but each harmonized with all the others when Gaia was healthy. Was Gaia healthy? So far, but disturbing incidences like this indicated an attack of some kind. There was always somebody wanting to feel powerful.

Speaking of power … I summoned a vision of Valgren astride the rock, sword aloft, maneuvering terrifying amounts of magic with ease. It was obvious he was a powerful being. I may have been a teensy bit guilty of prejudging when Dorian had called him a Rider. So what? I could ride too. Should have clued in when Angus had treated Valgren with such respect – an equal, in fact. I folded my legs in a meditative position and gave a deep sigh.

"What's the matter?"

"Nothing."

"Maybe you should give that honesty thing another try."

I canted my eyes to the side. "I'm beginning to realize what we're up against and I haven't a clue what I'm doing! The only thing I can see me helping with is creating a catastrophe." I chewed my lip.

Valgren's hand moved to the back of my neck where gentle fingers massaged. *Oh, man! How could that possibly feel so good?* I glimpsed a smile as I heard a moan. I'd like to believe the moan was his but suspected not.

I struggled to get my mind back on track. "You need to stop doing that!"

"Why?" He continued.

I had trouble coming up with a *why*. It felt so good! My bones turned to jelly.

"You worry much too much, Raven. If Gaia was weak, life would've disappeared long ago. You don't need to do everything – just your own small part."

"If Gaia doesn't need help, why are we doing this?"

"I don't think Gaia is so concerned with which life forms thrive as long as some do."

I struggled to keep up with the simple conversation. I licked dry lips. "So this is a self-serving enterprise. Keep humanity alive." My vision blurred as my head drooped.

"Not just alive but as the dominant life form. We complain about how bad humanity is but they're a cake walk compared to some of the other options." He gave a final rub and slid to his feet. "We have some more stops to make. Ready?"

Ready? I wasn't sure I could walk! I blinked and got my feet onto the grass where I waited for my head to clear. I peered up at him through narrowed eyes. "How do you do that?"

"Do what?"

"You ... *get* to me. That's never happened before. What is it about you?" I felt the cool forest again as he looked deep into me.

The tips of his lips curled upward. "I'm not only a servant of Gaia, I'm an extension of her. Sensuality is a strong attribute of Gaia therefore it's strong in me, and your own Gaia energies make it natural for us to be drawn to each other. I realize you have cultural inhibitions so I'll refrain from compromising your ... social integrity. I understand it may cause unpleasant repercussions for you."

"You don't want to cause me problems so you ... will keep your distance from me."

"That is correct."

"You think I can't control myself?"

"Evidence would indicate otherwise."

Shit! Right again! I heaved a deep sigh, stepped around him, and headed to Moonlight. Whose stupid idea had this trip been anyway?

Now I understood my attraction to Valgren (sort of), I was better able to control it, though not without difficulty. It was as if my body had a mind of its own when he got close. As we settled onto Moonlight, I asked if his attraction to me was as strong.

He said he felt a pull but restraint was not difficult. As an extension of Gaia he had opportunities to … blend with others.

If I hadn't known better, I'd have said I felt a twinge of … jealousy at that little tidbit. As Moonlight's ears swiveled my direction I suspect he heard my jaw flex.

We stopped at two other sites where I practiced opening the portal, allowing the magic to flow. His expectation that my magic would blend well at ley line intersections was proven correct. Now that I knew how to move the magic, I could get the same effect anywhere and my spells would be more powerful. Considering what we were up against, I was grateful for any advantage.

Shadows skimmed along the ground and a golden light filled the countryside as the air cooled. I was feeling less anxiety about riding a flying horse hundreds of feet above the ground so was making progress with the vertigo thing. Maybe practice helped. Then again, maybe it was my companion's warm grip.

The sky presented a glorious show of reds and golds as Moonlight tipped to begin the descent to Cumulos. Welcoming lights twinkled in windows as a band of deep indigo widened in the east. We flew over the high walls of the courtyard to make a graceful circle as we dropped toward the grass. Without the slightest jar, Moonlight galloped a few steps before halting next to the large outer doors.

I stirred, but Valgren held me close as his breath caressed my ear. "Perhaps another time . . ." he said softly as warm lips brushed my skin.

My heart slammed.

"Another time for what?" Dorian, arms crossed, leaned against a pillar.

For some reason, I gave a guilty start. Valgren remained calm, holding me against him. He glanced at Dorian who stepped forward. "Another time to do further … exploration. Raven is a talented mage."

If he hadn't told me he had all the female companionship he needed, I'd have said he was exhibiting masculine territoriality. Good thing I knew better.

"Dorian!" I said, trying to quash the irrational burst of guilt. After all, nothing had happened with Valgren. Did fantasies count? If they did, I was doomed.

Dorian reached up. "I'll catch you."

Valgren gave a gentle squeeze before releasing me. I lifted my right leg over the front of the saddle and slid into Dorian's grasp. In an unusual gesture, he tucked me beneath his arm and looked up at Valgren. "I trust your experiment is finished."

Valgren flicked a look from Dorian to me. "I haven't decided." Then he nodded at me (I swear he winked), spun Moonlight and, in a few short strides, they flew into the air, made a circle, and headed toward the setting sun.

I didn't know quite how to respond to Dorian's arm around me. Was it because of Valgren? … or me? I grinned up at him and cocked an eyebrow. "Miss me?"

He narrowed his eyes. "What's the story with that guy? Seemed a little … familiar with you. What kind of experiments was he talking about?"

So it was Valgren. I slipped from beneath his arm and stood with hands on hips.

"What is your problem? You don't like that a man pays attention to me? I have news for you! You don't own me! We've always been just friends. Unless that changes, and maybe it never will, I have the right to see anyone in any way I want! I don't expect to see another demonstration like that!"

I was so angry I spun on my heel and stomped into the castle. If the damned door hadn't been so heavy, I'd have slammed it to make my point!

Chapter 22

I was cuddled in a chair in Frost's suite. A cheerful fire licked at logs in the small kitchenette as Frost proffered a silver pot.

"More tea?"

I took a bite of butter scone and shook my head. Frost poured for herself and settled into an easy chair. "I hear you met a Rider today," she said after a careful sip.

I was horrified to feel heat rush to my face but Frost gave a faint smile. "It's all right, my dear; all magical females are drawn to the Riders. You should've been forewarned."

I rested my chin in a palm, elbow propped on the soft arm of the chair, "So how do you handle it? The attraction, I mean? Is it just … physical? You … ignore it?"

The smile still tugged at the corners of her mouth. "You don't have to ignore it, Raven. Riders are wonderful lovers. They're gentle, aware, sensuous … and they have *amazing* stamina."

My right eyebrow inched upwards. "That sounds like the voice of experience."

The smile widened. "Any woman would have to be dead to ignore a Rider."

After sharing a chuckle, I returned to my book where I was soon immersed in the memorization of defensive spells. I was visualizing a complicated sequence when Bluescale's voice blasted into my head.

"Raven! Raven! Can you hear me?"

Hot tea spilled onto my knee. "Of course I can hear you! My head will be ringing for hours! What's up?"

He sounded smug. *"Mydryth is my new best friend!"*

"Does that mean you're not going to eat him?"

"Not today. He bought the story of Angus threatening to send me back to the stream."

"What's his plan?"

"With my help, he thinks he can attack Cumulos – and he's promised to release all the dragons afterwards."

"Do you believe him?"

"Do I seem stupid to you?"

"Just checking."

"Anyway, he's called in reinforcements of the dark variety. They don't like me much. Not often they meet someone who

can turn them into a puff of smoke; and he's added soldiers for a direct assault."

I frowned. "Soldiers wouldn't be able to get through the spells around the castle. Why would he do that?"

"*He has three mages to take down the shield. And he'll send a mage with the soldiers to deal with localized spells around the exterior wall. I attack from the sky with fire, soldiers break through the perimeter, and Mydryth goes after Angus.*

"Think he can do it?"

"*Don't see why not.*"

"When?"

"*Next week.*"

"So we've got one week to get him into the stream. Thanks, Bluescale. We owe you."

"*I believe that's three.*"

"Good to know you can count."

I relayed the conversation to Frost who insisted on speaking to Angus. "He'll want to know even though it's late." We hurried down the hall toward a heavy wooden door carved with Celtic runes.

As Angus, in a green plaid robe, paced before a fire, he stroked his chin and listened, interjecting with quiet questions.

"That's the gist of it," I concluded. "We don't have much time."

"That is so. Let's sleep on it and talk in the morning. I'll inform Talon."

The next morning at breakfast, I updated a still standoffish Dorian. His attitude made me think of Valgren which made me wonder if Gaia would have any interest in saving the unicorns. Perhaps Valgren could serve as an emissary of sorts. It was a semi-formed idea I determined to work on later.

I flicked a look at Dorian and decided not to bring it up. I sensed he may not be receptive to the idea of me looking for Valgren. I recalled my attitude toward Nightshade with a touch of unease. That was different. She'd been a traitor. At least, that's what I told myself.

A movement caught my eye and I choked when Valgren strolled through the door, acknowledged Angus then locked eyes with me. My throat closed until my lungs got desperate. He slid into a chair opposite me and gave Dorian a short nod of greeting.

"I hoped you'd be here this morning, Raven. I'd like to go over some ideas later if you have time."

Dorian dropped knife and fork onto his half-empty plate with a clatter. "I need to see Cash about something."

With a glance at Dorian's stiff retreating back, I turned to Valgren. "You realize he thinks you're invading his territory."

"It only matters what you think."

True. Wasn't that what I'd told Dorian last night?

"I need to see Angus. We'll talk later."

As I watched Valgren stride away, I felt like I was about to get flattened by a steamroller and didn't know how I felt about that. Then I remembered Frost's comment. She was right. I should lighten up. Being pursued by a Rider was something any woman would dream of, and Dorian was in no position to object. He'd had plenty of opportunity. Although I tried with heroic resistance to prevent it, a smile worked its way onto my face.

A council of war was underway. I sat between Dorian and Valgren as Talon outlined the need for info on Mydryth's strategies in case we were unable to neutralize him in the streams. The dark mage would have to counter the shields of Cumulos and we needed to know how he planned to do that.

Angus, from behind his massive desk, looked over at Valgren. "What do ye think?"

Valgren rested an ankle on the opposite knee. "Gaia could get me inside Mydryth's castle but there'll be layers of defense. It would help to have another person – someone who can also channel Gaia's magic." He glanced at me.

Dorian caught his look and straightened. "No way! You're not taking Raven! I have the same magic she does. If anyone goes, it'll be me!"

Valgren cocked an eyebrow at Dorian. "Your magic is not exactly the same. Yours is male. Female magic will complement my own."

"I'll bet!"

I thought this would be a good time to intervene. "I'll decide if I go!" I shot a narrow-eyed look at Dorian and turned to Valgren. "Tell me more."

Although I floundered in a few places, his explanation made sense. He was of the magic of Gaia and, as such, could move through any part of the earth. Since I had the same innate ability (although I really didn't believe that), having me along would intensify his perceptions. After I'd waded through his explanations, I settled on the idea that I'd be fulfilling the role of a spare battery and, as long as he was touching me, I'd be alright.

Dorian's frown deepened at this little bit of information overload. Not only did Valgren propose taking me along on a dangerous mission, he planned to be touching me for most of it. I didn't know if his concern was that Valgren was putting me in danger or if he felt threatened by the Rider's interest in me.

The discussion continued until lunchtime but, in the end, Valgren's plan was the most viable. We needed to get into Wickness to find out how the mages planned to collapse the shield around Cumulos.

I closed my eyes and focussed on Bluescale's essence. A couple of minutes later, the dragon's over-cheerful response blasted into my head. *"Raven! You wouldn't believe the creatures that live in King's Loch! Some are even bigger than I am!"*

"Bluescale! Could you turn it down? I'm not deaf – yet!"

"Sorry! Just caught the juiciest fish! A marvelous chase! Almost sorry to eat him."

I decided the dragon's stomach must be bottomless. "Could we ... focus?"

"Sure. I'm finished for now. What would you like?" With me as translator, Angus and Valgren outlined the plan. *"Sounds like fun! I'd love to get back at those three old geezers! I vote we dump them in the stream with Mydryth."*

"Causing you problems?"

"*Nothing I can't handle. For some stupid reason they don't trust me.*"

"Does Mydryth?"

"*Mydryth doesn't trust anyone but he's willing to work with me.*"

"We want to get started. Do you know of anything that could cause a problem tonight?"

"*The old guys will be in the library with their charts and chants. I swear they even smell old. Be careful though; they don't have a single drop of charity amongst them – and they're powerful mages. Don't underestimate their skills.*"

"What makes you say that?"

"*Let's say I'm growing some new scales and leave it at that.*"

"Oh … okay, then."

Valgren and I would leave at midnight. As the group scattered for lunch, Dorian left the study without a word or backward glance.

"Raven, if you don't breathe, you'll pop a blood vessel."

Valgren's hand tightened on my wrist. The strange darkness of the surrounding soil had me convinced there was no air to be had even though Valgren had assured me he'd matched our frequencies to Gaia. There was plenty of air. He placed my hand on his chest in the dimness. "Feel. I'm breathing. It's okay."

As every fiber of my being protested, I inhaled a little then more. Valgren was right. There was air.

My body must wonder about its driver. A convulsive intake swept through me as I was kicked out of the driver's seat and oxygen flooded in. That was better. Not so much the threat of imminent death.

Moonlight had dropped us on a rocky shore at the base of the high cliffs to the south of Wickness. After the Pegasus had departed into a blustery wind, Valgren had led the way straight toward a cliff where my body over-rode my instructions and took over the reins. In an effort to convince me I couldn't walk into solid rock, my feet refused to move.

Valgren took one look at the sheer terror on my face, swept me into his arms… and walked straight into the rock wall. I loosened my hold after he pointed out that now *he* couldn't breathe. A few minutes further on, he'd commented that, although he appreciated our closeness, he didn't think he could carry me all the way to the castle. Perhaps I could walk. I must've agreed because I now tagged along at an alarming pace considering I couldn't see much.

"We don't need to see everything, Raven. We can move through anything."

"Sorry. This is new to me. I've never waded through solid rock before."

"The only thing you need to remember is to keep touching me. If we get separated, even for an instant, you'll be sealed here forever. Even though you have the ability to stone-walk, you don't believe you can, and that lack of belief would kill you."

I was torn by that comment. Should I be insulted he didn't trust me to think, or happy he'd taken that responsibility? Perhaps I'd shelve the question for now.

A soft glow appeared in the shadows ahead. Valgren slowed and peeked into a dim corridor lit by flickering sconces.

I followed suit and almost fainted at the sight of his head sticking out of a tunnel wall. It was even worse to realize I was the same. Claustrophobia clutched at me and I began to hyperventilate. Valgren's mouth quirked as he pulled me into the corridor.

"You'll get used to it," he said. "The first few times can be unsettling."

Unsettling! I'd just stepped out of solid rock! That was more like mind-blowing! The bits of magic Dorian and I had played with were nothing compared to what went on here. I felt like the dumbest kid in Kindergarten.

As I worked to normalize my breathing, Valgren checked the corridor. He slipped the map from his pocket and held it up to the dim light of a sconce, traced lines on the map. With a satisfied grunt, he refolded and returned it to an inside pocket. Then he grasped my hand and set off down the corridor.

I struggled to keep up. "I thought you didn't need to touch me if we weren't in rock."

"I don't." He continued at a swift pace.

Oh.

I wasn't small but his legs were longer. The floor acquired an upward slant and it wasn't long before I was puffing and sweating. Valgren, of course, looked like he was out for a stroll. He stopped at a junction in the corridor and held a finger to his lips.

Have you ever tried to breathe quietly when you're out of breath? Not possible. I took great gulps of air and tried to hold it then let it out silently while the rest of me screamed for oxygen. My heart pounded in my ears – more evidence that I needed to work out regardless of how many stairs I climbed in a day.

Valgren turned his head as if listening, squeezed my hand at the unmistakable clank of metal and heavy treads. With a finger to his lips, he pushed me into the rock wall from which he peered into the corridor. As I followed suit, I realized I could see and hoped nobody could see us.

Regular marching grew louder. Eight soldiers in full battlefield garb rounded a corner and marched past without a glance. They could've been clones of the guards I'd outrun not long ago.

As they disappeared down the hall, Valgren pulled me back into the corridor. By this time, I felt like a sack of refuse. When I pointed it out, he said it wouldn't be long now. We started down the corridor again but this time he left me to follow.

A dilapidated door set into an alcove made us wince as it protested with a loud screech. We slipped through into utter darkness. I whipped out my wand, lit it, and sucked in a breath in absolute horror.

We were on a creaky wooden stairwell that wound around the inside of a tower. Visions of hanging in the darkness held only by Dorian's grip flashed into my mind as I flattened against the wall. Now would be a great time to hide inside the rocks! I'd be good with that!

Valgren looked puzzled. "What's the matter?" I told him in halting sentences, my stare glued to the bottomless shaft.

"I understand," he said. "Good thing Dorian was quick and strong." I nodded. He gestured up the stairwell. "We still need to move. Stay to the inside." He clasped my wrist. "Even if we fall, as long as I'm touching you, we'll just fall through the floor. Nothing will happen."

"Are you sure?" I peered into the blackness again.

He gave me a warm smile. "I'm sure, Raven. I'll keep you safe."

There it was again. *I'll keep you safe.* Why did that statement catch me so off guard?

Valgren's wand lit the entire tower. I couldn't imagine how much magic that would take. With a rueful grimace at my paltry light, I pocketed my wand with a sigh. Turning mine off didn't make the slightest difference. But I was gaining an education in the power of real magic. What had I gotten myself into?

I kept up as best I could but it wasn't long before I was huffing and puffing. I pulled to a stop, gasping for breath.

"Okay! How does everybody here do that?"

Valgren glanced back from a step above. "Do what?"

"Do you not see any difference between you and me at this moment?" Sweat trickled down my back and my lungs heaved.

His gaze flicked over me. "Of course."

I rolled my eyes. "Not that! I mean, how do you climb stairs all day without turning a hair? How does that work? I want to know! I'm tired of being tired, especially when no one else is. What's the trick?"

His brows rose. "It's a spell. You reduce your weight to something negligible. It's simple. Children learn it. I thought maybe you were just – you know – working out like some humans like to do."

My legs trembled and I collapsed onto the stairs. "It never occurred to you I might not have chosen this?"

It looked like he didn't want to embarrass me. "Well … it's something everyone learns almost as soon as they can walk. It never occurred to me you wouldn't know . . ." He trailed off. It was the first time I'd seen him uncomfortable. Might even be worth it to see him squirm. Maybe I was being bitchy but he was just so … perfect and in control … and I never was.

My neck was getting a crick from staring up at him. I ground my teeth. "Tell me how to do this … spell thing and we'll forget this ever happened." I wobbled to my feet, glared up at him.

Thirty seconds later, I floated up the stairs with minimal effort. That's how long it took to learn and apply – seconds! I felt like an idiot. My face must've been flaming (I blame it on my ancestors for passing down fair skin) but our progress was faster now.

How could anybody assume I was working out? I mean there's a time and place, and invading a hostile castle was neither! I didn't know whether to be relieved I finally knew or pissed that no one had thought to tell me before.

I still seethed when Valgren stopped beside a small door. Keeping a tight grip on my wrist, he opened it and slipped through to a narrow corridor that came to a point much like the one Dorian and I had explored at Cumulos though it was higher. Still, Valgren's hair brushed the ceiling.

A finger touched his lips. "We're coming to the library," he whispered. "We'll have to watch for magical alarms set by the mages."

"What're we going to do?" I whispered back.

"We move into the wall, watch and listen."

Okay. *I could do this.* Visions of being incinerated by three old mages flashed through my mind. *I could do this.* Maybe they'd just hang us in a dungeon. *I could do this.*

I was the last person Valgren needed. Almost anyone else would've been better but, for some reason, Angus had agreed. Maybe he thought I'd actually be of some use. I don't know what he saw in Dorian and me but, if I were him, I'd have sent us home weeks ago.

Valgren inched toward a soft glow. He did something and the rock thinned until we could see into the room. Sure enough, three old men occupied a room lined with books stacked in shelves to the ceiling. Volumes were piled all over the floor. Wow! What I wouldn't give for a few weeks in there!

The geezers worked in silence and, after a time, I got antsy. Valgren, of course, like a forest, could wait forever.

Finally an old fellow with a bald pate tottered over to one of the others carrying a book that looked too big for him. He plunked it open on the table in front of a thin, bespectacled little man with hair that hung in greying tatters to his shoulders. A threadbare coat that looked like it used to be brown hung on a thin frame. Sharp, mean little eyes glanced at the page.

"What?" rasped the second man.

A bony finger pointed. "There!" A voice, dusty from lack of use. He waited, obviously expecting his motion to mean something to the other who's thin, cracked lips pressed together and bristly brows met between deep folds of skin. I'd never seen brows that long. If he combed them straight up, they'd touch his hairline – what was left of it. The wrinkled face began to collapse, morphing into something hideous. It didn't make me feel any better to recognize the caricature of a smile.

A third figure labored at a paper-covered desk on a second level reached by six worn wooden stairs. Two candles flickered to his left to spill meager light over his work. He glanced up through small round glasses as the other two waved him over. As he heaved to his feet, I noticed he was as short as Drughorn, his lack of height compounded by a hunchback. A wispy beard drooped from his chin, appearing to be a remnant of whatever hair used to cover a freckled skull. Heavy lips pulled at the sagging skin of his face.

Time didn't seem to be an issue. The others waited while he made his way down the stairs, placing both feet on each stair before accepting the challenge of the next. The first hurdle over, he shuffled between stacks of books, a podium, and other paraphernalia that blocked his path. In due time, he joined the others in staring at the item of interest. He perused the papers and nodded.

"This will work." His voice was surprisingly strong. He pointed. "We combine these." The other two nodded and locked gazes of satisfaction. "We can bring down the shield!"

We needed to get that book! How were we going to do that? I hadn't the slightest doubt those frail-looking old men would make mincemeat out of me and my meager bits of magic.

Valgren moved us further into the wall, pulled me against him in a warm embrace, breath soft against my ear. My traitorous body had an instant response to his masculine warmth as I inhaled yet again the scent of wildflowers and forests.

"That book contains the spells to collapse the shields around Cumulos," he whispered. "And probably a lot more. Angus would find it valuable."

Making an effort to ignore my body's response, I suggested that maybe now they'd go to bed. After all, it was after one in the morning.

Damn! It was hard enough being close to Valgren without being plastered against him – but I didn't move away.

Minutes passed. Heat was swirling through me when I felt a light touch beneath my chin. Looking up, I caught the passion in his eyes. We locked gazes before warm lips descended to mine.

Of all the places for a kiss! I melded into the man, his warm sensuality flowing through me in a wild torrent as my arms crept around his neck and the kiss deepened.

I was jarred back to reality when he pulled away, stroked my hair back. "We'll have to continue this some another time," he said. The three old mages were making their way out the door in single file. The door closed behind them with a rusty squeak.

In a desperate attempt to regain my sanity, I scanned the room. "Can we get in without setting off an alarm?" I hoped focusing on immediate danger would get my hormones under control. So far, not so successful.

Putting a finger to his lips, Valgren stepped into the room, pulling me along. He made a strange motion with his free hand and a bubble formed around us. I didn't know what the bubble would do but, at this point, doing what I was told seemed best – not that I'd ever liked that option.

We scurried to the desk where Valgren inserted a sheet of paper to act as a bookmark then tucked the heavy volume under his arm. As we turned to leave, there was a flash of movement.

The biggest and ugliest dog I've ever seen leaped from behind the desk, teeth bared in a vicious snarl. The hair on my neck and arms stood on end. Guess non-magical defenses were also effective.

A scream echoed through the room as I slammed my forehead against solid stone in an effort to wade into it. As I bounced back, a brilliant light flashed accompanied by the blast of an alarm. Pounding footsteps sounded from the other side of the door and the snarling, barking dog was upon us.

"Valgren!"

I don't think the guy has had a single worrisome thought in his entire life. "The bubble was supposed to prevent the alarms from activating," he said, with a puzzled frown. "They must have augmented their defenses."

The bubble disappeared as the door slammed open to admit soldiers – lots of soldiers who kept very good care of their very sharp weapons. Roaring in unison, they came after us.

For some reason, the dog was leery of Valgren and stopped inches from us, snarling and drooling. His glare at me hidden behind Valgren indicated I didn't share my companion's immunity.

There was a sharp tug and I was inside the wall trying to keep up with Valgren who, I discovered, can run very fast. As we darted through walls and across corridors, I lost all track of where I was. All I could think about was keeping up – until we burst through a heavy door and into the tower shaft …

I couldn't begin to stop the scream that erupted when Valgren leapt straight into thin air and we fell, my wrist still in his grasp.

Maybe I wouldn't feel it when we hit bottom. Maybe I'd skip the dying part and go straight to being dead. As the paving stones shot towards us, I scrunched up my eyes. What a stupid way to die!

Chapter 23

"A little more speed, Raven?"

What? I wasn't dead? I opened an eye. Lordy be! We were running again, not splatted against the stone floor as any normal person would expect. I'd been so preoccupied with being pursued by soldiers I'd forgotten what Valgren had told me about the spell.

I was grumpy about that. I don't care how magical you are, your body is going to argue if you jump into a hundred feet of space with only a stone floor at the bottom. That was a huge leap of faith I was nowhere near ready to make. But I'd have to deal with that later. I put on a burst of speed.

After what seemed like forever, Valgren stopped and lifted a hand, palm forward. There was a brief blur – and we were on a narrow ledge above monstrous waves which crashed against jagged rocks. An icy wind whipped my hair and chilled my sweat-soaked body. I slammed against the wall but, try as I might, couldn't mould into it.

As the piercing cry of a shorebird filled the air I was surprised to find it came from Valgren. I didn't see how performing bird imitations was going to help but figured now was not the time to criticize.

Nothing happened for a while. No surprise there.

I was fast becoming chilled and cranky when I caught a movement in the distance. The shadow solidified into Moonlight. Perhaps a rescue! Considering our precarious position though, I didn't see how it was going to work since my levitation abilities were far from dependable. I examined the thin ledge we were on – no more than eight inches thick. The view of crashing waves below made me slam back against the rock again. Why couldn't I stone-walk like Valgren?

Valgren, of course, was relaxation personified. He flexed his knees as the Pegasus neared then, with perfect timing, leaped to land with flawless grace onto the animal's back. Moonlight tipped to avoid the rock wall and curved into a slow circle. Now I truly was terrified. I was alone on the ledge!

As they turned and approached my position, I looked down and gulped. If Valgren thought I was going to jump for it, he had another think coming. I couldn't move a muscle.

Valgren extended an arm. "Jump!" he called. "I'll catch you!"

Yeah, right! But I couldn't see another way out of the situation. Sooner or later, I'd fall anyway. On the second pass, I heard Valgren shout that dark-ghosts were coming.

Correction. Dark-ghosts would suck the life out of me first.

I gritted my teeth, stopped looking down, and watched as Valgren approached. "Trust me!"

I did trust him for some reason. I flexed my knees, timed Moonlight's approach and, heart in mouth, leaped into space. There was a moment of pure terror before I felt arms like steel bands go around me. Our mount tipped to avoid the cliff and, a moment later, I straddled the saddle in Valgren's tight embrace. I didn't know if I'd ever breathe again.

Moonlight's strong strokes soon had us over the cliff face and above the rolling landscape. Glancing back at Wickness, I perceived dozens of pursuing shadows.

"Can they catch us?" My voice had an embarrassing quaver.

"No. Moonlight's fast. We'll be snug in Cumulos before you know it."

About then, I didn't think I'd ever leave the place again.

The sky in the east had a rosy glow as the welcoming lights of the castle came into view. Angus' study was ablaze so Valgren directed Moonlight to land on the walkway that joined the tower to the castle proper. Our approach was silent until we touched down onto the stones then the clopping of Moonlight's hooves echoed against the castle walls.

Valgren had wrapped his cloak around both of us to keep out the chill night air and, as he needed one hand to guide Moonlight, I'd taken over carrying the huge old book which was leather bound, reinforced with iron at the corners, and four inches thick. A heavy leather strap buckled at the front.

What secrets did it hold? Would Angus and Talon figure out the spell? What would Mydryth do when he discovered the book had been stolen? Speed up his itinerary? That's what I'd do. Don't give the enemy time to work out a strategy.

Moonlight clattered to a halt as Angus and Dorian stepped onto the walkway.

Valgren tossed his cloak back. "The three magi had an intense interest in this," he said. "I've marked the page."

"Well done!" said Angus. "Let's have a look!"

I lowered the book to Dorian who passed it to Angus before reaching for me. Valgren lowered me into Dorian's arms then slid to the ground with catlike grace. He murmured something to Moonlight who trotted to the far end of the walkway and soared into the night sky. Dorian didn't say a word but walked away with the others, leaving me to follow with Valgren.

Talon, Angus and Valgren, hunched over the open book, were probably unaware of my presence. Dorian had gone to talk with Cash and, as it sank in that I was safe again, I experienced an overwhelming sense of fatigue. I stretched out on the divan closest to the fireplace. Reveling in the warmth, my eyes grew heavy and muted conversations blurred. Before I lost consciousness, I had a vague sense that Valgren had covered me with a soft blanket.

I tried to block out the irritating voice that kept intruding but it didn't seem to want to give up. With a growl of resent-ment, I swam back to the world of the living.

The fire had gone out but I was warm under a plaid coverlet. I peered through bleary, heavy eyes. Nothing out there I wanted to see. I closed them again and fell off the divan with a thud as Bluescale's voice crashed into my head.

I grabbed my temples with both hands. "Down, Bluescale! Down! Not quite so much volume!"

"You didn't seem to be getting the message!" he retorted. *"Were you sleeping at this time of the day?"* Sounded like an accusation.

I struggled back to the divan. Sunlight poured in through a high window. Why hadn't someone woken me? I heard a soft sound and slanted a look at Angus' desk where he perused the pages of the book we'd snitched. I smothered a yawn, glad it was at least of interest, and pushed to my feet, feeling I'd barely slept.

"Good morning," he said, "I trust ye slept well?"

I'd opened my mouth to respond when a bellow blasted into my brain, causing me to collapse on the spot. *"RAVEN!"*

"Would you shut the hell up?! I'm awake already!" When I removed my hands from my head, I noticed Angus had a strange expression. In fact, his jaw was almost on the floor, eyes wide. As I attempted to collect my thoughts which were ricocheting around the inside of my skull, it occurred there may have been a miscommunication. I didn't recall ever seeing that particular expression on the Scot's face before.

I made my way up the two steps to his desk, rubbed my temples, and collapsed onto a chair. Angus watched me like he would a werewolf about to morph into something worse.

It occurred to me that he hadn't heard Bluescale's greeting. Ohhh … that would've sounded strange.

I pointed to my head. "Bluescale," I said. "In my head. Nearly blew my skull apart."

Angus closed his mouth with a snap and nodded. "I see," he said. I hoped he did. I didn't want to live the rest of my life as a toad.

I held up one finger. "Excuse me. He wants to talk." I let my eyes glaze over. "Okay, Bluescale, I can hear you now," I said both aloud and mentally. "What is it you want?"

Silence.

"Bluescale?"

Nothing.

Ahh … the silent treatment. I heaved a deep sigh. And I really meant it. I was far too tired for this. "Bluescale! Stop being such a ditz and answer me! If you felt it necessary to wake me, at least spit out what's so important."

He sounded sulky. *"I don't like it when you yell at me!"*

"Neither do I, so let's call it even. What did you want to talk about?"

He huffed out an injured breath. *"Mydryth will attack the castle at sundown tomorrow."*

"Tomorrow?!" I was suddenly wide awake.

"Tomorrow," he repeated. I envisioned his snout in the air.

"Don't be insulted, Bluescale. Valgren and I were pursued by dark-ghosts most of the night and you woke me from a sound sleep. Under the circumstances, don't expect me to be lucid." I heard a distinct "*hrrumph.*" Maybe he hadn't had his allotment of fish yet.

"Thanks for the warning. I'll let everyone know. I'm with Angus now so I'll contact you in a couple of hours." I gathered he was still in a snit as he didn't respond.

After I'd explained, Angus stared at me for perhaps two full minutes, his thoughts miles away. Then he sat back, materialized dozens of small transparent disks, murmured something, and the disks vanished.

"What were those?" I asked.

"Notices. We need te speed things up."

An hour later, Talon, Frost, and a dozen others were gathered in the library at one of the long tables, the murmur of voices softened by the books that lined the tower. As people filed in, they settled at the table leaving a chair at the end unoccupied. Dorian was seated to my right when Valgren slipped in on my left. I felt Dorian stiffen but that didn't stop a cascade of tingling throughout my body.

Angus appeared from between two rows of books labeled with warnings, approached the table, and greeted the assemblage. As he spoke, frowns and expressions of dismay crossed a variety of features.

Cumulos could sustain considerable damage if Mydryth was able to shut down the shield. The dark mage wouldn't want to give us any time to prepare a defense, and the fact we'd taken the book of spells wasn't a guarantee that he didn't know the spells already.

When he came to the part Bluescale was to play, expressions of unease increased. All were familiar with the tumultuous history of mankind and dragons, and a flame-throwing dragon wasn't to be trusted. But, reluctantly for some, it became clear that Angus' plan was the only one with a hope of success. The world couldn't afford to lose the unicorns and, though Mydryth was prevented from killing them himself, others weren't.

The thought flashed through my mind that perhaps Mydryth's plan was to use Bluescale to destroy the herd. The more I thought about it, the more I worried that Bluescale wasn't bloodthirsty enough. Which, in one way, was good; in another, perhaps the mage would see through him and create a secondary plan to harm the friendly dragon. For the first time, I felt concern for the big lunk's welfare. I must've been getting soft.

"Bluescale! Where are you?"

As seconds ticked by, I thought he might still be miffed but his voice resounded in my head. *"Raven! You're awake!"*

"Of course, I'm awake! Why wouldn't I be … never mind. We need to meet. Sooner is better."

"Meet me where King's Loch meets the ocean. Great fishing there. I can eat while I wait." Good idea. I didn't want to meet with a hungry dragon who might forget we were friends.

I sat through the rest of the meeting in a froth of impatience and was first out of my seat as Angus concluded his overview. Since at least one of them would insist on accompanying me, I wanted to escape before either Dorian or Valgren noticed I was gone. I charged through the heavy library doors and skidded around the corner into the wide stone hallway. As I proceeded at a very natural walk/run, I still got some curious glances from magical folk. As the curved entranceway appeared, I muttered an incantation, my broom appeared, and I shot into the air.

The wind was gusty, piling up threatening grey clouds in the north. A flick of my wand brought me my heavy cloak. I pulled the hood down, did a transportation spell to get me close to the loch then urged the broom to maximum speed. Tears flowed from my eyes so I materialized a pair of old-fashioned goggles, the kind made of brass that make you look like an alien. I didn't think Bluescale would care.

A disturbed grey ocean appeared in the distance. It thrashed against a ragged coastline and strong wind gusts whipped whitecaps from high rolling swells. I searched overcast skies for Bluescale, remembered to look behind. Wouldn't put it past him to ambush me just for fun – especially if he was still a little mad. Probably wouldn't eat me though . . .

I floated to the lea side of a cliff to cut the wind as I scanned the ocean. I expected he'd erupt from the frigid water soon. Minutes passed. I was getting cold – or rather colder.

"Bluescale! Not everyone has an internal furnace! I'm freezing out here!"

"*Look out belooow!*" Bluescale's merry voice rang in my head and I glanced up. A speck in the sky grew into the dragon. He was in a vertical dive, wings flat to his sides. As the scream of air reached me, I snuggled against the cliff face to avoid being anywhere near his landing point – or perhaps crashing point.

I was cringed against the rocks when his wings shot out. I would've thought at that speed they'd have ripped right off but those fragile-looking things must've had amazing strength. He performed a tight turn and skimmed by me with inches to spare. "Show off!"

"Whoowee!" he chortled, did three rollovers then made a sharp turn to line up on my position. "Follow me!" He disappeared around an outcropping.

Who the hell knew what that nutcase was up to? I peeked over a pile of stones to see him fold his wings at the mouth of a cave.

He peered over his back plates. "What's the matter? I've already eaten." With a grin he tossed his head and strutted into the cave, sinewy tail snaking through the gravel.

I touched down on the flat area and peered into the gloom. "Bluescale? You there?" As a roaring orange ball of flame lit the interior, I ducked behind a boulder to escape the searing blast. After the noise abated, I remained behind the boulder. "Bluescale! Are you done?"

His booming voice echoed from the cave entrance. "I'm done! Come on in!"

I took a deep breath, wand in one hand, broom in the other, and followed the winding trail made by his tail along a passageway which led to a pile of red glowing rocks. I felt sheepish at my distrust. He was warming the cave! I squelched an unworthy suspicion that he could be heating the oven.

I inched close to the stones that threw off amazing amounts of heat, my fingers numb from cold. Bluescale settled across the mouth of the cave. *Okay, I'm not nervous at being trapped in here.* In feigned nonchalance, I perched on a rock, right hand on my wand within the folds of my cloak.

Bluescale adjusted his wings. "You really are a Nervous Nellie, aren't you? I'm stopping cold drafts with my body."

"I knew that." As he snorted in disbelief, I added, "Well, you're the one who pointed out your teeth were made for tearing flesh!"

He yawned. "I don't like the taste of people. Their diets are unhealthy. Makes them taste bad." He heaved a sigh and settled in, large green eyes on me. "Besides…I'm full." He flashed a fake grin.

I never quite knew how to take Bluescale and, though I thought I could trust him to be true to his dragon nature, I wasn't sure what that entailed. At the moment, it seemed he was being thoughtful by warming the place so I decided to relax and enjoy. I slipped my hood back and unsnapped my cloak.

"Thanks. I appreciate the heat. I was turning blue out there." I spread chilled fingers toward the stones.

"No problem," he said. "Now what did you want to talk about that we couldn't do telepathically?"

"I've heard some mages can use telepathy like you and I do, and I didn't want to take a chance on Mydryth overhearing. Angus can speak the old language so it's possible Mydryth can too."

Bluescale curled his tail around his haunches and shifted to a more comfortable position. "He's never done it with me but that doesn't mean he can't. In the times before dragons were ostracized, many mages could *dragonspeak* and some could communicate with telepathy. Of course, all dragons can *humanspeak* in any language."

"Why's that?"

"There are dragons all over the world. We pay attention." He looked at me as if I was mentally deficient, lowered his snout so his eyes peered into mine. "We … are … *te…le…path…ic!*"

Of course.

I slapped my forehead. "You're still telepathic as a . . ." I realized I didn't know what he was in the stream.

"As a bug?"

"I wasn't going to use that word but if that's what you are … were."

"It's not a technical term but it'll do. People think of all small squirmy things as bugs." He rested his chin on an outcropping. "What did you want to talk about?"

"I'm concerned about what Mydryth will do to you if he finds out you're not evil."

He gave a slow blink. "If you don't think I'm evil, why do I make you nervous?"

I rubbed my bottom lip. "I don't think you're evil. I'm just concerned you might be … hungry … at the wrong time. After all, as you've pointed out, you are a dragon."

He blinked again. "I'm centuries old – and smart enough to choose my food with care. Some of it will come back to bite you, so to speak."

"Like people."

"Like people." He rolled his eyes. "They never give up! It's like being pursued by a bunch of ants. For every one you kill, three more take its place. You get tired of stepping on them after a while. It's just not worth it!"

"Glad to hear," I said with a smidgeon of sarcasm.

"I suppose," he replied with a total lack of comprehension. "By the way, Mydryth wants to practice riding a dragon this evening."

A lance of fear shot through me. "You'd let him get that close?"

"I'm to drop him into the courtyard tomorrow after the shield is neutralized. I don't like it, but at least I'll know where he is." His lip curled. "I'd prefer to drop him from five thousand feet without a broom but that's not going to happen either.

"While Angus works the spell, I'll keep Mydryth from escaping. I do have magic of my own, you know."

"You do?"

Green eyes rolled towards me. "There are plenty of books about dragons, Raven. You should read some."

I felt stupid again – a familiar feeling. "Sorry. I've been distracted by the whole Mydryth-destroying-the-world thing. And up to a few weeks ago, Dorian and I thought we might be the only magical folk in existence."

Bluescale threw his head back and laughed until rocks fell from the ceiling. I popped a protective spell over my head. "It's not that funny." I gave an annoyed sniff.

"Yes it is," he guffawed, and went off into another paroxysm.

It's possible my face took on a sour expression at this point. The crunching sound I heard when he finally brought himself back to earth was my teeth shortening. At this rate, I'd need dentures before I was forty. Wouldn't have wanted my blood pressure taken about then either.

"Are you quite finished?"

Tears pooled in the corners of his eyes and he wiped them away with the backs of wicked claws, lips stretched in a grin that exposed a terrifying number of gigantic canines.

Fish … he eats fish … think about fish . . .

"Considering how much magic there is in the world, it's hard to believe anyone would think they were the only ones," he said, still chuckling. "I'm glad I didn't eat you. You make me laugh!"

I didn't know how to take that so reminded myself he wasn't human. "I just wanted to warn you," I said. "Mydryth will have a whole deck of aces up his sleeve."

He gazed down his snout. "I'm touched," he said, surprise in the gravelly voice.

"Don't let it go to your head," I growled. "I don't want to see anybody die but, if it has to be someone, I'd rather it was Mydryth."

Before Bluescale could respond, the air shimmered and Angus appeared. "Ahhh," he said, moving to the hot stones, hands to the fire. "Tha's pleasant!"

My protection spells fizzled and died as my attention lost focus. How had he known?

The dragon shifted his attention to the new arrival. "Greetings, Mage."

"Greetings, Dragon. My apologies for the delay."

My eyes flicked between them. "What are you talking about? What do you mean, *delay*? What's going on?" Suspicion and ire began to warm my belly as I spun to the dragon. "Bluescale? What's this about?"

Two more shimmers rippled the air on the far side of the stones as Dorian and Valgren materialized within seconds of each other. From the look on Dorian's face, he hadn't known Valgren would be there either.

"The others were also concerned about Mydryth listening in. This is a secret meeting!" said Bluescale, waggling leathery eyebrows.

I felt a flush creep up my cheeks. "Why did you let me think it was just the two of us?"

He rolled his eyes towards me. "I didn't know you thought that. I assumed you were part of the plan and first to arrive."

I turned narrowed eyes to the others. "Why wasn't I told?"

Dorian shrugged. "If you hadn't gone haring off like you did, we'd have explained after the meeting. Angus sent a message disk to Bluescale to meet to go over the details."

The dragon snout turned to me. "That's why I suggested here." He looked around. "It's cozy."

I felt a presence and glanced to my right. Valgren had moved closer and watched me from where he leaned against the cave wall. We exchanged a glance before he turned to

Angus. Dorian saw the glance, crossed his arms, and braced his legs in a wide stance.

"Dragon magic can overpower a mage if he's got the element o' surprise," said Angus. "Tis something many mages prefer te forget but will be verra useful in this case. We'll uncover the well near the edge o' the outer courtyard this evening. Since there are no children in the castle, it should be safe enough, and twill serve as a depository for Mydryth once he's enchanted. He must be immersed in water immediately or the spell will nae hold."

"I thought it had to be running water," I said.

"The bottom o' the well is fed by an underground stream that emerges about a mile east."

"What about Bluescale?"

"We'll fish him out downstream."

"How'll you find him?"

"Tis nae difficult. A small magic tag. I'll attach it today before we leave."

"The unicorns?"

"We have two goals: one, protect and return the unicorns and, two, reduce Mydryth te the stream where he canna cause harm. Frost, Talon, and some o' the others will cast an enchantment large enough te move the entire herd. In the confusion o' the attack, the creatures will be returned te their meadows.

"Although we've reinforced the shield around Cumulos, I've arranged for it te drop so Mydryth will assume he's done it, only I'll retain control o' it." He glanced at the dragon.

"Bluescale will soar about shooting flames, pretending te attack but I expect a lot of dark-ghosts will get in the way o' his aim."

A puff of smoke drifted from the dragon's nostrils as he slid a look towards Angus and I got a chill, once again confused about whether he was a big friendly puppy or an unscrupulous killer.

Dorian moved to a warm rock and sat. "No doubt Mydryth's army will have mages help them through the gates and, if the shield's down, how do we stop them?"

"We've backup spells and Cash and his men only need te hold them off long enough te isolate Mydryth."

A sense of the surreal enveloped me as the discussion continued. Was I really going to participate in a battle? Did I have the capability of harming anyone? And what would that make me? Could I ever go back? How many oh-so-important and countless battles had been fought and not even remembered? It seemed humanity was locked in one long struggle with short periods of exhaustion we called peace.

I shook off the anxiety that type of thinking produced and returned my attention to the matters at hand. We hadn't chosen this battle and countless lives would be imperiled if we didn't remove Mydryth from the scene. That would have to be reason enough.

As Bluescale took an active part in the planning, I realized Angus trusted him though I couldn't imagine why.

Valgren could summon Gaia's assistance. I marveled at how he brought such profound power to the table yet exhibited such calm balance – an odd juxtaposition. I guess the truly powerful had no fragile ego to protect.

By the time everything wrapped up, I was clear on the sequence of events. Since Dorian and I had the best chance of surprising Mydryth with our magic, we'd be stationed near the well. We were the "wild cards" – the unexpected advantage that might make the difference in the effort to transform the dark mage into something a lot less dangerous.

Chapter 24

Bright shafts from a setting sun illuminated the spires of Cumulos as somber shadows spread in the valley and courtyard. The unicorns grazed, tails dislodging insects intrepid enough to try a sip of unicorn blood.

As Dorian and I paced the ramparts behind the crenellated walls in silent companionship, I experienced a sense of nameless agitation, the kind you feel before a summer storm hits.

As the orange globe in the west slipped from sight, dusk filled the hollows, and night encroached upon the floating island. As I leaned my elbows on the outer wall, Dorian moved beside me, his shoulder against mine. A flock of evening swans flew by headed for a nearby lake accompanied by the haunting notes of an owl.

"Beautiful, isn't it?" I said. Dorian made a sound of agreement. "Makes you wonder why we can't enjoy Gaia without feeling the need to destroy one another. What is it that gives us such a relentless drive for conflict?"

"Fear," said Dorian. "In all its nasty disguises."

"Too bad people haven't figured that out."

Dorian turned to face me. "We can't solve it all at once, Raven. One step at a time, but removing Mydryth from the mix will get a powerful player off the field."

Sounded a lot like what Valgren had said. I didn't have to do it all, just my small part. I sighed and stepped back. My eyes were heavy and tomorrow would be stressful.

"I should get to bed. Won't sleep much but at least I'll get some rest. We both should."

He lifted my chin with a finger. "Are you alright?"

"Not really, but I'll get over it."

"Don't take any more chances than you have to tomorrow," he said. "There are others to share the risk."

"I'm not that brave."

"I wish I believed that." He gave me a thin smile and walked away.

A black, suffocating mist surrounded me with darkness. Bony fingers with a thin covering of cold, grey flesh groped towards me, latched onto my wrist. I began to fall … from darkness into deeper darkness, my magic useless.

There was a thump and my eyes flew open to fasten on the dim glow of a low fire. I was flat on my back on the floor twisted into a bundle of blankets. It'd been years since I'd fallen out of bed. Groaning with the effort, I extricated myself and pushed to my feet, sorted out the bedding, and crawled beneath them to fall once again into a fitful, disturbed sleep.

After the sun rose, I staggered to the kitchen where I noticed the room was filled with more witches, wizards and mages than usual.

Dorian strolled in behind me. "Good morning."

I looked up. "Good morning."

He glanced at me and flinched.

"What?"

"Ahhh … you look a little … tired. Didn't sleep well?"

"The gigantic blue bags under my eyes your first clue?" I knew I was grumpy but was grumpy enough not to care. I pulled out a chair and flopped into it. "Maybe I'll look better after I eat." I thought I heard something that sounded like, "hope so" but didn't have the energy to take the bait.

I shovelled bacon, eggs; three slices of toast, orange juice, and shredded potatoes into myself hoping to lighten my mood. Maybe I was cranky because of low blood sugar. On the other hand, perhaps it was the thought this could be my last meal.

I steered away from that idea, remembering a spell that said, "What you think about comes about." I hoped that was wrong but just in case … I'd think about something else.

Dorian returned to his old shuttered self. Can't say as I blamed him. There was a lot to think about and prepare for. I scanned the room for Valgren who, for some reason, had chosen not to show up. Perhaps he was on a mission but it seemed doubtful he'd miss this.

I stirred cream into a second cup of coffee as Angus rose to his feet. He wanted to go over everything one more time to ensure we were all on the same page. As he itemized each plan within a plan, I was impressed by his thoroughness. My hopes rose. Perhaps all was not lost after all.

I paid close attention to our parts. Angus and Mydryth were a close match so Dorian and I would lend our magic at the last moment. Bluescale was another card in our deck that should catch the dark mage by surprise.

When Angus at last took his seat, Cash motioned Dorian over and they were soon deep in a discussion. At loose ends and too unsettled to read or study, I tramped up the stairs to the ramparts, leaned my elbows on the outside wall, and stared to the north.

A chill wind whipped my cheeks and tied knots in hair that had come loose from its braid. I fingered the wand in my pocket and summoned my broom. Perhaps a quick flight would settle my nerves. If Bluescale was right about the time of the attack, we had all day to get ready.

But I didn't believe Mydryth had gotten as old and as powerful as he was by being stupid. And I doubted he'd take chances or fall into the trap of predictability. I couldn't help but think this had been too easy – and the whisper of my intuition was deafening.

A thin cloud had formed in the north. I frowned. Rain usually came from the east or west. I made counter-clockwise gestures with my wand and uttered an incantation. The centre of the circle cleared and the cloud expanded. Still kind of fuzzy. I made another adjustment … and my knees wobbled.

The cloud consisted of hundreds of dark-ghosts. The large form leading them must be Bluescale. He probably didn't dare warn me the timing had changed in case Mydryth noticed the communication. So the dark mage had lied to Bluescale. Why was I not surprised?

I leaped onto my broom and shot straight to Angus' tower window where I rapped so hard my knuckles bruised, made frantic gestures until Talon and Angus looked up from poring over an old tome.

As Angus hurried across the floor, Talon folded his arms and sat back in his chair. I didn't care what he thought. As Angus unlatched and swung the window wide, I darted in to hover in the middle of the room. Somewhat incoherently, I blurted out my news.

"Of course, he'd keep his own schedule," snapped Talon. "He'd never tell anyone his real plans!"

"It was fortunate we anticipated such an eventuality," said Angus with maddening calm. He made a smooth gesture and dozens of four-inch disks appeared. With his forefinger, he inscribed a message on one which appeared on all. Seconds later, they disappeared. "The others will be ready," he said. "Come, Talon!"

They scurried from the room leaving me feeling superfluous. By the time I opened my mouth to ask what they wanted me to do, they were gone. Now it was my turn to scowl. Against castle rules, I exited via the window but closed it behind me. I didn't want to be the one responsible if a raging storm soaked the books or some of Bluescale's flames went awry.

Maybe I should find Dorian. I'd last seen him with Cash. I shot over the castle wall straight up the hill to the giant's cottage where Dorian was saddling a griffin. Cash's dragon, the only other flying dragon in existence, was almost ready. Too bad it couldn't shoot fire.

The area was a beehive of activity as soldiers loaded two wagons with weapons prior to transporting them to the castle gates.

Dorian glanced up. "We got the disk, Raven. You should get into position. There isn't much time."

I felt like my thunder had been stolen. I'd been the one to notice the attack and here I was being marginalized. I huffed and left without a word. It didn't help that he was right. *Did I mention I hate it when he's right?*

I shot back to the castle to check for the anticipated arrival of Mydryth's soldiers. Nothing yet. There was activity along the walkways beneath the castle overhangs but the unicorns grazed throughout the courtyard oblivious to the machinations of humanity.

I landed in the grass and scurried to a wide pillar next to the well, flattened myself against cold stone, and performed an invisibility spell. It wouldn't fool Mydryth for long, but maybe he'd be too busy to notice.

Shadows ducked and scurried throughout the courtyard but, in minutes, all except my thundering heart was still. Glimpses of dream skeletal monsters and a fall into an abyss flicked through my memory. I hoped it wasn't precognitive. I took a deep breath then another to calm myself.

Didn't work. No surprise there. My wand trembled and my palms were slick. Did anyone else feel the same? I hoped my breakfast wouldn't turn out to be a last supper. I realized my internal babbling was getting out of hand so focussed on the furtive movements around me.

Silence descended. Even the unicorns were calm. Foals stood by their mothers, ears perked at their surroundings. Perhaps the unicorns were more aware than we gave them credit for. One of the mares folded her legs and settled onto the grass for a nap. Then again, perhaps not.

Time stretched. I hoped it wasn't a spell – or perhaps just the normal spell of anticipation. I glanced skyward as I felt the shield flutter. It flashed a couple of times … and collapsed. Although it wasn't visible, I always sensed its presence. Now I felt exposed; the castle naked. The hair on my arms lifted as I reminded myself not to get distracted, that Mydryth was the target.

Since Mydryth would never tolerate another leader in his world, everyone with him would be a follower and, if they lost their leader, they'd break apart. At least that's what we hoped.

A blast of flame shot over the top of the castle followed by Bluescale clothed in reflective armour. Mydryth must've wanted to make an impressive entrance. The mage was seated in a padded leather seat with additions that curved over his legs to hold him in place. Bluescale, with his rider brandishing an oversized wand (*no surprise there either*), made a sharp dive into the courtyard before pulling out the other side.

The dark-ghosts that trailed in his wake veered toward the unicorns. As flashes of magic flew from behind the stone supports and incinerated the first wave, the creatures broke ranks and shot toward the witches hidden in the walkways. A burning odour filled the air as defensive spells flashed time after time. When the dark-ghosts glanced off the shields, they changed strategies to attack from behind.

With shocking suddenness, thick blue beams shot out to form a gigantic triangular corral around the herd. Talon was busy at his task to save the innocents. Say what you will about Talon, one could never call him a coward – a lot of other things – but not a coward.

Two dark-ghosts dove at him but a covering spell formed by two witches flashed before they connected. Frustrated, they bounced off the curved shield and swung around again. Others continued to dive at the unicorns enclosed within the gigantic triangular blue shield.

As the smell of ozone mixed with the stench of incinerated dark-ghosts, my ears caught the sounds of guttural grunts and the clash of metal from the direction of the high metal gates. Mydryth's soldiers had arrived.

High above, Bluescale made a wide sweeping arc. The first pass had been to guide the dark-ghosts to the unicorns which he knew were protected. Although good at sucking energy from living things, the dark-ghosts didn't seem too bright.

In fact, I wasn't sure they were alive at all. Maybe they were giant viruses following a food source.

I watched Bluescale approach and had readied a protective spell when my attention was caught by another flying dragon ridden by a giant, followed by a griffin and rider. Cash and Dorian! Moonlight and Valgren skimmed over the castle walls behind them and all three took positions equidistant around the castle walls.

I glanced at the unicorns, mentally urging Talon and the others to hurry as their protection spells drained vital resources. We couldn't protect the unicorns *and* defend the castle much longer. And where the hell was Angus?

A deep hum started which gained in volume and pitch. I closed my eyes against a brilliant blue flash – and the courtyard was empty of unicorns. The dark-ghosts created a vortex with their smoke forms and howled at the loss of the promised treat.

My invisibility spell must've flickered because one shot towards me, leaving scant seconds to conjure a protective shield. The dark-ghost's grotesque features were further distorted by rage as it slammed against my shield again and again.

I flicked a glance toward the aerial battle. Dorian, Valgren, and Cash on their agile mounts ducked and dove to avoid Mydryth's bolts of energy as well as Bluescale's blasts of flame. I couldn't pay much attention to it all as I was pinned down by the determined dark-ghost until Talon blew it to cinders.

In spite of the dark-ghost swarm, I focussed on what was happening above as our people, with deliberate coordination, drew Mydryth lower. It gave him the illusion of winning as the mages and witches withdrew. He threw bolts of energy in every direction while Bluescale made a great show with bursts of flame. The dark mage was too busy to notice the dragon never connected with anything other than dark-ghosts.

At this point, it occurred to me to realize what an awful lot of *noise* a battle made. All the yelling, smashing and roaring were deafening! I don't know why I was so surprised. After all, it was unlikely such an event would be quiet.

Angus appeared above Mydryth. As predators ourselves, we seldom look up, and Angus took advantage of this weakness. Frustrated dark-ghosts had returned to Mydryth to add to the swarm around their leader. My heart squeezed at the sight of one behind Dorian but Valgren disposed of it with a well-placed blast of green energy.

There was so much going on by then, I lost track. To add to the confusion, now that the unicorns no longer needed protection, witches shot into the air to blast every dark-ghost they encountered. The clash of swords rang as Mydryth's soldiers materialized in groups of four in the courtyard, broadswords in hand. Those old mages had been a busy trio.

At a sound from behind, I turned to see a newly-materialized set of soldiers. My hasty spell froze them in place but it wouldn't last long; there was too much wild magic about.

I ducked in time to avoid decapitation by another soldier then rolled into the courtyard and brought my wand to bear. Before I could use it, the advancing soldier stiffened and fell. Talon flicked a glance at me from behind a pillar.

I groaned. I owed the odious little creature another one! I nodded my thanks and rolled to the stone fountain where I could watch and wait.

I could see when Mydryth realized he might lose. He must've ordered Bluescale to blast an opening through the defenders because the dragon gave a mighty shot of flame and darted through the resulting hole. He sailed high above the castle and Mydryth must've been confident in his escape when the dragon turned and plummeted straight towards the courtyard. Angus ducked behind him.

I took a deep breath and held steady. No room for error. The words of the enchantment rolled through my head like a mantra.

Mydryth hadn't spotted the danger yet as he blocked the bolts of energy thrown at him. When he was fifty feet above the well, Angus intoned a loud incantation.

I saw shock and panic on Mydryth's face as understanding registered. He was about to leap from Bluescale when the dragon reached around in a lightning move and grabbed the mage in his mouth. I cringed in anticipation of a juicy crunch but Bluescale held him just hard enough to keep him there.

The flicker of orange dragon-magic enclosed the mage. Mydryth, screaming with fury, was about to target Bluescale when he was shaken like a rat until his wand tumbled to the ground.

My turn! I shot upwards to create a modified protective shield next to Bluescale and Mydryth. Dorian did the same on the other side. Valgren had added Gaia's energy when I felt a sharp pain in my shoulder which caused me to drop my wand. I glanced up as I fell; saw I'd received a glancing blow by a dark-ghost, enough to suck my magic.

As Bluescale shot past me towards the well, I experienced the strangest sensation. I thought I saw Valgren reach for me – almost as if he'd dove head first off of Moonlight. The shock must've caused me to hallucinate because a person would have to be crazy to do that in the middle of such a magical maelstrom. As I sank into a spinning dark vortex, I could've sworn I felt strong arms wrap around me.

Ice-cold water closed over my head and sucked me into blackness. I struggled against whatever was holding my arms to my sides, frantic to breathe as my world became a tumbling, suffocating blackness. As my lungs were about to burst, I realized I could hear Valgren's voice in my head.

"Breathe, Raven! Breathe!"

The infinitesimal portion of my brain that wasn't preoccupied with that exact problem wondered why he'd say anything so colossally stupid. And why did he sound so calm?

"You've been changed, Raven. Open your gills."

My *what!?*

"You're going to pass out if you don't breathe."

Too panicked to think, I wondered why he didn't understand. But a warm sense of comfort came from somewhere and the panic subsided. I had the sensation of coming home, wherever that was. It didn't matter anymore. I relaxed and let my lungs fill – only they didn't. As something moved on the sides of my neck, the vise around me relaxed.

"It's okay, Raven. I'm here. You're safe."

You're safe. Those two words were like an "open sesame" to my heart. Could I be primitive enough to crave the safety of a man? Sounded like dangerous introspection.

Somehow I could breathe but the rushing darkness continued. Was I dead? Was I going to the light? Was this it? All she wrote? Done with life this time around?

But I wasn't ready! I had things to do, lots of things! I'd planned to get my hair trimmed next week and I'd found a lovely new robe in deep maroon. How could I wear my new robe if I was dead? How would I pay for it? And what about this thing with Dorian and Valgren? I wanted some romance in my life! I'd practically become a virgin the past few months! I wasn't ready to die!

I'd refuse to go! That was it. I'd simply refuse. But I couldn't stop a pale light that had appeared in the distance from brightening. Was this the light all those people who came back from the dead talked about?

"Raven! Look at me!"

It was Valgren's voice but when I turned to where the voice originated, all I saw was a trout – a big trout swimming along. I tried to blink but couldn't.

"What's happening, Valgren?" My voice sounded weird, my head wouldn't move, and I couldn't look down at all.

"You were caught in the spell to trap Mydryth. Don't worry. We'll only be fish for a few more minutes."

"We're what?!"

"You're a trout – a fish. Look around. You're in an underground stream that's about to come to the surface."

Seconds later, a gush of water tossed us both into the air which, strangely enough, made me feel as if I was choking. I gasped as I submerged again. The other trout, with a quick flick of its tail, shot back to my side.

"Valgren . . .?"

"It's me."

"We're fish?"

"We are."

I stared at my surroundings. There were living things everywhere – and they were big. Are we … big fish?

"Minnows more like."

But you look … huge!

"Matter of perspective."

Monstrous water entities swam by, multiple legs churning. Beetles soared amongst plants that dwarfed the tallest trees, their bodies as long as I was. The serpentine shape above us was a water snake and tiny evenly-spaced dots on the surface belonged to a water strider, a delicate insect able to run along the surface. The stream seemed as deep as the ocean and miles wide.

Life I'd never imagined busied itself in a kaleidoscope of colour and action. Some flowed, others swam with jerky movements but everything was going somewhere and doing something. All that purposeful action reminded me of a city. I'd never imagined such complexity of life in the stream.

I now understood see why Bluescale enjoyed living here and why he wanted to move to the waterways of the Americas. The opportunities for exploration of this fascinating realm were unlimited and a great place for a dragon to spend a few centuries waiting for the maturation of humanity (okay, maybe more than a few centuries).

Mydryth! My fins sprang out and I stopped relative to the gravel beneath. Valgren, caught by surprise, shot ahead but swam back.

"What's wrong?"

What's wrong? Where would I start? I was a *fish*, for crissake! I peered around as best I could. "Where's Mydryth ... or rather ... what is Mydryth?"

"See that salamander with feathered gills?" He turned his fish body to point his head to the right. "That's Mydryth. He won't remember much and won't recognize us."

I wouldn't recognize us! Why should he? I scanned the creatures around us. "Where's Bluescale?" I couldn't see anything that looked like it used to be a dragon.

"Ahead. Angus will pick him up and restore his memory."

"Why do we remember?"

"I modified the magic as we fell. Since we didn't expect you to go into the stream, you had no tracking device."

"You mean I could be stuck like this forever?"

"Not now. I can get us out. The likelihood of finding you otherwise would've been ... well ... slim at best."

I was horrified when Valgren explained he too could've been lost in the stream if he'd made the slightest mistake.

Neither of us would've retained any notion of who we'd been. I didn't know what to say to that.

After drifting along in the turbulence a while longer, I asked him what was next. He said he was waiting for something and to enjoy the scenery.

Sometime later he closed the distance between us. "Are you ready?"

"For what?"

"To regain your form."

"Will it hurt?"

The answer was a blurring of my vision and the oddest sensation of stretching. It felt like a heater had turned on inside me and then I was spluttering and coughing, splayed on hands and knees in the stream, water running off me in rivulets. Valgren knelt next to me, calm and collected, of course. I felt something was amiss but was too focused on learning to breathe again to figure it out.

I rasped, "Holy hell! That was a bizarre experience!"

Valgren cocked his head as if listening then smiled.

"So what were you waiting for?" I grumbled, still out-of-sorts.

He gestured to a grassy slope that bordered the stream. "For Angus to extract Bluescale and for the stream to carry us here."

"Bluescale's already out?" My eyes widened.

"Angus took him five minutes ago. They're on their way to the castle."

"What about us?"

Valgren's gaze softened and flicked over me. "This meadow is very secluded."

A horrible suspicion came over me. I looked down to discover my clothing consisted of goose bumps. So that's what'd been missing! We were both stark naked!

Upon reflection, it made sense our clothing wouldn't fit the fish we'd become. Our garments, along with my wand, floated somewhere in the stream. It wasn't Valgren's fault. If he hadn't come to my rescue, I'd have been drowned – or remained a small fish until, of course, I was eaten by a bigger fish.

As his gaze wandered over me, he spotted the goose bumps – among other things. "Let's get out of this cold water," he suggested. "The sun looks inviting."

True. I was getting colder by the second but was embarrassed to stand in front of him in my current state of undress.

A corner of his mouth quirked as he correctly assessed my hesitation. "I'll go first."

With perfect ease, he flowed to his feet and waded across the stream. I couldn't tear my eyes away, my mouth dry. I had the sinking feeling I'd have trouble walking away from this one. Frost's comments about Gaia's Riders came back to me. She'd have been cheering me on. A sigh escaped. I was a weak woman.

Valgren stepped onto the grass and turned to face me. "You're turning blue. Do you need help?"

I shook my head, swallowed my pride, and lurched erect. My fingers were indeed blue. Now that would be attractive, I thought with resignation. Why didn't I look as perfect as he did? No wrinkles in his fingers, I'd bet; hair already drying to delightful messiness. I felt like a drowned rodent.

"You could turn around!" I growled.

He smiled and shook his head.

"Did you plan this?"

He watched me pick my way over the slippery stones. "I planned to save your life, that's true."

Conflicting emotions warred within as I waded to shore, a combination of embarrassment and excitement tinged with a dollop of pure cussedness. I couldn't shake the feeling I'd been manipulated but couldn't see how. And it wouldn't be fair to take it out on the man who'd just saved my life.

I stopped to regard him. What was it he always said? *To Gaia, sensuality is as natural as breathing.* Pieces fell together. Valgren was an extension of Gaia. Then I realized I too was an extension of Gaia. And Valgren had never forced me to do anything. Perhaps it was time for some brutal honesty. It wasn't Valgren's sensuality that had me so tied in knots. It was mine.

I came to the realization that no matter how I'd tried to avoid it, I'd been contaminated by the strangling morality of the belief systems of the Americas. Whether you believed in them or not, they oozed like rot, sending black tendrils of guilt into your life, twisting the beautiful pleasure of Gaia into a perceived evil. Even though I guarded against such things, I'd been influenced. It wasn't Valgren who was wrong here. The only question was whether I could be honest enough to admit I wanted him.

Valgren remained still, his gaze magnetic. Self-consciousness fell away like a dirtied garment. Our eyes locked as I reached warm grass, aware only of the invitation in moss-green.

I stood before him, looked up. His eyes flashed a brief question, answered by my own. The corners of his lips lifted as he tucked a strand of wet hair behind my ear. Gentle hands cupped my face, tipped it upwards. I raised myself onto my toes and, as warm lips claimed mine, I moved against his warm chest, felt my arms slip around his neck and my insides melt to warm butter.

Time stopped. Perhaps literally. He *was* Gaia, after all.

I'd never imagined a kiss could be so … open … and yet so intimate. He took his time, gentle and welcoming. Something metaphysical happened then – something I could never have imagined. Valgren's soul, scented of sage, forest and fields of flowers, opened within *me*, and any residual defenses I'd harboured dissolved into nothingness. In seconds, my essence had been cleansed and glowed with purity to match that of Gaia.

A moan came from someone. Perhaps it was me; perhaps both of us. My toes curled into warm grass. *Holy cow!*

Chapter 25

Sunlight skimmed tree tops at an oblique angle. The surreal glow of the meadow could've been either the imminent sunset or the result of my newfound perception. As I lay in the grass with my head on Valgren's shoulder, his fingers stroked my arm in a gentle repetitive pattern as every cell of my body tingled with well-being and contentment.

Although loathe to break the spell, the air had cooled and we didn't have clothing. Instantly aware of my slight shiver, Valgren shifted until he leaned over me, elbows on either side, warming me with his body. The scent of meadow flowers intensified as he gazed into my eyes and smoothed tangled green and raven locks with gentle fingers.

The incredible sensuality of opening to Valgren/Gaia caused a catch in my throat. Could one ever get used to this? He lowered his head and gently kissed me until I thought my insides would turn to jelly. Time fled once again. When he lifted his head, our eyes locked and the corners of his mouth lifted.

"Your eyes are the colour of the sky," he murmured. "A man could get lost in them."

I slipped my fingers through his hair, gave him a languorous smile, and pulled his unique scent into my core. "And yours are filled with life."

The green seemed to move, the ebb and flow of Gaia herself. He smiled, gave me a quick kiss, and rolled to his feet. "I'll make us something to wear. Moonlight will be here soon."

In Valgren's embrace, it never occurred to me to be afraid as Moonlight sailed over the castle walls to touch down in the courtyard. A light kiss brushed my neck and then, with the soft rustle of a grass loin cloth, Valgren was on the ground. He reached and I slid into his arms.

"I'll be back tomorrow," he said. After a toe-curling kiss, he sprang to Moonlight's back and, in a few swift strides, they were over the wall and gone.

I huffed out a deep breath and smoothed my scanty woven tunic. The stones were cool against bare feet as I approached the main doors. They opened a crack and Frost motioned me in.

"Best be quick," she said. "The others are searching the castle for left-over dark-ghosts and soldiers."

I must've flushed an alarming shade of red because she put a hand on my arm. "There's nothing to be ashamed of, Raven. There's no way your clothing could've gone with you but sometimes it's better not to be too obvious about spending an afternoon with a Rider sans clothing. There's only one way *that* ends."

I flushed again. "How did you know I was here?"

"I saw Valgren go after you. If anyone could bring you back, he could, so I set a spell to alert me of his return. Let's get you to my quarters."

I glanced at the empty sky then followed my roommate.

As I watched a tub fill with warm water, the scent of my woven tunic mixed with the dampness that swirled upward. I was reluctant to wash the scent of Valgren from my body. I didn't know what to think of that sentiment. The experience was branded into my soul.

But I needed to remember he'd soon be gone – or I would. I squared my shoulders and cranked the tap to hot. With one last inhalation of mysterious forest, I stripped out of the tunic, stepped into the steaming tub, and reached for the soap. Some experiences couldn't be held, only remembered.

Ten minutes later, I sipped tea with Frost, hair in a towel, and wrapped in a thick terrycloth robe. A message disk popped into the room and Frost's brows drew together as she read it.

"What is it?"

"We're to convene with the other mages at midnight. They want to talk about Bluescale."

"Now, there's a surprise," I said. "A lot of people will object to removing him from the stream as per the agreement but, without him, Mydryth would still be a threat. We owe him, and he hasn't asked for much in return."

"I'm inclined to agree." Her lips firmed as she glanced at me. "Perhaps you and Dorian could transport the dragons before the meeting convenes? After it's done, it's not like anyone will be able to find them."

I charged to my room to dress and, minutes later, was headed out the door.

"Angus is in his study," called Frost as I tore down the corridor. "And no one else knows you're back."

When Dorian and I nearly collided at Angus' study, I was startled by his pale, shuttered expression. As his gaze fastened on me, I saw both shock and relief. Then he gathered me into such a crushing embrace, I couldn't breathe. *This was a surprise. How was I supposed to respond?* As he stepped back, I looked up into his eyes; decided silence was safest.

I could see him fight for self-control as he leaned against a wall and let out a long, slow breath. "I've been trying to accept that you might be dead. When did you get back … and how?"

"Less than an hour. Valgren rescued me from the well."

His face tightened. "I should be grateful, I guess, but the guy's interest in you is obvious."

"Is that a problem?"

Dorian looked at the floor then back at me. "Time and place," he said. I nodded. This was neither.

Angus was behind his desk surrounded by stacks of books. "Take a seat," he said. "It won't be long before the others arrive and we need te be done before that."

We reclined into comfortable chairs next to a cold hearth. The sun had set and a chill had crept into the room. A roaring fire burst to life as Angus joined us and Sin, who'd been curled in front of the cold fireplace, looked relieved. He spotted me and, with a squeaky, questioning mew, strolled over and looked up. To avoid his clumsy attempts at accessing my lap, I picked him up.

He sniffed at my face, perhaps thanking me – or complaining about where I'd been. He made a few turns before settling his fifteen pounds with a satisfied sigh. At the moment, I didn't mind. He was a thick, warm blanket and only the occasional claw extended to prick my skin.

Angus glanced at the cat. "Sin seems te have taken quite a shine te ye, lass."

I suspected the cat had identified the most comfortable lap which I didn't find flattering. "Seems to have," I said and gave the wide back a pat. Sin looked up and seemed to smile. Or was that a smirk? I narrowed my eyes at him. With an indifferent shrug, he heaved a sigh of contentment, turned towards the flames, and his body began to vibrate. As I scratched under his chin, the purring became furious.

Angus waved his wand and the ceiling disappeared long enough for Bluescale to sail in. I have to admit I was impressed by the dragon's ability to squeeze into a small space without knocking anything over – well, almost anything. A couple of vases crashed to the floor as he curled around the desk.

"Sorry about that," he said. "Room's not made for dragons."

"No harm done," replied Angus as he reassembled the vases.

Bluescale turned to me. "I see you're still alive. How'd you do that?"

"Valgren," I said avoiding Dorian's glance.

"Good thing he's quick. I thought you were a goner."

Not wanting to dwell on it, I turned to Angus. "So what's the plan? How do we get the dragons to the Americas?"

"Bluescale has alerted his companions te be ready within the hour."

On a marble table next to his elbow was an object draped with green felt. He removed the fabric to reveal a box blackened with age, every inch of its surface carved with runes. Six inches by five by four, two brass bands encircled the rectangular shape. Brass clasps were locked with tiny padlocks which sprang open as he touched them with his wand. As he lifted the lid, I saw four clear cubes.

"As ye can see," said Angus, "we've room for four dragons. Bluescale will have te fly which means you'll need te do his reduction in the stream near Denver."

"Won't he be spotted?" I asked. "Americans are paranoia personified. Their radar covers every square inch of the continent, and he's big enough to show up."

"A time compression will nae trigger radar."

I felt my eyebrows rise. "Time compression?"

"Aye," he said. "Ye used it te get here."

I slipped back to the night we'd gotten to the east coast much too fast. I hadn't realized we'd been compressing time. How about that? I felt pretty good.

"Bluescale will carry all of ye."

"What about the transformation back to the stream?" asked Dorian. "How do we do that?"

Angus handed him a packet of oiled paper tied with string. "Make sure the dragon is *in* the water along with the cubes before ye do the incantation. And say your goodbyes before reading the spell aloud as he'll shrink at the final word."

Pain lanced through my heart as I realized – this was goodbye. Would we ever be able to come back? I glanced at Dorian who watched me, the same thought probably going through his mind.

Valgren! I had to say goodbye! I couldn't just leave! As I surged to my feet, the cat hit the floor with a thud and a yowl. It stalked to a braided rug near the hearth where it curled up and stared at me out of narrowed green eyes.

"I need … I need . . ." I glanced at Dorian, turned to Angus. "I need to talk to Valgren before we go."

He nodded. "I will alert him."

Meanwhile, there was nothing to do but pack. I returned to Frost's quarters to collect my meagre belongings and thought of a dozen people to whom I wouldn't get the chance to say goodbye. Cash, Frost – even Talon. But Bluescale and his friends depended on us.

I stuffed spare clothing with unnecessary force into my backpack. The few things I couldn't bear to part with went into a pile on my bed. I pulled out my wand and muttered an incantation. The pile glowed then disappeared, hopefully to materialize in my living room at home. *Home*. Denver didn't feel like home anymore.

I grimaced and sucked in a deep, steadying breath. What a difference a few weeks could make!

I heard a sound and turned to see Valgren in the doorway, his perfect hair looking rumpled, sleeveless jerkin accentuating powerful arms. He wore snug trousers with high, worn boots and, as the scent of forest drifted into the room, I knew I'd remember him forever this way. I didn't want to forget a single thing.

Swirling moss-green drew me and I flew across the room into his arms. I trembled as he crushed me to him, face buried in my hair,

"I thought we'd have more time," I choked out. "I knew it couldn't last, but a little more time . . ."

He remained silent, held me against him and, I could tell, breathed in my scent. He pulled back to look into my eyes. "Will you return?"

"I don't know if I can. Perhaps we can make arrangements with Angus but having us here was an exception. Our magic is alien to Cumulos."

"But it is of Gaia, and she is strong in you. You have great power."

"Since I don't know how to use it, I doubt that counts."

He smiled and stroked my hair. "You will learn."

I bit my lip. "Can you ever … come to the Americas?"

"Gaia needs me here. There's much to be done." He pushed an errant strand behind my ear. "But the world is a wondrous place, my White Raven. Gaia may not yet be finished with the two of us."

"What do you mean?"

"I'll say only that we're … connected at a deep level, and our relationship doesn't feel complete."

The backs of his fingers stroked my cheek and he felt warm and alive. I couldn't let him go like this! I rose on tiptoes, whispered against his lips, "We have a little time . . ."

A sensual smile lit his face and the aroma of wildflowers once again filled my senses.

"We do indeed . . ."

The air had a chill and a light misty rain fell. Night birds huddled against the dampness and, except for the gurgle of water and patter of raindrops, the forest was silent. I tugged my travelling cloak close as Bluescale banked beneath us and executed a graceful landing in the inky darkness. I was astonished the dragon could see at all but apparently his eyes were more like a cat's than a human's.

Angus sailed to a smooth landing next to us, lit his wand, and strode to the edge of the stream. Dorian and I slid down Bluescale's side and followed, our wands pushing back the darkness.

As we reached the water, Angus took the cubes from the box and set them on a rock in the stream then raised both arms and turned his face into the falling mist. A blue glow began to emanate from his body and an eerie incantation filled the area. Four small blue lights glowed on the bottom of the stream, there were simultaneous flashes, and the lights transferred to the cubes.

I leaned to inspect them. Each contained a small water creature. Those were dragons? I found it hard to equate Bluescale with such a tiny creature.

He didn't, though. A gigantic snout pushed me aside as he peered into the cubes. Communicating with his friends, I suspected.

"Are they alright?" I asked.

"They're fine. Excited to be going to America. My mate would rather have flown as a dragon but I told her it wasn't allowed."

"Your mate? Bluescale, you never told me you had a mate!"

He blinked. "You never asked."

"Who are the other three?"

"My sons and daughter."

I wanted to bang my head against a rock. I had to be the most insensitive, inconsiderate dolt on the planet! But I also understood how difficult it would be to control five dragons if they didn't want to cooperate.

I stroked his snout. "Someday you'll be dragons again."

He pursed his lips. "The world is full of temptation for a dragon. Perhaps after humanity has grown and, like Elvis, has left the planet . . ."

Angus handed me the box with the cubes and I slipped it into a deep pocket.

. . . And it was time.

I turned to Angus. "I don't know how to thank you. Will we see you again?"

"The world is a magical place, lass. Nothing's impossible. Besides," his eyes twinkled. "I'd still like te explore the Rocky Mountains. Perhaps Denver could use a visit?"

I laughed. "It could indeed!" I gave him a great hug, surprised to find moisture in my eyes. How could I leave all this? How could I go back to my normal life?

Dorian and Angus clasped hands. "If you ever need us . . ." said Dorian.

Angus smiled. "Gaia is uneasy these days. Perhaps we'll meet sooner than ye think."

My thoughts flashed to Valgren. I hoped so.

Thunder rolled and streaks of lightning lit the meadow. As I turned to mount Bluescale, I thought I saw something move. Lightning lit the shadowed figure of a man – a man at one with Gaia. At the next flash, the meadow was empty. Had it been my imagination?

Dorian followed my gaze. "See something?"

"No, it's … just a shadow."

He boosted me onto Bluescale and climbed up behind me, slipped an arm around my waist. As the dragon's powerful wings lifted us into the night sky, I murmured, "We'll be back." I leaned into Dorian's warmth. "Somehow … we'll be back."

The End

CPSIA information can be obtained
at www.ICGtesting.com
Printed in the USA
LVOW11s0542060217
523321LV00001B/1/P

9 781773 023052